JOHN ANTHONY HENRY ADVENTURES
Saving Fort Henry

JOHN ANTHONY HENRY ADVENTURES

Saving Fort Henry

A. H. Henderson

PALMETTO
P U B L I S H I N G
Charleston, SC
www.PalmettoPublishing.com

John Anthony Henry Adventures: Saving Fort Henry
Copyright © 2023 by A. H. Henderson

First Edition

Paperback ISBN: 979-8-8229-2612-7
eBook ISBN: 979-8-8229-2613-4

CONTENTS

Introduction to the World of Fort Henry

This story took place in the 1990 and it is a parallel universe to a real story, in real time, in real space. There are no such things as space and time when it comes to love. Space and time are only a human condition. Space and time to provide humans with the necessary subsistence to stabilize their existence.

This book was written to honor the purple finches that fly under the soaring literary eagles.

Welcome to Fort Henry and the many adventures of John Anthony Henry on his return to his homeland. John Anthony Henry was not born in Fort Henry, but his heritage, tradition, and ancestry are tied to Fort Henry. Will John Anthony Henry be able to save Fort Henry from the vile entanglement choking the life out of this town?

CHAPTER ONE

THURSDAY

Through the Fog

There was a deep purple emptiness staring back at me, obscuring the road and life. I felt virtually alone as the wipers battled the enclosing weather. The mist, the fog, was extremely heavy and thick as the wipers fought vigorously against the elements desperately trying to keep the windshield clear. My world was now fashioned in headlights bouncing off this blinding wall of purple and gray. I could not see the road nor my future. I was blind to all.

The fog in my mind was as bedazzling to my future as the fog concealing the road. I was looking for more than road markers obscured by the fog. I was looking for life markers to forge my way forward. How many miles had I traveled in this treacherous tormenting weather? More importantly, why was I doing this? Why not stop? But where? The rain had stopped some time ago and no matter how hard it had rained, this fog, this mist, was far worse. I was having trouble seeing the road or any road markings. What road was this?

Turning the car lights off was of little benefit, for the world would become a light gray blanket encompassing me. I had turned several times on side roads looking for a main highway, a town, or anything to give me a bearing of where I was, but where? It had been ten or twelve hours of driving with a failing memory in this miserable weather. I knew where I was going because I had been there many times. But it was a lifetime ago.

Weariness was setting in; I had to stop, I had to sleep. But where? Where was I? Oh, this nasty weather, as my first wife would say in a nagging fashion, "This place is in the middle of nowhere. Why do we have to go? Why don't you go by yourself? There is nothing for me to do." My first wife and I were separated long ago. Why was I thinking of her now? We were divorced about twenty years ago and the only contact I had with her over the years was because of our children. There are a son and daughter from the marriage. They were and are the proud gifts of our marriage. Our son is living in Anaheim and our daughter in Orlando.

The only recent time I had seen my ex-wife was at my son's wedding about three years ago. Why was I thinking of her now, I must have been incredibly weary, if not delusional? I still hoped everything was going well for her.

There were a multitude of causes for the breakdown of our marriage: youth, school, work, service, going different directions, diverse tastes, and much more. One thing our marriage had was love and lust. We cared about each other but living together was not an option.

Here I was this fogged never-ending road traveling alone, traveling toward the place my first wife would never consider home. I was going to fall asleep soon at the wheel if I did not stop - but where?

I was in desperate need of somewhere to get off this road, a parking lot, a drive, a path, anywhere. I was exhausted from driving for hours in this quagmire of weather. Stopping was not an option. It was a necessity, I had to rest. I could hardly see the road, let alone a way off the road. My speed was slow, sometimes twenty miles an hour and many times even slower. Out of nowhere, an opening. It was a drive. I slowed to a crawl and aimed toward this opening in the fog. Whatever it was, I left the road. Sleep was upon me as I turned off the key.

I awoke in a few minutes or hours. I could not tell which. It was too dark to see my watch even if I could get my eyes to focus. The fog was covering my vehicle like a blanket. I could see only a few inches. I was still very tired and a bit confused. I was to shut my eyes and sleep captured me again, leading me into a world of dreams. The weather surrounded me in a tunnel of darkened despair; was I never to awaken?

Awaking again the fog was lifting a little. I could barely make out a house, but it could not be...the house stood out from my childhood memories. It was the house where my grandparents lived. This is where they lived before, they moved into town. Shutting my eyes again, I fell into a deep slumber. In my sleep or unconscious reality, I could hear the back door of the house opening. The springs on the screen door were creaking as usual. This was music to my ears. The sound was so familiar, I could see my Granny Ruth standing at the door, waving.

Granny Ruth was the center of my life ever since my parents and younger sister died in a car accident. Granny Ruth took me in when I was eight and raised me until I was an adult or at least I thought I was an adult. When Granny Ruth sent me off to college there were tears in her eyes. Granny Ruth made sure I had a solid education. Every day after school, she would make me work on school assignments, no matter if there were school assignments or not. When I opened my eyes again the house was gone, but the memory of the dream lingered in sweet contentment in my mind.

There was a tap on the window, an angry tap. Out of the fog a face appeared. The face... my mind was searching for recognition of the face. "Who are you? Why are you here?" the face said through the watered stained glass; I did not answer. My mind wrestled for recognition of this face staring at me. It came to me. This was a face from many years ago, but the same face. How could it be? It was the face of Poke Sally.

She said, "I know you, welcome home, I knew you would come" and she disappeared. I was sure that I was awake and not dreaming, but Poke Sally? It was hard to see Poke Sally through the fogged stained glass, but she looked the same as she did twenty plus years ago. She had been my very dear friend when I was a boy. She had helped me out of some intriguing tricky situations. Poke Sally? Was I dreaming or was I home?

It took me some time to focus on reality. During this time, the fog started to dissipate, and a vision of home was upon me. Looking through the water-streaked windows I could see the remnants of the Henry farm. I was home. Most of the buildings - the house, garage, barn, and out-buildings I knew in my youth - were gone. A Tornado came through about sixteen years ago, when my Granny Ruth and Grandfather Jason were in Carrollton. Carrollton is a town about twelve miles from Fort Henry. The tornado leveled the house, barn, garage, and outbuildings in a moment of devastation; all was lost. My Granny Ruth and Grandfather Jason were safe.

After the tornado my grandparents took what few belongings they could find, and moved into town, to the house my grandfather's father had built. The house in town had been vacant for a few months since my grandfather's sister had died. It was a grand house: two stories with, six bedrooms upstairs, and downstairs was living room, a dining room, a parlor, a bedroom and bathroom off the dining room, a large kitchen with a wood burning stove, a bedroom and bath off the kitchen, a large pantry downstairs, a front porch covering the whole front of the house, and a side porch off the kitchen. The house sat on six acres of land.

My body was sore from driving for hours and sleeping uncomfortably in the car. I got out of the car and walked around stretching and getting the kinks out. I walked to the northeast corner of the farm, as I had many times as a boy. There it was still standing tall, my red oak tree, nestled among a small forest of Red oak trees. It was important I show respect and awe, for this tree once caught me.

After spending time in memories of years ago from my happy youth, my mind was starting to focus on today. It was time to go home. I drove into town, the town I knew so well, but did I know this town? How would the town appear to me? Was I driving into Brigadoon or was I driving into reality? My tiredness was paying its price on me. I was too weary to challenge how I arrived at this location through the hours of the rain and fog. I was here. Here is where I needed to be. My son Bret had located me after a few weeks of searching. He found me at my favorite fishing camp in Canada. He left a message with the owner and friend Bob Williams. The message stated that I was to contact my son immediately for he wanted to talk to me about Granny Henry's death and the possibility of losing the Henry estate.

It was urgent that I speak with my son. On contacting my son, he informed me of the death of Granny Ruth, who had died suddenly. My son told me if I did not appear at the county courthouse quickly to identify myself as alive and complete all the necessary paperwork. It was possible the Henry estate would be sold for taxes. My son said that I have had enough time to feel sorry for myself. It was time to start thinking about others, like my daughter, son, and the Henry estate. My son was becoming my father or at least giving me a good kick in the pants.

I drove into Fort Henry following the road as it was curving onto the main road of town. The main road is called Henry Way. I found a place to park on the main street of town. Fort Henry was unchanged after over twenty-eight years. At least unchanged through my youthful eyes. It needed some paint and cleaning, it was beautiful. I know the town has changed since I was last here, but my childhood eyes and youthful mind did not see all the changes. My mind's illusion was manifesting what I wanted to see. Tomorrow was soon enough to distinguish, from what was and what is.

I had a few days to reach the county courthouse and save the Henry estate, but first I needed some food and rest. Tomorrow was time enough to take care of all the commitments and paperwork. I was hungry, very hungry, because it was yesterday morning since I had two donuts and a small black coffee. I questioned myself what was I in for on returning to Fort Henry? Fort Henry is filled with my childhood memories, most were incredibly good, but some have haunted me to this day. Why had I not returned to Fort Henry other than short visits before this? What was I afraid of after all these years?

CHAPTER TWO

FRIDAY

The Bully Falls

T he eyes of my childhood spotted a restaurant, the restaurant I remember having five cent Cokes and the occasional ice cream soda. Now my focus was on food, real food. I was extremely hungry. The restaurant is now called Sandy's Café. As I approached Sandy's Café, I noticed a dog sleeping near the doorway. It was a young good-looking chocolate Labrador retriever. The dog opened its eyes and wagged its tail. I said, "Good girl" as I bent down to pet the chocolate lab. The double-screen-doors entrance door almost fit, I pulled the left side of the door. It screeched as the door opened the springs were playing some sour notes. The door slammed behind me. I was in.

Looking around the restaurant there was a center aisle leading to a front counter splitting the restaurant into two sections. The counter on the left was guarded by round red vinyl backless stools. An ancient richly decorated cash register was on the right counter. There were more round swirl stools standing at attention beneath the register. The red vinyl stools were dressed to look like leather. There were ten or so tables on both sides of the center aisle. On the left people were seated at a table next to the wall toward the door of the restaurant. On the right a man was sitting at the third table on the center aisle. Another man was sitting on a stool on the right next to the wall. There was an aroma of bacon and coffee.

I sat at the front right table, facing the majestic cash register. Normally I do not sit with my back to the door, but I was hungry. I was forgoing my usual scrutiny. An attractive woman whose name tag read Sandy gave me a one-page menu. She asked me what I wanted to drink. I was hungry, so I placed my order without waiting to read the menu. I said, "three eggs over, home fries, bacon, and wheat toast should do it for now... oh yes, black coffee." It was late in the morning. Lunch was not an option, for my body was on breakfast time.

The coffee came quickly, and I took two sips. The sips of coffee startled me but did not fully awaken me. This was not a dream. I was just starting to enter reality. It was essential for me to come to Fort Henry immediately, after my son contacted me. Talking to my son, he informed me that I had to go to Fort Henry at once or the Henry estate and all the family holdings could be lost. Our family could lose everything, it was up to me. I was to quit feeling sorry for myself because of the loss of my wife Jacquelyn and do my family duty, saving the family estate. I was ready and willing to protect the Henry name and the Henry estate.

My breakfast came, and I started to eat, I was well pleased, content. My world was shaken as someone burst into the restaurant. A loud boisterous voice was bellowing from the back of the restaurant. The chef Mike Rogers said to Sandra Martin, the owner of the restaurant "trouble just walked in the door." Sandra looked out the kitchen serving window with Mike and said, "Why does Butts insist on coming to my restaurant?"

Someone placed a hand on my shoulder and said, "This is my seat." Without looking up I picked up my plate and coffee and moved to the front left table near the wall. I continued my focus on eating. I did not hear the sneering remarks or laughter, for I was busy feeding my hunger. I'd almost finished eating and I was finding myself pleased and satisfied, but something was disturbing my peace. Why? Why? Reality struck as my ears started to hear. It came from the bag of wind. He was trying to disturb my breakfast. He was now trying to disturb my peace.

Mike Rogers the chef said, "There is going to be trouble, Butts is looking for someone to pick on." Sandra Martin, "He may find more trouble than he bargained for." Mike was looking at Sandra with a questioning expression.

I turned to see a mountain of a man and a little side-kick, obviously a hanger-on, standing over an older gentleman who was consumed with eating his breakfast. The old man eating his breakfast in peace was wearing a Vietnam hat.

My attention was focused on this bullying in action. My heart increased its beating. Something deep inside me was climbing to get out. I told myself this was none of my business. I was squeezing hard on my fork and turned away, but my body and mind forced me to turn back and watch this bullying encounter.

The bag of wind, a dominion of a bully, was standing over this Viet Vet, saying, "It is time for you to leave, you piece o' shit." The man sitting said something to the effect of "Forget you" or words to that effect. The would-be bully grabbed the vet's hat and threw it toward the door. The Vet was trying to stand up, but the overgrown bully pushed the veteran down.

Someone said, "Leave him alone" then the restaurant went still, as if we had moved into a different dimension. All stopped, all eyes turned. Why were they looking at me? Why? I said to myself, "Just finish your breakfast and go out in the clean fresh air. This is none of your business."

Mike Rogers the chef said to Sandra "Is that guy crazy? Does he know who he is messing with?"

Sandra Martin said, "It is Butts, who doesn't know who he is messing with."? Mike looked at Sandra questioningly.

The bully turned and smiled. Fresh blood, someone to play with. I was not in a playing mood. The bully jabbed his sidekick and pointed toward me; he was thinking about how he was going to enjoy this morning. The sidekick smiled with a mouth full of dirty teeth and a small laugh. The sidekick knew someone was going to get a beating. The sidekick was going to take pleasure in seeing pain inflicted and blood flowing. He had seen his buddy so often beat people up for no reason.

The sidekick was excited because his buddy was ready to do it again, to this old stupid man. This was a stupid old man, who did not have enough sense to keep his mouth shut. Jim was going to shut this old man's mouth; the little buddy could hardly wait.

"Should I do something about this jerk?" I said to myself, as he walked toward me. Again, I said to myself, "This is none of your business so keep out of it." The bully was approaching me. His intent was menacing. My mouth again spoke, "I don't want any trouble...you jerk." Once again, I was pouring gas on a fire. I would never learn.

I was tired but satisfied after finishing most of my breakfasts. Why? Why? Was my mouth doing this to me again? I had promised myself never, never again, but he was a Viet vet, a brother.

Chef Mike Roger said, "Maybe we should call the sheriff, Butts is going to kill that old man."

Sandra Martin: "That is not an old man, it's John Henry."

Chef Mike Roger said, "Who's John Henry?" Sandra Martin said, "He is Butts' worst nightmare."

The bully was hovering over me. Butts said to Sandra and Mike as they were watching through the serving window "What's your problem?"

Sandra replied, "Butts you best leave and take your little pain in the butt with you."

Butts said, "I will take care of you as soon as I finish with this old man. I'm going to teach him some manners." He placed his hand on my shoulder; this was a big mistake.

I said, "This is your lucky day... take your hand off my shoulder, apologize to my friend and leave this place in the next thirty seconds, no harm, no foul... or"

The bully with size twelve feet and a size four hat did not remove his hand from my shoulder but started to squeeze my shoulder. I grabbed his left thumb with my right hand pulling his hand down hard. His fingers exploded as they hit the edge of the table. I continued pulling his thumb until his jaw hit the table making a crunching sound. I was sure as his jaw hit the table that some of his teeth were being knocked loose. I kicked his left leg out from under him as I grabbed his farmer bib overalls with my right hand pulling his face down hard on the table again. My right hand continued to pull him down. With his head on the table this motion torqued his shoulder out of its joint.

I pushed my chair back and stood up. My elbow came down on the back of his neck, and again his face kissed the table. His left hand grabbed the table the best it could as he was trying to regain his balance. As his left arm straightened, I provided a powerful blow to the back of his straightened left arm. There was a sickening cracking sound. His left arm was broken. His mass ended on the floor next to me in pain. He was no longer a bully. On the floor he was squealing like a male pig after it had been castrated. It was easy to persuade the bully to get up; this took a little force and no menace.

After breaking three of his fingers, dislocating his shoulder, knocking a few teeth loose and breaking his arm, I helped the bully, whose name I found out later was Jim Butts, to his feet. I directed him to the door. Utilizing his bulky soft unconditioned body, I maneuvered him to the door and showed him out. His sidekick was also eager to exit the restaurant. I said to the two of them, "I am in town to stay, I never want to see the two of you in my town again." Looking outside I could see the chocolate lab raising her head, as if to say. What is going on.

The bully and his side kick slowly moved across the street to a rusty blue pickup truck. The side kick helped the dethroned bully into the passenger's side and then the side kick quickly ran around to the driver's side. They were gone in a cloud of black and dark-gray smoke. They were headed toward Carrollton, and probably to the hospital.

CHAPTER THREE

FRIDAY

The Chocolate Lab

I reentered the restaurant. To my surprise all the people were turned toward me with a flabbergasted look on their faces, as if to say, "What just happened?" I moved up the aisle to regain my seat to finish my coffee and the remnants of my breakfast. Someone approached me and said, "Way to go." I heard someone say this at a distance, but he was beside me. Turning to my right I saw the Viet vet standing there, again he said, "Way to go," with a smile on his face. I said, "Yes."

The Viet vet said, "Thank you, but he would not have hurt me."

"You are a brother; they should not mess with brothers. You are a Viet vet?"

The Vietnam Veteran said, "Yes, I am a Viet vet, and you know what they say about us: 'You don't step on Superman's cape, you don't piss into the wind, and you don't mess with a Viet vet,' but still."

"I know, I know. I overreacted." I was looking into the gray blue eyes of a man about fifty with graying hair. He was fit, and I could see with his physique and posture that he could handle the bully. His face was marked with lines that told of the hardship and experience he had lived.

"By the way, my name is Byron Keats, when were you in the Service?"

"A few years back, I am John Henry, pleased to meet you."

"Are you the John Henry of Ruth Henry?"

"Yes, Ruth Henry was my Granny." There was excitement in Byron's voice as his eyes brightened.

"You were in Vietnam?" Byron said questioningly, as if he already knew the answer.

"Yes, I was in Nam." I was answering a fellow veteran with respect.

Byron said, "And you have come back to live in the Henry house on Oak Street?"

"I guess so." I Looked at this Vietnam veteran wondering what he knew of the Henry house.

"We're neighbors, I live next door to the Henry house."

"Hello neighbor." I thought to myself that it would be good having a fellow veteran as a neighbor.

"Your grandmother was a remarkably close friend and she often spoke of you. She was worried for you the last couple of years before her death, something about you going off the deep end. I told her; you would be OK. I was sure you would find your way back." Byron said with compassion.

"Yes, I am mostly back. I'm sorry I missed my Granny's funeral."

"The whole town showed up, your grandmother was truly loved." This was even more troubling to me because I was not to attend the funeral.

He was named by his mother who loved Byron, Keats, and Shelley. Of course, Byron's middle name was Shelley. Byron's mother loved the three poets, so, her son was named after them,

Byron Shelley Keats.

Byron Keats: "I could see in your eyes as you turned toward Jim Butts that Jim had picked the wrong man. I had not seen that look since Vietnam. Your look told me you have seen some serious action. I have been looking forward to meeting you with all the stories your grandmother and the townspeople have told me about you. Well, I must get back to the homestead, but we need to talk. Your grandmother was a wonderful person. She did so much for me."

"Nice meeting you," I said as Byron slowly turned and left the restaurant.

The waitress came over to my table and freshened up my coffee. The coffee was full-bodied with an excellent bouquet. The waitress brought me a second breakfast. She was wearing an off-colored rose dress with a white apron. Her blond hair was in a ponytail, and she looked lovely.

She said, "Byron doesn't much talk to people; I'm surprised he was talking to you."

"Byron and I speak the same language." The waitress was standing across the table after she poured the coffee, as if to get my attention.

"John, you don't remember me?" I took a second look; the recognition was seeping into my brain. Many years ago, Sandra and I were in the same class, and we were friends, good friends. Sandra Martin was an important part of my life after the death of my sister Alice and my parents.

The electrons in my brain were firing on only two cylinders as I was energizing them up for the recognition from when I was young, incredibly young. Yes, I was vaguely remembering Sandra, when my family and I visited the Henry farm, Fort Henry, and my grandparents. The memory of Sandra came into focus. She was an important part of my life after my mother, father, and Alice my sister were gone. I needed a friend. I was eight. I remembered seeing Sandra off and on during the summer on my visits to town; she was dazzling. Her curly blonde hair was shining in the sun almost like a halo. One moment on a hot sunny day, she was the vision of my little sister Alice. I was not able to take my eyes off her. I looked for her every time I was in town.

School started in September. To my surprise Sandra was seated next to me in our third-grade class. Mrs. Sanderman was our teacher. I wondered if Mrs. Sanderman placed Sandra next to me to be nice or was it just fate? I daydreamed often which made me seem withdrawn and distant. I had no friends with me in school; Wobble, Boso, and Sally were not with me, and this made me sad and lonely. I was alone; I only had my daydreams to comfort me. Boso was a puppy my Granny gave to me a week before school started. Boso was so little, and he tried to follow me. As he followed me, he looked wobblier than Wobble.

Wobble was a lame young goose that followed me everywhere, for I had saved Wobble from the pack of domestic geese on the Henry farm. The geese were about to kill Wobble when I intervened. I explained to the geese that Wobble was my friend and the geese were to leave Wobble alone. After that Wobble would follow me everywhere. I was Wobble's friend, mother, protector, etc. Sally Kasey, who many called Poke Sally, was about ten years older than me; she came to live with Granny on the Henry farm a couple of years before I came to live with Granny. Sally was sad and alone, so she understood when I came to live with my grandparents that I, too, was sad and alone. Sally was always there. She was my friend and protector. Sally was always watching over me but never confining me.

For the first two weeks of school, I would ride the school bus to school and sit in my classroom seat all day, saying nothing. At recess and lunch, I would sit by myself. School was no fun. The school bus would drop me off at the farm after school and the day would start. I was with friends. They were waiting for me. Wobble and Boso were extremely excited to see me, and Sally would stick her head out to see if I was OK. I was alive and happy after school until bedtime. I was starting to hate bedtime for I would cry myself to sleep thinking of missing my little sister and that I would have to face another lonely day of school.

One day at lunch, I was sitting alone. This young, very pretty girl who sat next to me in class walked over and sat down beside me. She said, "I am Sandra Martin" I nodded and said nothing. She continued, "You are John Henry; you live on the Henry farm?" I still did not answer. I guess she knew my story and she said, "I would like to be your friend." I said nothing. She said, "Did you hear me; I want to be your friend."

I said, "OK" and from that day forward we were the best of friends. With Sandra sitting next to me in class and with us eating lunch together and playing during recess. School was great. I was up early and ready for school an hour before the school bus would arrive, school was exciting, I looked forward to school and going to school each day. Sandra was at school with her curly blonde hair that shined in the sun. She was my friend.

We were exceptionally good friends. I had a crush on Sandra since I was eight. She saw me as only a friend.

Coming out of my memories of the past, as my recognition of Sandra Martin reached my conscious mind I said. "Sandra, it has been a long time. Great to see you."

Sandra Martin: "John it is good to see you again, I'm sorry about your grandmother passing. She was such a dear woman, and she was always good to me. I'm busy right now, but if you are going to be around town for a while, we need to talk."

"Thank you, I'm home for good, and I would love to talk with you, any time." I said, as Sandra turned and headed for the kitchen. She was as beautiful today as she was over thirty years ago.

She paused at the kitchen door, talking to herself "I wonder where my niece Jean is, she should have been here by now."

I was working on the second breakfast Sandra served me. It was delicious, I truly needed this second serving, not for the food, but the time. It was as if Sandra knew that I desired time to slow my heartbeat and regain my calm. Once my composure was obtained and most of the second breakfast consumed, it was time for me to leave the restaurant and find the Henry house on Oak Street. I took a napkin and wiped the blood left by the would be bully when he so graciously kissed the table. It was the least I could do for Sandra since she had been so exceptionally kind in providing me with a second breakfast and time.

I slowly stood up from the table taking with me some toast and a few pieces of bacon. I headed for the cash register. The cash register was an old-fashioned register gilded in bronze ornamentation. Sandra rang up the exceptionally large breakfast for $3.00. It was a true bargain, so I gave her a ten-dollar bill and did not ask for change. Outside, I stopped. I took in a deep breath of fresh air. I was in control. I moved over to a bench at the edge of the high curve leading to the road. The cement sidewalks on both sides of the street were about eighteen inches high with steps conveniently placed to step down to the road.

I was going to call the chocolate Labrador retriever. Looking down she was by my side. The chocolate Labrador was healthy and well-kept; surely the dog belonged to someone in the restaurant.

CHAPTER FOUR

FRIDAY

Fort Henry is My Home

I t was becoming a hospitable and bright day. The rain and fog were gone.

The pleasant warm sun was upon my face. I bent down to feed the chocolate Labrador the bacon and toast I obtained from the restaurant. The chocolate Labrador retriever was most appreciative. This was, thankfully, a friendly dog. Looking around the town I observed a hardware store across the street. I'd spent many hours in the hardware store, just looking. I was fascinated by so many items the hardware store carried: fishing rods, lures, knives, BB guns, and tools. Hours and hours of looking and looking. These were wonderful memories. The old general store down the street was closed. The building was boarded up and in sad disrepair. The general store was where most of my clothes came from when I was young.

During the summer, the town provided free movies in the field behind the general store on Friday and Saturday nights. It was a real treat. There were two bars one on each side of the street, an antique shop, a small grocery, a bank, the post office, the city hall, the fire station, a gas station at the far end of the street on the right, a variety store, a hotel, a discount store and on and on. Though the town had changed over the years in many ways, it was the same through my eyes dusted with memories. I came to town often in my youth, for it was only a two-mile walk from the Henry farm. The elementary school was in town just about a half a mile east of downtown and the school bus would drop me off in front of the Henry farm. The high school was about halfway between the farm and town. I usually walked to the high school because I was involved in many after school activities and sports.

The town's name Fort Henry was born out of a fort built in 1763 called Fort Hutchins after Bretish General William Hutchins. This fort was acquired by Great Bretain from France following the 1763 Treaty of Paris. United States claimed this region after the 1783 Treaty of Paris that ended the American Revolutionary War. John Anthony Henry a Major during the Revolutionary War, for his valiant efforts during the American Revolutionary War was granted twenty-two thousand acres of land including Fort Hutchins. Major John Anthony Henry was to use

Fort Hutchins as his base of operations and headquarters when he moved to this region.

Fort Hutchins was changed to Fort Henry. This happened once Major John Anthony Henry was established in the region. He named the fort after himself. From what people have told me. It was not much of a fort, just an earth mound, which still exists and a few wooden buildings, now gone. Fort Henry was rebuilt in the fashion of a frontier fort in the 1920's to encourage visitors to visit Fort Henry. The earth mount, the frontier fort and the Memorial Park of Fort Henry are located a few blocks from the downtown area. There is a statue of Major John Anthony Henry proudly shadowing the remains of Fort Henry near the earth mount and the pavilion in John Anthony Henry Memorial Park of Fort Henry.

One interesting note about Major John Anthony Henry: he loved red oak trees. He planted many red oaks on his vast land. Some of these red oak trees are still standing today. I believe the oak tree that caught me and kept me from going to heaven was planted by my great many times grandfather Major John Anthony Henry. This thought was comforting to me, that my great-many-times grandfather planted the seed that not only was the lineage to my ancestry but also my angel who caught me and kept me from falling.

The slight history of this little-known fort is more folklore than fact. There were some amazing stories as a boy, and I would enjoy listening to each story. One story was of how Fort Henry helped win the American Revolutionary War with nineteen backwoods men holding off seven hundred British soldiers and Indians. I believe the truer story was that three farmers traded a pig and two chickens with the British for a parcel of land. Defeating seven hundred soldiers and Indians was a far more imaginary and stimulating story to a young boy.

My Granny Ruth was proud of Fort Henry because every visitor to our town and the Henry farm would be taken on a tour of Fort Henry, the earth mount fort, and John Anthony Henry Memorial Park of Fort Henry. She would spend an hour or so giving a detailed history of Fort Henry and its importance in American history, of course including the importance her husband's family played. Granny was always telling visitors that one day, Fort Henry would be restored at the earth mound to its original state per a drawing from 1816. I am not sure the drawing is accurate, because Major John Anthony Henry died in 1811.

I guess it was now my turn to take visitors, show them John Anthony Henry Memorial Park of Fort Henry and tell them the wondrous history and importance of Fort Henry. I guess it is my responsibility to take over for my Granny and provide the color and history of Fort Henry to all who would listen. This is my home. Now it is time I start bragging about Fort Henry and the history of my family. *What are some good fabricated and fascinating stories I could manufacture about the history of Fort Henry? I wondered?* The Labrador retriever was looking at me as if I was demented. I said to the chocolate lab "It is OK, if I brag a little about Fort Henry?" I waited for her reply; she was silent.

The next large town to Fort Henry was Carrollton. My grandparents and I only traveled to Carrollton once a week at best. Going to Carrollton about twelve miles away was a great adventure. I would look forward to going to Carrollton all week, saving up the few pennies I could gather, with the anticipation of some magnificent, and fantastic purchases. The expectation was exhilarating. Carrollton had a five and ten cent store with an overwhelming assortment of merchandise for a young man to gaze upon. Granny would always give me a nickel or dime to match my few pennies, so I could spend an hour or more making a precious selection. Yes, these memories of great adventures filled my mind, and I was pleased.

I started to walk east on Henry Way to revisit my memories. Beside me was the chocolate Labrador, walking step for step as if we had always walked together. A couple of older gentlemen were sitting on a bench outside O'Day's Bar. I am not sure if they were enjoying the morning sun or waiting for the bar to open. I said, "Good morning." They were nice enough to nod as if they recognized me. The Labrador and I continued our walk saying good morning to the few people we met. It was like I was eleven again. What great adventures were we going to encounter as the

Labrador, and I strutted up the avenue. We passed Mel's grocery store and the Fort Henry Bank, and across the street was Henry Hotel and Bar. The Henry Hotel and Bar had a tarnished history of being the only place in the county to serve liquor during the prohibition. It has been said that President Roosevelt that is Teddy stayed here one night on his way to Yellowstone. Many stories are told about Fort Henry, some exceedingly questionable.

There was an antique store, on this side of the street. I was here about three years ago for a quick visit, but I spent little time downtown. Fort Henry was my world of adventures over thirty-five years ago. Now I felt young again walking around the town with this chocolate Labrador by my side. The gas station owned by Kirt McKennon on the other side of the street was where I would play the pinball machine in the back room when no one was paying attention. It was fun. I used to rack up many free games on that machine. The fire station and the granary grain elevators were a little further up the road. The granary is where we would bring our corn, beans, and wheat during harvest so many grand memories. I could almost smell the wheat pouring from the back of our truck as it drained into the floor of the granary.

The chocolate Labrador and I wandered the town for about an hour, my memories and reality intermixing. Was it today or thirty-five years ago? The chocolate Labrador and I returned to Sandy's Café, and I was admiring the town from the front of the café when someone or something had forced me from my memories, pushing me into reality just when I was enjoying my youth again. I heard a female say, "Leave me alone."

CHAPTER FIVE

FRIDAY

A Trio of Trouble

Standing on the sidewalk outside of Sandy's Café, looking into a hazy reality, I saw her standing behind a red Ford pickup. She was trying to retrieve something from the back of the truck. Her strawberry hair was shimmering in the sun. A young incredibly attractive girl wearing cutoff jeans and a pink blouse was in a quandary. The vision was frozen in time and place. Was I seeing Alice, my little sister? But this girl was grown. My mind, my memories, this town, I was now seeing what I wanted to see. Reality slapped me in the face. This was not Alice my little sister, but a young girl calling out for help as Alice did when she was five when a rowdy bunch of kids were harassing her. Three creepy guys were giving this beautiful young girl a tough time.

The young girl said, "Leave me alone." The three boys were laughing and having a good old time. They were inflicting unpleasant anguish upon this attractive young lady. They were playing grab ass with her. She was not a willing participant nor was she enjoying the game at all. I could tell this was not the first time these clowns had harassed this young lady. If I had my way, this would be the last time. No longer able to protect my little sister, I could damn well protect this radiant young lady who rekindled the memory of my little sister.

I said to myself. "Don't do it" but I never was a good listener. Something inside of me was erupting. In a very polite fashion, I said, "Leave Jean alone." My guess was that this young girl was Jean, the girl Sandra Martin was talking about in the restaurant. I found out later that Jean was Sandra's niece, and she was on early release from school.

These were not boys, but well-developed young men nineteen to twenty-two or so. They were dressed in what seemed like dirty clothes, a kind of cowboy look but with baseball hats facing the wrong direction. All three were wearing jeans. One had on an orange plaid shirt. The other two were wearing blue jean shirts. My request was gaining their attention. They did not seem so happy at my suggestion. The first indication my proposal was not taken well was when one man said, "Old man get lost." Another guy said, "Let us teach this old fart a lesson." At least my outburst took their concentration away from the girl. Their total focus now was on me. Part of their bold behavior was gained from the beers and shots they had consumed.

Looking at these three despicable characters troubling this young attractive strawberry blond female my mind was flashing back to the kids picking on Alice, my little sister. I saved my little sister of five from the kids pestering her. I told my sister I would always be there to protect her. My sister died, and I was not there to protect her. This young girl across the street was the image in my mind of what Alice would look like now if she had lived.

The three poorly behaved young men interest was moving little further from the girl, and they started focusing in on me. Pouring a little gas on the fire, as I said, "If you want to grow another day older, you'll leave the girl alone." Their awareness of me was changing from curiosity to action. They strolled across the street in a column of pure contempt. They were laughing and smiling as they came. They were in town to drink, have fun and cause trouble. Jean could wait, as they chose me for their current pleasure.

The entertainment and excitement they were looking for was across the street from them. I was to be their three-ring circus of amusement for the day. They looked at me as if I were a cool refreshing watermelon on an extremely hot day. They planned to smash this watermelon and enjoy its pieces. I stepped down from the high curve to greet this approaching trio with no consideration of menace. I did not believe this was going to be a cordial reception. The chocolate Labrador was beside me, standing her ground, ready for action.

It was not my intent to cause trouble only to interject a moment of civility. Civility is a word these despondent lowlife creatures would surely not understand. It was my desire to rescue this fair maiden without causing a confrontation. I knew I was deluding myself into thinking that my few words of distraction would cause these bumbling reprobates of humanity from discontinuing their harassment of this young girl without a price.

To my surprise their attention quickly moved from this young girl in distress. This was not my true intention, but it did get results. I could tell these three upstanding citizens had been drinking by their conduct. It was early in the day, yet they showed signs of an alcoholic stupor. Because of their alcoholic state I felt it would be easy to distract this trio of trouble from the young lady, however I had not thoroughly thought through the consequences of gaining their attention. They seemed to first huddle as if they were devising a football play, I had a feeling I was to be the pig skin in a one-sided game.

This assembly of a masculine courageous trio was enhanced by their morning consumption of beers and a shot or three of Jack Daniels. They were moving toward me. They came at me not in a single file but in discombobulated motions of three overgrown boys who were under the influence of spirits. They were loud, vulgar, and amused by themselves. I was in a state of pure contentment being home. I felt no compulsion to enter a physical altercation with these unmannered low lives. I prided myself on avoiding conflict; it was not an intelligible way of solving problems. They approached. My desire of entering an enlighten conversation on the proper social graces and behavior with young females was not a tactic I believed would be well received.

The two who looked like brothers came at me slowly with blood in their eyes. The only weapons they possessed were four clenched fists. They stood aside making room in the center for the third dressed in orange plaid shirt. He was a bit older, a rough looking guy. He was coming at me with a knife. He was far more dangerous. In his hand was a knife with a six-inch blade, more than I wanted. I hate knives, but that is another story. He came dancing slowly side to side, with the knife constantly moving. This was something he had done before. I could feel the guy on my left side was ready to attack. This was a no-win situation. If I turned to face the guy at my left, the guy with the knife would stab me. If I continued to face the guy with the knife, the guy at my right would jump me. This action would result in the guy with the knife stabbing me. I could feel the knife piercing my stomach and I did not desire another knife scar.

Just then I felt the chocolate Labrador by my left side. She growled. She was ready to take on the guy to my left.

If the dog attacked the guy to my left this would provide me with the option of taking down the guy on my right, then the one in the center.

As luck would have it, the guy with the knife in the center of the two brothers said, "Who the hell do you think you are?"

"I'm John Henry and this is my town." As quickly as my name was said all the fight when out of the three. At that moment, I could tell there was to be no fight. Why I did not know, but I was thankful.

The one with the knife to save face said, "This was none of your business and it is nothing to die over." I said nothing. I was just wondering why there was such a change in their despicable behavior. The guy with the knife said, "You stay out of our way, if you know what is good for you." The guy with the knife put the knife away, tapped each of the two and spoke. "Let's go we don't need any more trouble."

The three of them were staggering across the street to a dark-blue pickup. They were gone as soon as they were able to get all three of them in the pickup. A crowd gathered in wonderment of what was going on. I looked down and the chocolate Labrador was by my side. I said, "Thanks. I could not have done it without you."

I looked up at Sandra and Jean standing together at the entrance of the restaurant and I said, "Whose dog is this?"

Sandra replied, "It looks like yours."

"What is her name?" I said looking down at this beautiful dog.

Sandra Martin: "I'm not sure the dog has a name. She has been hanging around town for a couple of weeks."

In appreciation I said to Sandra, "She is a great dog. She helped save my life."

Sandra Martin: "Jean, I want you to meet John Henry. Many years ago. John and I went to school together, when he used to live with his grandparents."

Jean Jefferson, "Sandy, my aunt has told me about you, and I guess the stories are true."

"Hopefully just the good ones. Well, I guess it is time for me to go to my Granny's house before I find any more trouble. Good seeing you again, Sandra. Nice to meet you, Jean." I said with the sun in my eyes from the reflection of a store window.

I started to cross the street to my car, I heard Jean say, "I wish the Grimm boys would leave me alone."

"Don't worry they will not trouble you anymore," Sandra Martin said with reassurance.

"Why?" Jean questioned her aunt.

"Because John Henry is back in town" Sandra Martin said with a smile.

I opened the car door. There was something pushing against my leg. It was the chocolate Labrador. I said, "Get in" and without hesitation the chocolate lab jumped into the front seat to the passenger's side.

Beer, a dog, and luck had saved the day for me. I was lucky. The fight would have been one sided because of the beer the trio had drunk, and the chocolate Labrador had been ready to attack one of the guys. This was a reminder to mind my own business because luck should only be pushed so far. I'm not as tough as I think I am. In fact, I am more stupid than tough. This adventure of saving damsels in distress was happening way too often. I was thinking slaying dragons would be less adventurous and dangerous for me to pursue. The main reason was there being incredibly few dragons, at least I have not met any this year and there are way too many damsels in distress.

Peace and quiet was what I desired as the dog, and I drove toward Granny's house. How much has Fort Henry changed, the town I remember as a peaceful, loving, and friendly town?

CHAPTER SIX

FRIDAY

Granny Ruth's House

I had been on this main street called Henry Way many times when I was young, but then I was usu-ally walking. Now driving, everything seemed different, distant movie like, not real. My Granny's house, I guess, now mine, was just two short blocks from downtown and, a right on Oak Street. The house sat at the end of Oak Street on the left side or as the farmers would say the east side. There were only nine houses on the street, five on the left, the east side of the street and four on the west side. There was plenty of space between the houses and all the neighbors knew each other.

Some of the neighbors have lived on this street since I was a child. As I approached the house, I remembered the house as larger; it was a two-story house built by my great-grandfather around 1900 to 1905. It was white with grey trim, and it looked like an overgrown Victorian style house. There was an exceptionally large semi-circle drive to the south of the house with many large red oak trees in the center of the semi-circle. My newfound friend Lady and I pulled into the semi-circle drive, and I stopped. A flow of memories grasped me sending me back into my youth.

My great-grandmother's house was the largest house in town and the most expensive of its day. The house stood on six acres of land; it was impressive. On the outside was a porch running the whole width of the front of the house. I remember there were eight rocking chairs and a three-person swing hanging from the porch ceiling. The front porch was the social center of the neighborhood during the summer. There were warm memories rushing over me as I looked through the open car window, gazing at the Henry house.

An addition to the rear of the house was added by my great-grandfather about fifty years ago. This was at the request of his wife. The addition included a kitchen, a large pantry, a small bedroom, an indoor full bathroom, and indoor plumbing. It was the wonder of the day. On the south side of the addition was a porch, large enough for two chairs and two rocking chairs. My great-grandmother was known to exit the kitchen and step onto the porch when the kitchen was too hot. My great-grandmother cooked on a wood stove and on sizzling summer days the kitchen was like a furnace.

The downstairs had been remodeled sometime later, a full bathroom and a decent sized bedroom were added. The addition was for convenience but did not take away from the size of the dining room, the parlor, or the living room. The house was huge.

The upstairs was remodeled about sixteen years ago around the time my Granny and grandfather moved into this house. The six original bedrooms were converted to five bedrooms and a full-size common bathroom. One bedroom was made into a master suite including its own full bathroom and a walk-in closet. Closets were not part of the original house, so a closet was a big deal, at least to my Granny. Grandfather Jason was to remodel the bedroom and bathroom off the kitchen. This bedroom was convenient after my Grandfather Jason passed, as

the bedroom provided convenience and comfort for my Granny.

The original house was built with no running water and without indoor facilities. The old kitchen had a well water hand pump by the sink; it was the only indoor running water. There were two outhouses to the back of the main house, one for men and the other for women. When I came to visit this house as a boy the outhouses were still standing.

I decided it was going to take some time to make this house my home. I was here to stay. This house and the surrounding property were to become home in time.

I was not sure how long I sat in the car looking into my memories. The chocolate Labrador nudged me, and reality awakened me as if the blanket of memories was lifted.

"Yes, we are home" I said to the chocolate Labrador as she looked up at me questioningly. I said, "What is your name?"

The dog turned her head "I must call you something. You are a beautiful Lady" again the dog cocked her head.

"Yes, Lady, is that your name?" The dog sat up and gave a low groan and a soft bark. "Yes, Lady it is."

Lady, and I exited the car and headed to the side porch. The porch was about eight feet by sixteen feet with two rocking chairs on the right side of the door. The porch was located on the rear south side of the house. The porch floor was newly painted a light gray color. The house seemed well taken care of by someone. Lady was at the kitchen door, sitting waiting while I looked around the yard from the porch. The memories were flowing again like a waterfall. I could see the past that was so vivid, so enjoyable, and so real. I could almost taste the watermelon from summers' past, smell my great-grandmother Bertha's cooking from the kitchen and hear my Granny Ruth humming.

I did not live in this house, only visited. The Henry farmhouse about two miles from town is where I grew up from the age of eight until I left for college. My life with my grandparents was wonderful for they nourished and loved me after my parents and my little sister died. They did everything in their power to fill the void of missing my parents and little sister. Even with all their love and compassion, I cried myself to sleep most nights. A bark from Lady, pulled me from my warm daydreams. She was sitting at the door waiting. I said, "Waiting for me?" Lady was looking at me as if to say "Yes."

I did not have a key; I was wondering how to enter the house. I tried the kitchen door, it was unlocked. Unlocked doors were a way of life when I was young, but why now? I stepped in; the house smelled great as if it had just been cleaned. Granny Ruth had passed only a couple months ago; I was told she lived in this house to the end. I was wondering if she kept the house closed-up when she lived here. Not my Granny, I thought to myself. The house would have been open and welcoming.

Looking around the kitchen I was delighted to see my great-grandmother Bertha's wood stove. I remember my great-grandmother in her nineties cooking on this wood stove. She would fire up the stove at about four-thirty in the morning and keep it going all day and into the night, no matter how cold or hot the weather. I was wondering if I could cook on this stove or even get a fire started. My Granny Ruth was a bit more modern; Granny had an electric stove, refrigerator, and indoor running water.

The meals my great-grandmother would prepare on her wood stove on many warm Sundays after church brought a wonderous taste to my mouth. These were fond recollections. In the summer, we would set up tables and chairs outdoors on the lawn on the great semi-circle drive for Sunday dinner. When I was old enough to do more than just gather eggs, I would catch a hen or two on Saturday night and place them in a coop. On Sunday morning before church, I would kill the hens, clean, and pluck them and ready them for dinner. My grandparents and I would deliver the prepared chicken to my great-grandmother's house as we picked her up on our way to church. She would prepare the chickens after church for Sunday dinner.

The Henry house's lower floor was the way I remembered it when my great-grandmother Bertha Henry lived here. I walked through each room taking inventory of my memories. There was a mixture of extraordinarily strong emotions, both sad and happy. My great-grandmother Bertha Henry was delighted with every inch of this house. In the living room was a painting my great-grandmother Bertha would gleam with pride for as she showed each item to guests visiting Henry house. She would take me to this painting and say, "This is our history."

My great-grandmother Bertha married into the Henry family, and she became more Henry than the Henry's. She was prideful of the Henry name, family, history, and town. One Sunday afternoon when we were all visiting the Henry house. I was about twelve and my great-grandmother Bertha took me to this painting and told me a story about Major John Anthony Henry, whom I was named after. She said he was a great and courageous warrior, before, during and after the American Revolutionary War.

He was a kind and noble man with immense concern for his fellow men, women, and children. He was forced to fight in many Indian wars trying to bring peace to this land. He was not fighting against the Indians, but for his people and the friendly Indians. He was a part of George Washington's Civilization Plan. The plan believed the Indians were equal and the Indians should be given equal rights. He understood the fate of the Indian society; it was a downhill slope. If they continue to fight with the white man, they were doomed. Major John Anthony Henry's efforts were a "civilizing" process to share with the Indians the many advantages he possessed.

After Major John Anthony Henry settled in Pike County and renamed Fort Hutchins to Fort Henry, he was to marry Oklane. Oklane was a half Shawnee Indian. She had blue eyes and deep blond hair. My great-grandmother believed Oklane meant "blue" or blue sky in the Shawnee language. My great-grandmother said she believed Oklane was a relative of Chief Blackfish and because of her relation to Chief Blackfish Fort Henry and Pike County were safe.

They had three children; Great-grandmother Bertha said you are a descendant of John Anthony and Oklane Henry. Oklane was to change her name to Anne. The name change made it easier for the people in the settlement to accept her. The Indian nations were always welcome in Fort

Henry. She said something happened in the late 1700's and early 1800's. The Shawnee Indians was move to Oklahoma in about 1830. She was not sure why. Great-grandmother suggested it was important sometime during my life that I travel to Oklahoma and search out information about Oklane and my people. Two years ago, I was in Oklahoma, but that is another story.

The chocolate lab was becoming impatient with my lapses into memories, as she sat next to me waiting for me to reenter reality.

I was incredibly pleased to see my Granny's China displayed in a glass cabinet in the kitchen. My Granny was not much into material items. Almost all her possessions had utility written all over them electric stove, sewing machine, washer, dryer, tables, and chairs. A few items with little or no utility gave her immense pleasure. Her China cabinet with her cups and saucers was most treasured. These were a very few of her remaining treasures, the glass cabinet with her fine China cups and saucers and her white oak kitchen table. Granny was to lose most of her precious treasures in a tornado sixteen years ago. The tornado hit and destroyed almost everything at the Henry farm; the Henry farm was located two miles outside of Fort Henry. The precious items were handed down from her mother, grandmother, and great-grandmother. Her most treasured possession she had brought with her when she married my grandfather and came to Fort Henry. Many of these valued items were lost due to the tornado sixteen years ago. I know the loss was a heartbreak to my Granny Ruth, but she never complained of the loss. Granny Ruth was an extraordinarily strong courageous woman.

Granny Ruth was married to my grandfather Jason. They met during the Henry family vacation outing on the white sands of Lake Michigan. Granny at the time was living in Holland Michigan. She was sixteen years of age. Granny was with some friends on the beach of Lake Michigan enjoying a warm summer day, when her eye caught a glimpse of my grandfather fishing in the surf. She told me it was a fine statue of a man, the best she had ever seen, so she walked down to the edge of the water where grandfather was fishing, and she said to him "Catching anything?" His response; "Nothing yet."

Granny said, "Would you mind showing me how to fish? I would like to catch something." He showed her how to fish and they spent the afternoon fishing. Granny would say "Grandfather did not know it but I caught a big one." They exchanged addresses and corresponded over the next year; it was the start of something beautiful.

The next summer the Henry family was on their family outing on the shores of Lake Michigan and Granny was there with her mother and father. By the end of the week Granny and Grandfather were engaged. They were married the next summer on an extremely hot day in a little church in Holland Michigan. Granny Ruth moved to Fort Henry and the Henry farm. She was happy, for she not only caught the big one, but she also reeled him in.

My Granny only stood about five feet tall; she was a tower of strength, strength that I was leaning on often after the loss of my parents and little sister. What I am today comes from the strength and love of my Granny Ruth. She was the heartbeat of my life. When I was young after the loss of my family, I did not know how to go on, how to live. My heart was empty. Granny Ruth filled my empty heart with love and smiles.

Granny Ruth took me in her arms of love when my parents and sister were killed. She raised me as her son. She never wavered as she raised me. She embraced it as a gift. I know the hurt, the devastation of losing her son and granddaughter ripped her soul apart, but she never showed tears, only smiles. It was as if Granny Ruth knew something or someone that gave her a greater inner strength. My Grandfather Jason became my father. He taught me many wondrous things: how to fish, hunt, track, shoot, and farm; carpentry; masonry; how to repair almost anything; and on and on. The most important of his teaching, was he taught me how to become a man what it is meant to be a man and the importance of knowing right from wrong.

I will always miss my parents and my little sister, always. The love and caring of my grandparents smoothed the deep despair of my loss and filled my body with nourishment and my soul with love. I was, and still am, an incredibly lucky boy.

I was only seven and my little sister was five when some older neighborhood kids were picking on my little sister. I fought those boys picking on my sister like I was possessed. They all ran in fear from that crazy boy. I promised my sister I would always be there to protect her. She died; I was not there to protect her. I was not there for my sister. I would cry myself to sleep for letting her down, it was my fault.

Lady was by my side. She groaned and put her right paw up in a waving action. "Yes, you must be hungry, but there is no food here. Off to the store." Lady was out the door and standing by the car before I could get off the side porch. I was starting to wonder. How smart is this dog?

At the store Lady carefully selected her food. I chose a toy or two for Lady and lunch meat, cereal, bread, milk, and beer for me. On returning to the Henry house there was a car parked in the circle drive. Entering the kitchen Sandra Martin was sitting at my Granny Ruth's white oak table with a smile on her face.

"Hello Sandra," Lady and I greeted Sandra with pleasure. Her hospitality was welcomed.

"It's Sandy; no one calls me Sandra anymore," Sandra said firmly.

"You will always be Sandra, my best friend." For I have known Sandra Martin since the third grade. Her name was and is Sandra. Sandra had grown into an incredibly attractive lady. She was dazzling.

"I thought you could use some food, but I see you went shopping." There were containers of food she had placed on the table.

"Yes, Lady was hungry so I when to the store to buy some dog food." Looking at the food Sandra had brought, I said "Thank you Sandra, you are very thoughtful, and especially after the commotion I caused in town. You know I am not usually so much trouble."

Sandra Martin. "You forget. I knew you well, years ago and you were always a commotion in motion. You were always up to some kind of mischief. You were in the school office so many times they were going to start charging you rent.

"Come on Sandra, I wasn't that bad."

"It is good to have you back and I hope you are here to stay. Now come, give me a hug."

"Thank you for caring, the food and your friendship is appreciated."

Sandra hugged me as if we had not seen each other for years. Sandra spoke. "You can thank Mary, Susan, Cheryl-Ann, Sally, Byron and me for preparing the place for you. We were hoping that you were coming home." The names were overwhelming, but they could not be the same, as, my protector, my neighbor, my first love, my adopted sister, and my ex-wife.

"Thanks, I will have to have a party and thank all of you for your help," hoping these were just friends of Sandra.

Sandra Martin: "You remember Mary and Susan; we all went to school together. Talking about together, CherylAnn is here, she has been here for a couple of years. Well, I must get back to the Café Sandra headed out the door and back to her restaurant, saying, "See you later."

As she reached the door, I said, "I am going to find a bed and sleep for a couple of hours." But how could I sleep with Mary and CherylAnn in town? With all this on my mind, this was becoming more than I could take. This was a wild homecoming. It was turning out to be more like a kaleidoscope of emotions.

Lady ate the food she had selected at the store, and I ate the food Sandra so graciously delivered. It was a great late lunch. After lunch, Lady and I climbed the stairs to the second floor, and we entered the master bedroom. It was enticing. The bed was comfortable and without removing the blankets or my clothes, I laid on the bed.

Sleep was welcomed. I awoke and checked my watch; it was 3:47 p.m. It was time to get up. I swung my legs off the bed to the floor, and almost stepped on Lady. "Good girl, I guess we should get moving." I went through the house checking out all the rooms, closets, drawers, etc., taking inventory of the house and my memories. They were both in good order. The house was full of furniture; beds, chairs, tables, rugs, everything. The kitchen had a refrigerator, stove, microwave, and table and of course my great-grandmother's wood burning stove. All the appliances seemed to be in good working order.

I was awestruck at the notion that this could be the cleaning and preparation of Mary, Susan, CherylAnn, Sally, Byron, and Sandra, my new guardian angels. Outside the house with Lady, we checked out each side of the house. Thanks to doing a few flips in my time, I knew what I was looking for as I inspected the outside of the house. The house and windows had been painted in the last couple of years. The house, though old, was in good shape. The roof and chimney were good. The foundation showed no major cracks. The yard had been cut recently. Yes, the house was in incredibly good shape for being about ninety years old.

Next to the garden. Wow, it was excellent. No weeds and a vast variety of vegetables growing nicely. Now to the outbuildings. There were five outbuildings: a decent sized barn, a two-car garage and three outbuildings. They all seemed to be in good order, but they all needed some TLC. Some projects were taking shape for the summer. Yes, a fruit cellar or tornado shelter was in the middle of the semi-circle drive. The doors to the fruit cellar were in bad shape, needing replacement, but the stairs going down looked good. I stopped at the top looking down, but without a light I could go no further.

Back at the house, Lady and I were searching for a flashlight or a candle. In the kitchen, I quickly found a candle and some matches, and went back to the fruit cellar. Lighting up the candle halfway down the stairs, the light also lit up memories, as I moved further down the stairs. Yes, I was here now or was it thirty years ago? It was like my Granny was here holding my hand leading me down these stairs. There was nothing here, only empty shelves, and my memories filling the cellar's earth walls. Back in the daylight Lady was waiting. Her face was questioning where I had been, but quickly changed to a smile. I asked myself "Can a dog smile?" but I swear Lady was smiling.

The outbuildings would have to wait for another day or two to determine their shape. It was about 5:40 p.m. when I decided to walk downtown with my mind wondering what Sandra said. Lady was by my side. I was not sure if I was going to take care of Lady or if Lady was going to take care of me. A warm feeling was filling my body as I looked down at Lady. It had been a long time since someone or something had cared so much about me. I knew Lady was by my side, just as Boso had been in my childhood, and a great comfort came over me. There was no leash on Lady. She was free to come and go. It was her decision to walk next to me step for step on our way to town.

Lady and I were walking toward town with a sense of mystery of what adventures waited. Our legs needed stretching, so we walked all over town. Fort Henry is not a large metropolis. There are neither traffic lights nor even a stop sign on Henry Way, the main street through town.

A quick walk could take you from the eastern edge of town to the western most part of town in twenty minutes. It took us over an hour. I was moving slowly. I was eight years old again pulling a small wagon filled with a heavy load of memories. A few people stopped to say hello. The pleasantries were neighborly and cordial.

Lady and I returned to the Henry house at dust. We were refreshed and ready for a late dinner and bed. We were both looking forward to tomorrow.

CHAPTER SEVEN

Byron Shelley Keats

I t was a quarter to seven in the morning when Lady and I started to walk downtown. We made little progress for the house next to us sat a man on the front porch. It was Byron Keats. We stopped and talked for a few minutes. Bryon was a good friend of my Granny Ruth. He was a great help to my Granny Ruth, for example he would drive her to Carrollton to shop and visit her doctor. Byron Keats was a Vietnam veteran. He was drafted into the Army when he was in his twenties. Byron had served most of his time in the northern most region of South Vietnam, called I Corp. His Vietnam cap was showing front and center a red diamond. All those who had served in the Army, especially Vietnam, knew the red diamond was a unit that served well and saw its' share of action. Looking at Byron's face, it was marked with the deep crevices of a man who had lived a full and hard life. His gray blue eyes were soft like a small child's eyes. I could see in an instant the warmth and compassion my Granny Ruth saw in Byron's eyes.

Byron took some time to share with me his personal history. He was twenty-two when he was drafted. He was married at the time, and they had no children. After the Army he finished college, but working, going to college, and trying to make his marriage work was not a formula for saving his marriage. They were married one year before he was drafted. He loved her deeply. Looking back now, he felt she was in the marriage for security and social acceptance. Marriage was the thing you did back then because everyone got married. Byron on returning from Vietnam had the feeling his wife did not love him and he wondered if she ever did. Byron's time in the Army, especially Vietnam gave his wife time to grow up and grow away from Byron. She no longer wanted or needed to be married. It was nothing personal about Byron. After four years out of the Army Byron was a single man. He did not fit in anywhere, he was lost. His marriage failed, and failure was a way of life. Going from job to job, town to town, even being homeless from time to time, his life was crumbling.

Byron's short story filled with heart ache, despair and disillusionment is a common story of men returning from Vietnam.

"John you were in the service. What branch?" Byron asked.

"Army." I said with pride.

Byron Keats said, "I was drafted at twenty-two. You know I was perfectly happy on the outside, not in the Army. They explained to me that they could not fight successfully in Vietnam without me. I wished that I'd never heard of Vietnam, the death, the heat, the cold, the wet, the dry, the sand, the jungle, the rice paddies, the sweat, and the boredom when they were not shooting at you."

I said, "I understand."

"I know the coldness; I have never been so cold in my life as the fifth degrees during the monsoon, the monsoon which lasted for over three months it rained so hard, it was difficult to get your breath. Everything was wet, wet to the skin, Yes, John, I have a deep dislike for Vietnam." I thought to myself. Why on earth were we ever in Vietnam?

Byron Keats continued: "There were some electrifying moments in the Army before Vietnam. My first week in the Army I was assigned to basic training in Fort Knox. We were housed in some World War II barracks. These barracks were not only old and dirty, but nothing worked. We had five barracks in our company but only four drill sergeants, so guess what they did? Very unwisely they assigned me to oversee the fifth barracks. It was called the 'Mixed Barrack.' There I was, four days in the Army and in charge of the 'Mixed Barrack.' It would not be so bad, but about forty-seven guys came with the barracks. Do you believe it, forty-seven guys and me in charge?" Byron was happy to talk to someone who understood.

"That's the Army for you," I agreed with Byron.

Byron Keats: "We arrived in the "Mixed Barracks" late the first night. It took three hours getting our clothing, gear, and bedding. Our first duty was making our beds, sleep came about two in the morning. The Army was nice enough to wake us at five in the morning. We drilled all day until about eight o'clock that night. Sleep was going to be welcomed, but of course the Army had other ideas. I did tell you about the barracks being old and dirty; the Army does not like old and dirty and our barracks was the dirtiest and oldest of all."

"I believe it, I know what you are leading up to," I said smiling.

"Yes, at eight fifteen the first sergeant appeared and ordered that our barrack was to be cleaned, not just clean, but spotless. Talk about tired deflated troops."

"Yes, the Army way, always spotless," I reminded myself.

Byron Keats continued "There were three groups of draftees in the mixed barrack, back woods Tennessee kids, inner-city Detroit kids and a few bumbling older souls like me. The Tennessee kids were all white, the Detroit kids were all Black, and the other third were a mixture with some college and many worldly experiences. Once the first sergeant left our barracks, the whole barracks was in turmoil, ready for a complete rebellion. How were we going to clean our barrack? There was nothing to clean with no brooms, rags, cleaning fluid, soap, mops, etc. The place was empty of cleaning supplies, empty of everything except us."

"You were in a hard place without a rock, so what did you do?" I asked, showing my understanding.

"I looked over the impossible situation and came to one conclusion; to use the resources at hand. We were fortunate." Byron Keats was remembering like it was today.

"Fortunate with what?" I said with a little confusion.

Byron Keats: "We had talent. the inner-city kids could steal a hub cap from a car going fifty; the Tennessee kids could find their way in the dark without getting lost; and the other third could steer the first two groups astray. Everything was set. We huddled in a conspiracy to gain all the cleaning materials needed. I gave the instructions, not orders. The non-eager first week soldiers listened closely, and the excitement grew as I explained what we were going to do. This was going to be fun."

"What were you proposing, going over the wall in mass?" I said laughing.

Byron Keats: "Far better; I broke the troops into groups of three or four, about fifteen groups in all, and the interest was growing as I spoke. Each group was assigned the task of gathering cleaning materials, cleaning equipment, cleaning resources, everything needed to clean our barracks."

I said, "But, how at nine at night. Surely the supply depots were closed. Where were they going to get all the necessary cleaning supplies?" I asked in wonder.

"That was the easy part. Each group was assigned and instructed to go to another company area, two or more company areas away from our company. They were to enter a barrack and ask for whatever cleaning supplies or equipment they were instructed to gather. They were to state that this was for the orderly room, simple." Byron said smiling.

"And it worked?" I asked in amazement.

"By ten o'clock we were the best-equipped and-supplied barrack on the fort for cleaning supplies and equipment. We cleaned the barracks until midnight and when the first sergeant opened our barrack door at six in the morning, he was astonished with disbelief. How was this possible? All I said was, is our effort satisfactory?" Byron told this story with pleasure.

"Years of my wandering after Vietnam, something or someone brought me to Fort Henry; hungry, depressed, ready to give it all up. I stopped at a house and asked for food for work, and an angel answered the door. It was your grandmother," Byron said. "She fed my body and nourished my soul; she did not push the Bible or religion at me. She was goodness in action."

"I was a sorry looking specimen as a human being, standing at her kitchen door, but she looked past my disgruntled appearance and peered through my eyes into my heart."

'Come in,' she said to me, and then your Granny said she was lonely and needed some company and she knew her prayers were answered in me."

Byron Keats continued; "I walked into her kitchen, and I knew I was home. A feeling came over me, a feeling of warmth, comfort, and peace. I was home. She fed me, had me take a bath and provided me with a new suit of clothes. I was home. She took my broken spirit and breathed life into me. I was home, never to leave."

"She asked me to live in this house next to her house. This house that I am living in now. It was abandoned and in awfully bad shape. I spent over a year working on the house, bringing it back to life and making it livable. Each day as I made this house more livable; I was becoming more and more alive, more livable. She thanked me for taking this house from ruination to one of the best-look-ing houses in town." Byron Keats continued "This is not my house. I guess, this house is yours now and with Ruth gone...I will move along."

"You are my brother, your home is here, I need you as my Granny needed you."

"Your grandmother said I reminded her of you, and she hoped that where every you were wandering on this earth after the death of your wife Jacquelyn, someone was offering you a hot meal and some kind words."

"Yes, I fell apart after my wife Jacquelyn died. She was the one who was helping me put my life back together. She was the light of my life. With her, life made sense. Without her there was emptiness, loneliness, and despair. This was the third time in my life I was a miserable wreck. The first time was when my parents and little sister died in an accident. The second time was a combination of Vietnam and the divorce from my first wife. The third time was the death of my wife Jacquelyn. You remember we were baby killers. We did not know what PTSD was, only that we were broken. My first marriage failed, because I was a failure. I am happy Granny was here to help you. If I had any sense of intelligence, I would have returned here to the love of my Granny. I was too proud and stupid."

"John, I know you understand how low a person can sink after serving in Vietnam. Only we who have been wounded by the tragedy of war, understand. I am not sure how the veterans of World War II and Korea dealt with the heartbreak of war."

"Byron, I need you, for you understand. I need you to have my back. It is important that you make sure, that I do not do anything stupid, plus I need someone to talk to, who understands."

"John, I appreciate everything you are saying, but this is your house and."

I interrupted Byron, "This is your house. Granny intended that you were to inherit this house on her passing." A little lie, but brothers take care of brothers, nothing more was said.

"She would always talk about you. How immensely proud she was of you and wished you would come home more often."

I had not visited Granny Ruth since the death of Jacquelyn, my wife's death, over two years ago. This was weighing heavy on me now. Yes, Bryon was a special friend of my Granny for many years. He was the friend I should have been. The last two years I was deep in my own sorrow and self-pity. I felt empty inside as I talked to Byron about my Granny. She was always there for me when I was young, but I was not there for her in her days of need. Granny had died about two months ago, without any close family members present. I was traveling alone in my own anguish and misery. I should have been with my Granny in her last days.

Byron Keats said, "She died suddenly. She was in great health up to her death. It was a real mystery, a woman full of life one day and dead the next. If I had not known better, I would have wondered about foul play." Byron paused.

He continued, "If I find out there was foul play in your grandmother's death, I will…"

I interrupted again. "Bryon you were a true and loyal friend to my Granny, and I thank you, but if there was foul play… I will be the one to deal with it."

"Yes, I see that, but if you need…"

"Byron you will be the first one I call."

I was ashamed and saddened, that I was not here during the time of my Granny's death or for her funeral another weight of sadness I would carry along with the deaths of my sister Alice, my parents, and my wife Jacquelyn. I was sitting on the steps of Byron's porch. Lady came over and sat next to me, placing her head on my lap, as if to say. "It is alright, I am here."

Byron mentioned his good friend Sally, who was always there to help him and my Granny. I took it he was talking about Poke Sally.

Byron Keats said, "Sally had helped me restore this house, but she would never take any money for her efforts, only food, clothing, and tools. She talked about you as a boy. You should have seen her eyes light up every time she talked about you. You have a lot of people who care about you. Why did you leave? What took you so long to come back?" I did not have an answer for Byron.

I said, "Byron did you get your hat back?"

He said, "I really do not need my Vietnam hat, it is only a reminder of my difficulties from Vietnam. I use the hat more as a crutch than a hat. It gives me a sense of security."

After an in-depth conversation with Byron about my Granny, Lady and I continued our walk toward town. Sandra's restaurant was open with three guys sitting on the right side toward the front. Jean Jefferson, Sandra Martin's niece was wiping off a table on the left-hand side. It was quiet with only a low murmur of men's voices. Jean looked up and said "Hi" then a pause "Thank you…for yesterday's morning."

"You're welcome. Is Sandra around?"

"She should be back in ten or 15fifteen minutes, is there something I can help you with?"

"Coffee would be grand" as I sat down at a table on the rear right side. Jean came with a cup of coffee and a dog biscuit for Lady. The coffee was delightful and delicious. Who believed coffee with a pleasing aroma could be found in this small-town restaurant? I said, "Thanks," and I waited. I was anxious to see Sandra and catch up on old times. Sandra and I were inseparable during our childhood. She was the first girl I had a crush on. Sandra had always been a straight shooter, which means is she always told it like it is, no sugar coating. Sandra was one person I could always count on to let me know what was going on. I needed to know what was going on in Fort Henry. Fort Henry seemed to be tilted, like someone was pushing the town in the wrong direction.

CHAPTER EIGHT

The County Courthouse Red Tape

S andra Martin entered the restaurant about fifteen minutes and three cups of tantalizing coffee later. She spotted Lady and me and she said, "Are you two going steady?"

"Lady wanted to show me the town and I guess this is her favorite spot." I was happy to see Sandra.

"So, it's Lady?" Sandra stated.

"Yes, she selected the name, and it fits; she is a lady. Sandra, who did you say is in town?" I had a questioning look on my face.

"CherylAnn, your ex." Sandra smiled. She knew the name would get my goat.

"What is she doing here? If my memory serves me, she said she would never be caught dead in a small town like this. You say she is here?" I was astounded by this news.

"CherylAnn has been here for about two or three years. She teaches at the high school. She has asked about you." It seemed Sandra was toying with me.

"What a homecoming. Two altercations and now my ex is here. What next? Maybe I should get in my car and keep on traveling," I replied with reservation.

"You do and there is going to be another fight, and the fight is going to be with me. You, sorry excuse for a friend, this town needs you and I need you" Sandra placed her fists on her hips as she talked.

Sandra pulled a chair up across from me and said, "It has been an extraordinarily long time. What have you been doing?"

"Just traveling around seeing the country, nothing exciting."

"I bet, you and excitement were always hand in hand. What about the time you put the sheriff's car on the high school roof? They still have not figured out how you did it. They had to take the car apart to get it off the roof."

"Who said I did it?"

"Who else?"

"Well, I'm not saying one way or another."

"Yeah, right!"

"Sandra what have you been doing all these years?"

"After you left town, which broke my heart, I married Lew Jenkins from Middletown. It lasted three or four years and he was gone. I have one daughter Lisa, a wonderful child who is married and the mother of two. She now lives in Colorado. She gets home once or twice a year. You remember my sister Liz; she is the mother of Jean. Liz died about eight years ago of pneumonia."

"I'm sorry to hear that."

"I raised Jean, the image of Liz, such a delight; I'm not sure what I would have done without Jean since Lisa married and moved to Colorado."

"Sounds like you had it tough."

"It has been hard, but Jean and I are very lucky, we have the 340-acre farm Dad left me and this restaurant."

Sandra continued, "Jean and I have been renting out the farm since Dad died and the farm brings in good money. This restaurant, Sandy's Café, is my love. It not only keeps me busy, but I have fun visiting with everyone. We moved into town about four years ago. Jean and I live in the old Fuller house. What else could I ask for?"

"Sounds like everything has worked out."

"John, you remember the time we skinny dipped in the river..." Sandra said with a smile on her face.

"Do I remember Mrs. Grabtree saw me nude at the river and reported me to the school principal and Pastor Beck. You were hiding in the bushes, and she did not see you. If it were not for my Granny coming to my rescue, I would have been a marked boy for life. Granny said there was nothing wrong with a boy going swimming on a sweltering day. Granny told Mrs. Grabtree she should be ashamed of herself for gawking at me in the nude and stirring up such a commotion. And all you did was laugh every time you saw me for the next three weeks. Yes, I remember."

"We did have some great times together... how come we didn't wind up together?"

"You never took me seriously. I was just a friend."

Mike Roger the chef was motioning to Sandra that he needed her in the kitchen and Sandra said as she got up, looking me in the eye, "You are my best friend."

Sandra made a motion toward the kitchen "It is nice talking to you, but I have a restaurant to run. I hope you are going to stay around for a while, but now I have work to do in the kitchen."

"Maybe tomorrow I can ask you about CherylAnn."

"Sure thing."

At about 10:30 a.m. Lady and I were to travel to Carrollton and the county courthouse to present myself as alive and complete all the required paperwork. This was necessary to keep the Henry estate and fortune. It was 1:00 p.m. when I finished all the necessary paperwork, just in time for some lunch. I was carrying with me a couple of bowls for Lady, one for food and the other for water. During the hearing I found out that the Henry farm was mine including the house in town, the farming equipment, some land in the county, and a few buildings in town. In the will my Granny stated that I was not to sell the Henry farm to the Grimm brothers, for any reason. If I did not want the farm, then the farm and the Henry estate was to be given to the John Anthony Henry Fort Henry Foundation.

After completing my business at the county court House with the essential paperwork in toll, I returned to Fort Henry, with a smile on my face and Lady by my side. The town has not changed much over the years, the main street called Henry Way was much like years ago. Henry Way, the main street downtown was only two blocks with buildings on both sides. There was a barber shop (the center of gossip), a beauty salon (the second center of gossip), two bars (the places to pass on the gossip), a dry goods shop, antique shops, a hardware store, a laundry-mat, a bank, a post office, a city courthouse, a small grocery, a fire station, three churches and a gas station at the east end of the second block And oh yes, Sandy's Café. I was rediscovering many fond memories as I wandered around the town, visiting with friends both new and old.

The hardware store, for example, was where I'd spend hours just looking at all the amazing items. This was one of my special places. When I was young, the two things I enjoyed in town were the hardware store and the cafe' now called Sandy's Café. In the cafe', if I was lucky, I would be treated to a soda or "pop."The hardware store was a special place where I spent hours just looking at all the amazing items. These were wonderful memories. Lady and I walked around town for about an hour, and then we headed back to Sandy's Café. Food was on our minds. Sandra was gone for the day; Jean took our order. Lady was also hungry. Jean made sure Lady was well fed and treated. She served me the meatloaf special. It was delicious.

I asked Jean Jefferson. Where she and Sandra the only workers at the restaurant? Jean said, "There were three cooks and at least four waitresses also working at Sandy's Café. Plus, the customers help themselves. It is like a community kitchen and dining room."

"Well Lady it has been a long day. Shall we head for home?" Lady sat up with anticipation, she was ready.

At the Henry house I read for a couple of hours before I turned off the light's downstairs. I said, "What do you think, Lady are you ready for bed?" Lady gave out a soft bark and headed upstairs, as if she had lived in this house all her life.

CHAPTER NINE

SUNDAY

The Ex, the Ex, The Ex...

I awoke at six thirty raising my consciousness into reality. It dawned on me, I had no coffee or coffee maker. This was running through my mind as I laid in bed. Buying milk and cereal and food for Lady yesterday was important, but I forgot to buy coffee. Coffee is especially important to me in the morning, if not essential. There was soap, a razor etc., in my overnight bag, but I was not prepared to start the day without coffee. Gazing down at the side of the bed was Lady, looking up at me, with a puzzled look, as if to say, "Are you going to get up? and what are we going to do today?" Springing from the bed I showered, shaved, and dressed and headed downstairs. I was to find more than the coffee and coffee maker in the kitchen. A major surprise was in store.

I stepped on the last step leading to the first floor and, I smelled a wonderful aroma of bacon and coffee. Entering the kitchen, I saw standing over the stove CherylAnn Swift, my ex-wife the woman who would not live in a small town if her life depended on it. If she had to live in a small town, she was not about to cook, if she cooked, it would not be for me. There she was fixing breakfast singing to herself. This was going to be an incredibly strange day.

"CherylAnn what are you doing here?" I asked with my mouth wide open as if to catch flies.

"Good morning," she said as she turned.

"CherylAnn!" I started with a lack of ability to find coherent words.

"Sit down, the eggs are almost done." CherylAnn pointed to the chair.

I said, "CherylAnn!" still feeling overwhelmed.

"Eat breakfast first then we will talk."

"CherylAnn!" I said loudly trying to hide my expression of shock.

"Put your little buns in the chair, do you still drink your coffee black?" She took the coffee pot from the coffee maker and started pouring coffee. This was going to be an extraordinarily strange day. She was all dressed up in a flowing full dress of white and lavender. The dress complimented her brunette hair and hazel eyes; she was beautiful. For a moment I was dazed by her beauty, but just for a moment.

After a few minutes finishing my breakfast in silence, I said, "OK, breakfast is done. What's up?"

She said, "My second marriage did not go so well, I got a divorce after seven years, I kind of fell apart. About three years ago I stopped in this town for a quick visit with your grandmother and I stayed. The reason for my visit was to check on my divorce settlement. Would you believe my second husband Lou's family-owned land just outside of Fort Henry? It is a small world. The more I tried to get away from Fort Henry, the more Fort Henry was pulling me back. I thought my settlement was a small piece of land. I was planning to sell the land. To my surprise, it turned out to be 280 acres." She took a short breath.

CherylAnn continued. "I thought I was rich, until the banker explained that I owed about $130,000 on the land. There I was with little money, $130,000 in debt, no job, homeless and stranded in a town I hated. The land was muddled in miles of legal paperwork that would take years to work through. I could not sell the farm. I was at a stand-still. I was lost with nowhere to turn. Your grandmother helped me change everything, including myself. I did not know it at the time, but I was home. Your grandmother welcomed me to Fort Henry; she comforted me, supported me, and helped me get my life back, or better still, get a life. For the first time my eyes were opened. I saw Fort Henry, as I had never seen it before. I was home. Fort Henry is my home, thanks to your grandmother." CherylAnn paused.

Then continued, "Your grandmother helped me get my life back together. I substituted for a while at the high school, then I was given a full-time teaching job and here I am, little miss city girl."

"You're not living here; are you?" I said questioningly.

CherylAnn leaning in said, "I'm not sure if that is an invitation or dissent, but no I'm not living here in this house. I lived here with your grandmother for about six months when I first came to town. I now have a place on the other side of town. I heard you were back, and I thought we should talk."

"Talk about what?" My pulse was slowing, and my shortness of breath was subsiding.

CherylAnn was reassuring as she said, "Don't worry I'm not trying to get back together, but if we are going to live in this same small town, maybe we could be friends. It is important I live here. For once in my life, I am grounded and happy. Your grandmother and this town were responsible for breathing new life into me. This is not my second chance. This is my first chance, and I am happy. I never knew happiness until now__, no offense."

"None taken, but you were the city girl, never happy with anything I did, nor my love for this small town." I was still in a state of bewilderment.

CherylAnn continued for she had far more to talk about; "It is not your fault or mine. I lived with my parents until we got married, then I lived with you, but you were not around much with college, work, and the service. We were divorced, and I went back to my parents and of course I married again. I was never on my own. I was always under someone else's roof. After my second divorce, there I was again, living with my parents. Our children were grown, and they did not need me. Yes, I taught for many years, you remember I started teaching when we were married. My father died, and my mother went to live with my sister. There was no roof. My mother's house was sold. Your grandmother took me in and helped me change my life. The roof now over my head is mine."

"CherylAnn as long as you are here, I have wanted to talk to you for an exceptionally long time. I know our communication broke down toward the end of our marriage. There are a few especially important issues I have wanted to tell you. CherylAnn you were and are the love of my life. The first time I saw you was outside the university library in some kind of trouble. I fell in love with you. Yes, love at first sight. We dated and probably married too fast, but I wanted to be with you, with you every day, every minute. I know it was difficult during the first two years with school, studies, classes, work, and exhaustion." I stopped for a moment then I continued. "We were in love, little else mattered. After school, the service because of ROTC took me away from you for the best part of three years. My heart was always with you. I felt you were with me every moment. Then, Vietnam for two tours. The final tour lasted thirteen months, it was hard on both of us. I never would have made it without you in my corner. You were with me in Vietnam every day, every hour, every minute and every second. Vietnam was ever lasting. The seconds were like hours. The hours were like days. The days were forever. Without you in my heart, I would have gone crazy."

Again, a short pause then I started, "I was a mess mentally upon returning from Vietnam. The more I tried to hide from my problems, the more the problems grew. One day I was in Vietnam and the next day I was home. I tried to continue life after Vietnam as if Vietnam never happened. Vietnam happened and it changed everything__, you, me, and time. It took me years to deal with Vietnam; in fact, I am still dealing with Vietnam. I needed help, but I was too dumb to understand how much help I needed. Plus, there was no help available. My friends were trying to help me deal with my PTSD. They knew I was broken, and I needed help."

I paused to catch my breath, "You remember our last encounter when I asked you if I could come home after the week of self-imposed separation giving me time to think. I was not asking if I could come home from a week apart. I was asking if I could come home from Vietnam. I was not able to leave Vietnam behind. It was destroying me and our marriage. The two years after Vietnam were difficult, we did not talk. We were not close like before Vietnam. We were pulling apart. We were pulling each other apart.

When you put conditions on my coming home from my week of separation, it was more than I could handle, so I took my hurt and pride and left." There was a pause.

CherylAnn: "I understand."

"I'm not sure you do. I did not."

"You are correct, I did not understand then," CherylAnn said with deep awareness.

"It was not you or I, for it was bigger than both of us."

"I'm starting to understand all of this now, but what good is it looking back, for we are no longer the boy and girl who fell in love" CherylAnn said.

"Yes, you are right, but I have been wanting to say this to you for an exceptionally long, long time. A couple more things, I apologize for not bringing home from Vietnam the boy you married, and I apologize for not asking you if I could come home my first day back. It was wrong of me to assume everything was the same as before Vietnam." After finishing all of this, I sat back, a little exhausted.

"Thank you." She reached out her hand and said, "Friends."

We embraced with a soft tender cuddle. For a few moments we were trying to regain a lost moment in time. A love, a passion, a warmth, from the past we were not to regain. We pulled apart and stared into each other's eyes for an eternity. We were looking for the boy and girl we once knew. Where were they? Where was the love? We only saw before us a man and a woman older standing there. The distant memories would not bridge us to a future; it was a sadness that came over us as we stood apart.

I know it was only a moment, but it seemed like a lifetime, the embrace, the stare, the sadness we shared with each other. I moved forward to CherylAnn, and she put her hand out to stop me. She said, "Let's not ruin this precious moment, let us work on becoming friends." She was right, friendship was missing from our early relationship. Our early relationship was built on love and lust. We were consumed with love and lust when we were young. We did not take time to grow a friendship.

"I failed you, I failed our kids, I failed me, I failed us, for I thought my new normal upon returning from Vietnam was normal. My new normal on returning from Vietnam was like quicksand. I was sinking deeper and deeper until it covered my existence. It covered the blindness to our life together and all that was important. I was lost to myself, lost to everyone around me and most of all lost to you. You were my rock and when we parted I fell to pieces. I am still picking up the pieces, trying awfully hard to once again become a full person."

"You said a mouthful; is it possible for you and me to be friends after all this time?" she said with her head tilted down a little, showing some doubt.

"You will always be in my heart, but friendship is good." I reached out my hand. We shook hands, and I said, "It will be good to have you in my life again."

CherylAnn headed for the door saying "I have to go; I hear church bells ringing. I just wanted to say hello and that we all need you, even me. Hopefully, our talk will help both of us move on with our lives: Oh, by the way Mary is back. Bye."

CherylAnn and I have two children, Bret twenty-four, and Carolyn Twenty-two; they lived with their mother after the divorce. Upon the divorce CherylAnn moved to Florida to live with her parents, which meant I had little contact with our children. I would fly down to Florida and spend a week or weekend with the children, but the long-distance relationship with my children was strained at best. As the years passed, my children and I grew more distant from each other. This was another heartbreaking element of my life. CherylAnn was a good mother. She was always willing to share the children, but the distance was the obstacle. Three times the children were to visit Fort Henry during this challenging time. This brought much joy to Granny Ruth, but little joy to the children. They were city kids, and the rural farm life was not for them.

Bret lives in Anaheim; he married a wonderful girl named Jennifer about two years ago and they were both incredibly happy. I attended their wedding in the Anaheim area near where Jennifer's parents were living. This was about the only happy moment I had in the last two years during my despondence because of the death of my wife Jacquelyn. Bret and Jennifer are a lovely couple. CherylAnn and I even shared a toast to the new couple. Bret was employed with something to do with windmills and solar power.

Carolyn is living in the Orlando, Florida area close to where CherylAnn's parents had lived. She finished college and she was starting her career in something to do with real estate. Carolyn is beautiful. She is the image of her mother. Thinking back, I could see why I fell for CherylAnn, she was, and is, beautiful.

Our two children are living on their own, Fort Henry is not in the future for their lives. In talking to CherylAnn, we both believed our children would come and visit us here at Fort Henry. If we wanted to see our children more than once every five years, we would have to go and visit our children where they lived. I feel closer to my children now, even with the great distance between us, than I have since the divorce. The magic of Fort Henry was working.

I fell in love with CherylAnn in college. It was after Mary Campbell had disappeared from my life. The sadness of losing Mary put me in a stupor the second semester of my sophomore year. Barely functioning, my grades were falling__, then entered CherylAnn. She was to change my life. She was having trouble with an upper classman outside the library. I explained to the guy it would be wise to leave CherylAnn alone. Our next encounter was in a business management workshop. We were assigned a class project to work on together. Within a week of working on the project, she said, "If you are not going to take the project seriously and do your share of the work, I will ask for a new partner." She was serious. I apologized and asked for a second chance. It worked; we became a talented team. The project was completed on time with an A for the grade. We dated the last part of the spring semester. We were engaged, married, and setting up a life together in a crazed frenzy of five months. We were happy. I was happy.

We were young and in love, finishing our second semester in the gusto of lustful insanity that led our courtship into a late-summer marriage. During this very intense relationship, we were able to pass our classes with flying colors. The summer was the most wonderful time of my life, working all hours, stealing moments together, smiling, laughing, and loving. It was never going to end, the the junior and senior years. It was a tough time going to school full time and working almost full time. It took a toll on our marriage. Some of the magic was lost. I was in ROTC my junior and senior years, which helped with the finances, but detracted from our time together and our relationship. We were still in love, but all our outside commitments were wearing heavily on our relationship and marriage.

CherylAnn was pregnant with our first child during our senior year and Bret was born while I was in the service. On graduation it was necessary for me to enter the service. This was part of the ROTC program. This was the final part in my becoming an officer. The next three years of my being in the service were exceedingly difficult. We spent little time together. I was in the service hopping from base to base. CherylAnn finished college and moved back in with her parent. She needed support during the second difficult pregnancy. Only a few times were we together during these three years. The strain of separations and our lives being pulled in different directions were taking a toll on our marriage.

We were working together toward our future, our marriage, our family. I was to complete my commitment to the service in three years. CherylAnn, instead of following me from base to base with babies in hand, took a teaching position close to her family. Most of the last year the commitment of my service time was spent in Vietnam. CherylAnn and I were together only once in Hawaii on R & R during my last deployment to Vietnam. This did not help; CherylAnn was feeling alone, from me, from her friends, and from her family with two kids in tow. I was finishing up my third year in the service and by the time I was discharged, CherylAnn was not happy about my reentering her confused life. Happiness was not part of CherylAnn's demeanor. She was not happy with me, the two kids or her life. It was my fault, everything.

We again tried to regain or at least rebuild our relationship and marriage. It was an uphill battle. For every step forward, we were taking two steps backward. We tried for the best part of two years__, some ups, some downs;

we were not making any progress. CherylAnn left for her parents at the beginning of the seventh year of our marriage; it was over. Too much was asked of CherylAnn in the seven years of our marriage. I took my pride and hurt and became a lonely fool.

At this time in my life, I had nowhere to turn. In my thick-headed stupid thinking this is what I believed. Returning to Fort Henry to the love and comfort of my grandparents was not even a dot on my radar. I did not believe I deserved or wanted their sympathy, for I had failed. Years later, I encountered a beautiful woman named Jacquelyn Bonner in a café in a town called Easton. She told me she was waiting for me. She fed me, clothed me, and reached down into my soul and inspired me. During this fleeting period, I bumped into Tom Cotton, who was a county sheriff and a Vietnam veteran. Tom Cotton was in the Navy during the Vietnam War serving off the coast of Vietnam.

I met Tom Cotton at the same small café where I met Jacquelyn. I had stopped for breakfast. Tom was seated next to me at the counter, and I said to him since he was wearing a Navy Veteran hat, "Thank you for your service."

We carried on a conversation for about twenty minutes and the conversation changed my life. Tom talked me into applying for a position as associate deputy for his county. I applied and was accepted. These were the steppingstones to my future with my wife Jacquelyn. My position as an assistant deputy led to a full-time deputy position and then onto a teaching position in the local high school. I remained a part-time deputy as I pursued my career as a teacher, I was getting my life back.

Jacquelyn Bonner was a music teacher at the high school. She was beautiful with a warmth that mirrored my Granny's. It was love and there was no looking back. With Jacquelyn it was more than love, it was comfort and warmth, for Jacquelyn was breathing life back into me.

CHAPTER TEN

SUNDAY

The Henry Farm Can Be Deadly

W as I dreaming or was all this really happening? Was CherylAnn in this house this morning? Was she living in town? Was she happy? I was not sure if the last forty-eight hours were a dream or a nightmare. I decided, I would busy myself with the house, outbuildings, land, and paperwork and try to stay away from people, at least for today. Church was not an option today, but next week, yes.

Checking the outbuildings, I found that work was needed on the garage, sheds, and barn. I had all summer to repair these buildings. Making a mental note of where to start; the garage was to be the first endeavor a new roof, some structural repairs, siding repairs, and a new door. I estimated the cost was between one thousand and one thousand and five hundred dollars. The sheds would have to wait. The barn was in surprisingly good condition, some of the repairs to the barn were more than I wanted to do, so I would hire out most of the work.

In the barn was my grandfather's Ford pickup, an old Ford tractor, and a lot of miscellaneous equipment and tools. I would take an inventory of the barn and its contents another day; now, my pressing desire was to check out the Henry farm.

Lady and I hopped in the car and drove two miles to the Henry farm. There are 320 acres of prime farmland and a small house. This was part of my inheritance along with the house and properties in town, furniture, stocks, land, and money in the bank. The importance of the ownership of the Henry farm was not the wealth of the farm, but the wealth of the memories. I was aware of every inch of this land, since I had worked it as a boy and a young man. Gladly I was willing to give up all my inheritance, just to spend one more day with my Granny and Grandfather. They were my parents from when I was eight years old. They were the ones who raised me, since my parents and sister had died. There was a deep appreciation for the farm, houses, equipment, and money in my heart, because the farm was so important to my grandparents.

It was my privilege to honor the memory of my grandparents by keeping the farm in the family. It was my responsibility to make sure the farm operated at the level my grandparents would expect. The Henry farm, Fort Henry and citizens of our community were my roots. Now this was my reason for living. My desire to visit the farm made chills run up and down my spine. The Henry farm was especially important to me.

I was home after twenty-eight plus years. I was home to stay. I visited my grandparents from time to time over the years. Each visit was only a couple of days. Now I was home with an empty feeling inside, for I was home without my grandparents__, only memories.

Lady and I first stopped at Ben Stewart's house. He, and his wife with two children, lived in a small house on the Henry farm. This house was part of the Henry estate. Ben had been farming the Henry farm for the last twelve years since my grandfather retired from farming. "Ben is a good farmer and worker," my grandfather told me on more than one occasion. "Almost as good as me," I could hear my grandfather saying. Ben, his wife, and his children had returned from eight o'clock mass and Ben was in the garage/shed working on some equipment.

"Hello Ben" I said.

"Hi John. I heard you were in town." Ben seemed anxious.

"Yes, I got into town a couple of days ago. I felt I should stop by for a visit."

"I was a little worried when no one heard from you after your grandmother's death... I was not sure what was going to happen to the farm."

"Sorry about that. When the news reached me about my Granny's death; I headed to Fort Henry as fast as I could."

Ben said, "I kept on farming, hoping it was all right for me, to continue farming."

"Yes, Ben it is more than all right. I thank you for continuing to farm the Henry farm. I not sure what I would have done if you had not continued farming the land," I said reassuring Ben.

"That is sweet music to my ears. Do you want me to continue farming for you now that you are the new owner?" Ben almost did not want to ask this question, but he could not take the suspense any longer.

"Yes, Ben, I would appreciate very much if you continued farming, under whatever arrangements you had with my grandparents."

"We really did not have a contract. At the beginning of each year, we would talk about what was expected__ what we would plant, how much fertilizer, seed, when to plant, when to harvest, the split, you know." Hearing this from Ben was a little confusing to me, but if it worked for my grandparents, then it would work for me.

"Truly I am rusty on farming, so if you do not mind, I would like you to continue farming under the same conditions you had with my grandparents and when we have time to sit down you can bring me up to speed."

"Anything you want, but I have a wife and kids and I need to know," Ben said anxiously.

"Say no more; you did right by my grandparents and as long as you want, the farm is yours to farm," I said to a smiling farmer.

"Thanks. That takes a load off my mind. Do you mind if I go tell my wife? She was worried sick. Again, thanks." Ben shook my hand with much appreciation.

"I am the one who is thanking you. Say hello to your wife." Ben double timed it to his house with the good news, the news his wife was anxiously waiting for.

Lady and I left Ben's small farmhouse and drove a short distance to the Henry farmland where the house, barn, garage, and outbuilding had been before the tornado. This was the place I had luckily stopped a few days ago to rest when I was lost in the fog and mist. Lady and I got out of the car and started walking to the farm. I was lost in memories. I was twelve again, happily remembering the wonderful times of my youth that I used to have on this farm. The only structures remaining on the farmland was an old rusty windmill my father built when he was young and a grove of red oak trees on the northeast corner of the farm.

My walk took me to the grove of red oak trees. I stood in front of the tallest tree; I was here to show respect to the tree, the tree my great many times grandfather Major John Anthony Henry had planted. Next Lady and I walked to the tattered windmill my father helped build.

This windmill was used to pump water for the livestock. It was dormant with only five of the twenty-four sails in place. The sails were no longer moving, for the mechanism was rusty and broken. I walked over to the windmill and climbed the first few rungs. The view of the land was beautiful. When I was young, the windmill was in good running shape. I used to climb this windmill to the top and visualize my father building this windmill. This was my way of being close to my father. Rebuilding the windmill was not an option. I would make it like new so I could once again be close to my father. Rebuilding the windmill would serve no purpose other than to hold my father close. This was essential.

Once down from the windmill I walked over to an old hand water pump sticking out of the ground about three and a half feet. It too looked rusty and unkempt as I approached. There was a jar of water sitting next to the pump. *Could it be,* I asked myself. I picked up the jar of water, opened the top of the pump and poured water down the top of the pump. It was necessary to prime the pump to produce suction to make the pump work. I grasped the handle and started pumping. On my ninth pump, the water started flowing. Lady was happy to taste the water, so I bent down with both hands, tasting this cool incredibly refreshing water. I was a kid again. On many scorching summer days as a kid, this was what I would do.

After refreshing ourselves with the water from the hand pump which had to be over ninety years old, Lady and I started walking the land. It was a beautiful day with a few clouds in the sky. The sky was a rich deep blue. All was well. The red oak trees were still standing tall, and I went to them and showed my respect again. Lady and I were continuing our walk on the farmland. I stopped and picked up a handful of dirt, bringing it close to my nose. The smell of the dirt was exhilarating. My grandfather would smell the farm dirt each time he walked the land. I was becoming my grandfather. For the first time, the earth's smell, this farm dirt was alive with the aroma of richness, the richness of belonging. This was the aroma my grandfather would breathe in, and now I understood.

We were in the middle of the field when Lady pulled at my pant leg, as if she were attacking me. Lady's attack made me stumble to the ground, just as I heard a shot from a rifle. It was a very strange feeling that came over me as I hit the ground. I felt like something had hit my arm, so I lay still on the ground. The old Vietnam training was kicking in, and I laid there waiting.

CHAPTER ELEVEN

SUNDAY

Lady Saved Me

Lady hit the ground after forcing me down. She was lying between the shooter and me. She was protecting me. Lady and I were still hugging the ground for what seemed like an hour, thought. I am sure it was only a few minutes when a truck started up and drove off in a roar. Looking up I could see a dark blue Ford pickup heading west, toward Shaffer's Crossing. It was traveling fast. Lady was between the truck and me. She was protecting me; how did she know? There was no marking on the truck, and it was too far to see the license plate clearly. It was just a dark-blue Ford pickup. The window of the truck on the driver's side was down and I could see the reddish orange plaid sleeve of the driver. It looked like the same shirt from one of the three who I had an altercation within town the other day. It was not much of a squabble, and I could not believe the dispute would lead to this shooting.

Here I was with my face in the dirt kissing the ground, thinking that surely, the altercation with the three hot heads the other day would not lead to someone shooting at me. I was sure the shooting had more behind it, then a short argument. Someone wanted me dead. *This is not the first time*, I thought as I picked myself up off the ground. Gaining control from the excitement of the shooting, my heart was beating fast and my blood flowing. The last thing I was thinking about was the weather. It was a beautiful day. I realized that my blood was really flowing from my right arm. I was shot.

It was not the first time that I had been shot. I was wondering how long my luck would last. Was it used up? Lady had saved me, by pushing me down at an incredibly precious moment. Was Lady now my luck? My mind was racing__, not focusing, just racing. Lady gave a short growl and a small bark, as if to say, "let's get out of here." We headed across the field quickly to my car. My arm was bleeding, so I made a bandage type tourniquet from a t-shirt that I had in the trunk. I did not want to get blood on my nice somewhat clean car seat. It is funny how you think under stress. The bleeding stopped, at least temporarily and the wound itself looked like only a flesh wound.

Once I had controlled the bleeding and wrapped the wound, next was determining where to go to have the wound treated. I had passed a clinic at the north end of Fort Henry on the way to Carrollton. I was hoping that the clinic would be open. The clinic was much closer than the hospital in Carrollton. I was sure the clinic could treat this little flesh wound. Lady and I climbed in the car; she was looking at me with concern. I was asking myself. *Why would anyone want to shoot me. What have I done for someone to take such drastic action?* My mind was spinning.

"Welcome to Fort Henry," the sign read on our way into town. Yes, Fort Henry was welcoming me. It was my fourth day in Fort Henry and my welcome included two disagreements, a shooting, my ex-wife, inheriting a farm and house, accruing many questions, meeting old and new friends and a packet full of memories. My welcome to Fort Henry was starting to be a fantasy like in *The Christmas Carole*. I encountered the ghost of the past, who or what is the ghost of the future? The real welcome to Fort Henry was finding Lady, this beautiful chocolate Labrador. The look in Lady's eyes as she sat next to me in the front seat of my car was telling me everything was going to be all right.

I was not groggy or unsteady, just angry; I always get this way when someone tries to kill me. I did not want revenge, just an understanding of why it is that I was so disliked as to have someone try to kill me. Again, maybe it was not a dislike of me but something deeper and more cynical. I was a likeable easy-going person. I was not trying to cause harm to anyone, but I found myself once again the target of someone who wished me harm. I was not in a state of fear, more in a state of readiness__, but for what? For who was I the target?

Lady and I drove to the clinic just northeast of town. I was quite sure that my wound was just a flesh wound, and that the clinic would be able to treat the wound. The nurse or attendant at the check in counter looked more bored than helpful. When I removed the t-shirt bandage from my wound the person behind the counter perked up. The person behind the counter was not a nurse, only the receptionist. The red haired, freckled receptionist was quick to rush me into an examining room. The wound was treated quickly and professionally by what seemed like a noticeably young doctor, called Dr. Pickerham, and his nurse Nancy Tearnan. The doctor was young but seemed significantly confident as he treated and dressed my wound efficiently.

After ten or fifteen minutes of cleaning, stitching, and bandaging the doctor asked, "Was this a gunshot wound?"

"Yes, I guess someone doesn't like me," I said to the shock of the doctor.

"You mean this was on purpose?" The doctor said in a high tone.

"Yes, a little better aim and__"

The doctor interrupted me.

"I will have to report this" I did not answer as the doctor leaving the room said, "You will have to wait here while I call this in. Nurse, you wait here with the patient."

Within the hour a sheriff entered the treatment room, he looked familiar, but I could not place him, and he said "So, you're the one who was shot.... and accident or what?"

I said, "What.' Someone has it out for me and they only missed me by sheer dumb luck."

"What happened?"

I told my story in detail, and Sheriff Chad Bradford, who I remembered was a classmate, a year ahead in school, was writing everything down.

"So, it was a driver of a blue Ford pickup on the Fuller Road that shot you while you were walking the Henry farm? How long have you been in town?"

"Four days"

"Hum" Chad said busily writing everything down.

"I was just walking the Henry farm when I was shot, and I've only been in town four days. I would think that's not enough time to make any enemies."

"From what I heard you sure have ruffled some feathers in four days."

"Look Chad. None of this is of my own making. I did not go looking for trouble, I absolutely do not know why someone would want to shoot me. The bully in the restaurant was in an old rusty pickup, so I don't think it was him, but the three who were picking on Jean drove a nice shiny blue Ford pickup, maybe."

"I will check them out," Sheriff Chad Bradford said in a professional manner.

"Just remember that whoever it was, they meant to kill me."

"You said it was possibly only one guy who shot at you, not all three that you had a disagreement with."

"Yes, possibly"

"Did you see anyone else in the truck?"

"No"

"OK, stop by my office tomorrow and we will go over this again." Sheriff Chad Bradford left the room. Lady had waited patiently next to my bed. She only raised her head each time someone entered the room.

Lady and I left the clinic around four-thirty p.m. and headed home, yes, this was home. We were hungry, so I fixed dinner and we ate. After dinner we moved to the side porch, where I sat on one of the two rockers. We relaxed; it was cooler. I was going over in my mind the last four days trying to make sense of it all. I was not making sense of any of it. *Who, what, why* was all I could come up with.

Lady, sensing my concern, seemed to be in a very protective mode. Any noise and she would raise her head and sniff the air. I did not lock up as we went to bed; a 38 under my pillow gave me a feeling of security. The 38-caliber pistol was found with a box of cartridges in a bedroom dresser drawer. The pistol was found on the first day when I checked the bedroom furniture. I placed a couple of blankets on the floor next to my bed for Lady. I thought to myself, *I would need to buy a bed for Lady.* It was a comfort having Lady sleeping beside my bed. She had saved my life today and placed herself between me and the shooter. How did she know?

I was starting to wonder: *Is this the Fort Henry that I grew up in, the Fort Henry of peace-loving, friendly people?*

CHAPTER TWELVE

MONDAY

An Old Flame

I awoke, showered, shaved, and dressed. My arm was a little sore but workable. Going downstairs, I was greeted with the sweet smell of bacon and coffee. *Is CherylAnn here again?* I wondered. Entering the kitchen, it was Mary Campbell, standing at the stove. Seeing Mary for the first time in almost twenty-seven years, my mind shifted into overload. Was this a dream? Mary was my high school love. She turned and said "Hi" as if she fixed breakfast for me every day. Mary and I had made plans to marry as soon as I finished college. I was away at college too long and she did not wait. Mary was gone.

I had not seen Mary for over twenty-seven years, it was Mary,he same lovely Mary, the Mary who aroused me, the Mary that I wanted to spend my life with and the Mary who was now in my kitchen fixing breakfast.

Mary was dressed in a navy-blue skirt and a white blouse with navy heels, she looked very professional with her sky-blue eyes, and styled brunette hair with a tinge of red. She was now a woman not the girl I once knew. I was not sure if I should hop in my car and just start driving or sit down and have the breakfast that Mary was preparing.

I knew who Mary Campbell was, for I had much contact with her in my youth. The Fort Henry school system was exceedingly small. Mary was in a class behind me, and we had many encounters from when I enrolled in Fort Henry elementary school in the third grade until that evening in May. The evening in May was to change our relationship forever. For one evening in May, there was an awareness between Mary and me of what was and what was to be. We were bound, bound together by the chains of passion and love. We never spoke of the evening in May again. We were two souls hemmed in concert by a single episode.

I am not sure who needed who more, but together we became one. Our lives, our existence was one. Mary and I were on a double date for the junior and senior prom. Mary was not my date, but from that double date we connected. We were to talk on the phone most of the night after our dates. We were a couple. Christmas during my freshmen year of college Mary was delighted when we talked about marriage. I was not asking. We were only planning. I was happy. We were happy. I have asked myself every day since then. *What happened?*

My life was planned out, I would finish college and, Mary and I would be married. We were looking forward to making our two into one and sharing a life together. This dream came crashing down during my spring semester of my sophomore year, Mary was gone. She was to marry someone else. She had moved to Florida and married. She was gone without a word, a note, a call__ just gone. Her father was not going to give me her contact information. He said she had made her choice and I should live with it. She was gone.

I now was remembering that deeply lonely time, the time I was caught between two worlds, one missing Mary, for we were to be married and share our life together, and the other world of relief, for I was going on twenty and life was opening to opportunities and exciting choices. I did my due diligence in missing Mary and the life we could have had together. At the same time, I was thrilled by having my advantageous future back. Mary's disappearance was to change my life forever.

I sat at my Granny's white oak table in a robotic state lacking control as if this were the first time that I sat in a chair. Mary placed before me a breakfast plate of eggs, bacon, potatoes, and toast. She poured a cup of coffee and put it down in front of me, asking, "Still black?" She poured herself a cup of coffee, adding milk and sat down across the table.

"Mary" I said as my world stopped.

"Bet you never figured you'd see me again" Mary said with a small smile on her face.

"Mary" I said in bewilderment.

"We spent a lot of time around this table," Mary said running her hand on Granny's kitchen white oak table.

"Mary" I said, staring at Mary in disbelief.

"Quit sounding like a broken record, yes, I'm Mary."

"But, but" Words were not working well for me.

"I know it has been over twenty-seven years and I owe you an explanation. You were away at college, and you would not stop home for a weekend or even a week. Your heart was not here. I felt your heart was no longer mine. I was a small-town girl, and you were__" Mary said not finishing her thought.

"You never gave me a chance, you were gone." I said, like it was twenty-seven years ago, but it was today. I was in a time dimension of confusion.

"Too many things were going on__. You were off at college, you were coming home less and less, we had little or no time together... alone. You never touched me in that way."

"What?" I said in an almost demanding fashion.

"You never tried to make love to me."

"But__"

"No buts... I thought you felt sorry for me," Mary was to break eye contact as she looked down at the table.

"Mary, I loved you and I wanted to marry you and spend my life with you."

"You never said anything. You never asked. I heard you had found someone else at college and I took my broken heart and found someone else."

"Mary there was no one else," I said in a defensive voice.

"How was I to know?"

"But I loved you...we were to be married." I thought to myself. She knew I loved her.

"You never asked me." Mary looked me straight in the eye as she said this.

"I assumed you knew." I said more questioning than as a factual statement.

"Knew what? You were home for a weekend once a month and we were never alone."

"But..." Again, I thought to myself. *You knew I loved you, why are you saying this now?*

"It is water under the bridge, I got married, had two kids, divorced, earned a college degree, and taught for over twenty years. I'm now teaching at the Fort Henry High School, a full circle."

"But we were to get married."

"In your head. A girl can only wait so long on hope."

"I thought we had an understanding?" I was getting nowhere.

Mary: "What understanding? You would come home, maybe for a weekend, a week and we were never alone, and you did not make a move on me for almost two years. Great understanding. Hope ran out and so did I."

"But why did you leave town making sure I could not find you?"

"You know why. I could not stay here. No man in their right mind would look at me, after what you did... I'm not complaining, but I move to my aunt's home in Florida, started school, found a man who did not know, and got married."

"You were the most beautiful girl, and you still are. I was deeply in love with you. You broke my heart. You were gone, and no one would tell me where. You were just married and happy and I was to let it go."

"I'm sorry... I thought I was a burden to you, so I let you have your freedom."

She was not going to tell me why she left, so I decided to drop the subject. "You are living in Fort Henry?"

"Yes, full circle. My father left me the farm and the debt to go with it, back I came. You were not here, and I have made a good life for myself, so don't think of confusing my life. We can talk about this at another time. I must get going. We need you." she said as she walked out the door. I stared at the door for the longest time, until Lady put her paw on my lap.

I placed the breakfast plate on the floor for Lady, my appetite was gone. I said, "Lady don't get used to this" I was talking to Lady as if she understood what I was saying and I am not sure she did not. Lady looked up with appreciation, I swear Lady was smiling.

Sitting at Granny's white oak kitchen table I realized this was the table I had sat at since I was eight. This table was my Granny's pride and joy at the Henry farm. She had brought this table with her from Michigan upon marrying my grandfather; it was her great-grandmother's table. This table survived the tornado sixteen years ago along with Granny's glass cabinet and her teacups and saucers at the Henry farm, all else was lost, after the tornado, my Granny and Grandfather found only this kitchen table and a glass cabinet containing all of Granny's teacups and saucers. The house was gone. Only these two precious irreplaceable pieces of furniture were found standing as statue of serenity in the vast devastation which once was a home.

At this table Granny was in her glory either serving a delicious meal, entertaining guests or, what I enjoyed most, her telling stories. I had memories of sweltering summer afternoons sitting with Granny at this extraordinary table listening to her tell marvelous stories about Fort Henry, the Henry family, and her youth. The sizzling summer afternoons were an excuse for ice cream and stories, for there was no air conditioning and Granny loved ice cream and storytelling.

I was sitting at Granny's white oak table with a table-cloth she made by hand. It was linen with a crochet fringe and the tablecloth was covered with plastic. It was exactly as I remembered it in my youth. I could hear Granny so vividly telling me a story. I pulled my eyes slowly from the tablecloth to the other side of the table expecting to see my Granny sitting there telling me a story. A tear drop fell from my cheek. Granny was not here, but the stories remain.

I said to Lady, "If you are finished, let's go." Lady was outside the door and next to the car before I could get off the porch.

CHAPTER THIRTEEN

MONDAY

The Sheriff Calls

L ady and I were on a mission as we drove to Carrollton and found the Pike County Sheriff's Department. Lady let me know she was not staying in the car. Inside an officer said, "No dogs."

I said with firmness, "Lady is not a dog she is a witness."

The officer said, "A witness for what?"

"A shooting. Is Sheriff Chad Bradford here? He said to stop by this morning." The officer picked up the phone and told me I was to have a seat. In about ten minutes Sheriff Chad Bradford appeared and waved me into his office.

"How are you doing? How's the arm?"

"Fined, the arm doesn't hurt at all."

"You don't remember me, I'm Susan's brother. I was a year ahead of you in school. So, anything you need or want, just ask. What you did for Susan and the others will never be forgotten. Do you know people still talk about it?"

"Thanks," I said a little confused that he remembered.

"Whoever shot at you, if they knew you, I think they would have had second thoughts."

"Chad, whoever it was, they were a surprisingly good shot; if it hadn't been for Lady, I would be dead. I was lucky."

"John, I talked to Tom Cotton this morning and he told me about what happened to your wife."

"So, you know Tom?"

"Yes, Tom and I served in the Navy during Vietnam, Tom said, you were an auxiliary officer in his sheriff's department for many years. Tom said you were an exceptionally good one. He said duty and luck is your middle name."

"How did you connect Tom and me?"

"Tom and I have been friends for years. When I found out you worked for him, it spiked my interest. He kept me informed about you; it is a Susan thing."

"It is a very small world we live in."

"Tom asked about you. He was worried about you. Tom said after you lost your wife, you fell out of the world. He asked how you were doing."

"I'm OK. A bit lost for two years, but now I'm on my way back."

"Tom will be happy to hear you are OK. He said there is a job open with his office for you anytime you want it. He thinks especially highly of you."

"Tom's a good man." I was pleased that Tom Cotton was thinking so highly of me.

Sheriff Chad Bradford continued. "About a job opening, Pike County needs a good deputy. Would you be interested?"

"This is coming out of the blue. Why do you want me to be a deputy? You don't know me."

Sheriff Chad Bradford: "I know you like a brother. You see, I have followed you since what you did for my sister Susan, through high school, college, the army, deputy, and teaching. You know, very few men would or could do what you have done."

"I'm not looking for a job but thank you for the offer" I said with appreciation.

"John, I know you don't need us, but we need you. Let me tell you what's been going on." Chad took the next hour explaining all that was happening in Pike County. After Chad finished, I told Chad I would think about the position and the need. Chad was a little pushy. He insisted I take a 9mm pistol and a badge while I was thinking it over, if for nothing else than my protection. I was thinking to myself, *if someone is trying to kill me a legal pistol and a badge is of some comfort.* I told Chad that if I accepted, Lady would have to be a deputy too. Lady was lying next to me during this whole meeting as if she understood what was going on.

After the meeting with Sheriff Chad Bradford, Lady and I head home. I needed time to think. There was way too much on my plate and I needed time, time to work all this out. Working with my hands was always some help in clearing my mind. I went to the barn and started working on the old Ford pickup. It was a mesmerizing spell that I fell into remembering the many happy rides in this pickup with my grandfather. I was losing myself in thoughts and memories with my grandfather's wrenches in my hands. Grandfather was always working on something around the house or the farm. Lady was lying nearby watching me or watching over me. I was not sure which. There was no power to the barn (another project), so when I tired of working by flashlight, Lady and I headed to the house and bed.

On my way to the house, I saw a light from the far shed. I walked over to the shed and opened the door. Seated in a rocking chair was Poke Sally. Poke Sally's real name was Sally Kasey. She had a shotgun pointed at me and said, "Don't you believe in knocking?" I froze in place, not out of fear, but shock, Poke Sally had set up home in this small twelve by eighteen shed. She put her shotgun down and said "com'n." I stepped in, still very puzzled, Lady was already by Poke Sally's side wagging her tail.

"How long have you been living here?"

"Many years, your grandmother said it was OK."

"Yes, it is OK, but why not the house?"

"The house is too big, too close in. I would get lost in such a large house."

"Sally you are welcome to come and live in the house. You could take Granny's old room, it is just off the kitchen with its own bath, and you could come and go as you please."

"Too big, I'd be lost."

"You would be close, and you could watch over me like the old days."

"I will think about it."

Poke Sally__. Sally Kasey__ and I talked for about an hour. She was and is my connection to my youth, my grandparents, my parents, my little sister, and my life. Knowing Sally was here lessened my feeling of loneliness and isolation. There was comfort knowing Sally would be looking out for me. I now had two deep caring spirits in my life Sally Kasey and Lady. They were more than friends. They were the breath of life I so desperately needed.

I said, "Come on Lady, it is time for bed... See you Sally and remember the house is as much yours as mine, so please use the house any way you want." Sally was like a mother to me; she watched over me like a hawk. She was always there when I needed her, but she never interfered.

Lady and I were in bed after ten for we were tired from the day's efforts. Lying on the bed with Lady on the floor next to the bed. I was contemplating what tomorrow would bring.

CHAPTER FOURTEEN

An Old Friend

I n the morning after showering, shaving, and dressing, I was hesitant to go downstairs. Slowly step by step I moved down the steps to the first floor. Again, there was the wonderful smell of bacon and coffee filling the air as I reached the landing. I was not sure I could handle this again. Why was I afraid of breakfast? She was standing by the stove, I did not recognize the woman standing in my kitchen, until she slowly turned.

It was Susan, Chad Bradford sister, but why was she here? She was not an ex-wife or ex-girlfriend. She said, "Good morning, you do not remember me?" I remembered Susan as attractive; looking at her in my kitchen she was beautiful. She wore jeans and a pink plaid blouse. She was dazzling. Her long blond hair was resting on her shoulders as she leaned forward to serve a scrumptious breakfast. The light from the window was highlighting a halo effect upon her hair. She appeared as an angel.

Yes, I remembered her; she was my sister, my unofficial sister. She was a young girl of fourteen who I had adopted in my heart, as my little sister. The sister I was able to protect, since I lost my baby sister when she was six. I told my baby sister I would always take care of her; I failed my baby sister. I was not going to fail my adopted sister Susan.

Susan said, "But I will always remember you. I'm Susan Huff or used to be Susan Bradford."

"Yes, Susan, I remember you. Why are you here?" I was delighted to see Susan. She held a special place in my heart for she reminded me of my little sister Alice.

"I am here only because of you; you remember that night," Susan Bradford Huff said gratefully.

"Susan it is good to see you. It is genuinely nice of you to fix breakfast. Why not sit down and let us catch up on all you have been doing?" It was a pleasure, I always liked Susan. She was like a little sister, the sister I lost. She was three years younger than me. I had not seen Susan for many years. She told me she was married to Bill Huff, and they had three children. She and Bill owned the local hardware store as well as a farm outside of town. Life was good. Susan told me all she had been doing since I last saw her. She was happy. Life was good for her, her husband, and their children, that is, up to two or three years ago. Susan Bradford Huff was not about to unload her troubles on me, currently. I thanked her for breakfast as she was leaving, and she said, "We need your help."

Again, the door closed, I sat there pondering these four visits and their four requests for help. Was I in *A Christmas Story?* Was I being played? Was I confused? "Yes", was the answer to the last question. What help did they want? What help could I provide? Tonight, I may sleep in the barn on the ground level without steps. Maybe tomorrow there will be no breakfast, ex, friend, or request for help. Lady looked up at me as if I were eating her breakfast, which I was. Poor girl: she had to eat dog food. "Come on Lady let us enjoy the day."

Lady and I walked off the back porch toward the barn; I was planning to work on the old Ford pickup. A large pickup truck pulled into the semi-circle drive. There were three men in the truck. The truck stopped next to Lady and me. There was an eerie feeling in the air. The hair on the back of my neck stood up. I recognized two of the men as the Grimm brothers. Age was not kind to the two Grimm brothers. The three got out of the truck and came to stand in front of Lady and me. Lady was up on all fours with a soft growl, as if she were in an attack mode. "Lady, stay." Lady sat next to me, watching closely.

Darrel, the older brother said, "John do you remember us?"

I knew who they were only too well, but I said, "I'm not sure who you are."

"This is Jake Morrow, a friend, my brother Groch, and I'm Darrel. You remember the Grimm brothers; we went to school together," Darrel Grimm said with an anguished grin on his face.

"I think I remember. It has been a very long time," I said. No handshake was offered, and none taken. Our eyes met. The hatred was alive, from the depths of the past.

Darrel Grimm, trying to remain civil said, "I'm sorry to hear about your grandmother. We are here to help you. You inherited a farm north of town and we would like to buy it from you."

"You would?" I said, my hatred stirring inside of me.

Darrel Grimm: "Yes, we are able to offer you a great price, so you can sell the farm and move on with your life."

"Sounds interesting" I said, not interested in their offer in the least.

Darrel Grimm was starting to smile, but it was more like a smirk, as if he were thinking he was going to pull off a one-sided underhanded deal. Darrel said, "I believe the farm is about 320 acres."

"What is the amount we are talking about?" I said questioning Darrel, not out of interest in a deal but wondering. *How dare they come on Henry land and talk to me?*

Darrel Grimm was getting excited. He said, "320 acres at, let's say $2,000 plus an acre, would be about $700,000."

"Sounds very interesting" I replied with no interest, only contempt.

"Good $700,000 in your pocket and you can get on with your life where you came from." Darrel Grimm said with excitement.

"Very interesting" I said in a mocking voice.

Darrel Grimm with enthusiasm overwhelming him reached in his pocket and retrieved some papers. He said, "We have a deal" as he extended his hand.

I said, keeping my hand by my side "You are the Grimm brothers, right?"

Darrel Grimm said, "Yes" still smirking with excitement for a deal he believed was completed.

Not taking Darrel's hand, I said, "That brings up a problem, my Granny in her will, be stated that. I was not to sell the farm for any reason for ten years. Her will further stated that under no condition was the farm to be sold to the Grimms. As you can see my hands are tied. No sale. Have a lovely day." I was enjoying upsetting their little apple cart.

Darrel Grimms face turned four shades of red in anger as he and the others turned and started for the truck. Lady was back up on all fours and ready. Darrel looked back and said, "This is not over."

"Tell your boys not to cross my path again. It may be unhealthy." Darrel, Groch and Jake stopped in their tracks, turned, and looked at me in disbelief. They were deflated, as if someone had just pricked their balloon. They left without any other words or trouble; Lady again sat next to me as she relaxed.

"Well let's go to the barn and work on our pickup," I said to Lady. Together we walked to the barn as if nothing had just happened. The remainder of the day Lady and I worked on grandfather's pickup truck. It was a pleasant day. We only took time to stop by the clinic to have my wound dressed. It was not causing me any trouble. The clinic visit was just a precaution.

Working on my grandfather's pick-up truck with his tools in his barn caused a rush of memories. My grandfather was an incredibly special man who taught me much by his steadfast example and his stories.

There was a smile on my grandfather's face and a twinkle in his eyes when he told his favorite stories. I still can hear my grandfather telling his belove stories. I was about ten when my grandfather was telling one of his favorite stories. He said, "When I was about your age, they built the highway Route 17 from Fort Henry to Route 32, you know Route 32, it goes to Weston. It was the first cement roads in these parts. It was quite an undertaking; it took months of preparations and construction. It was back in 1918, the spring of 1918 to be exact. Remember it was built for Model T's, so it was not very wide. It was a continuous pour of cement, truck after truck filled with cement, pouring, and pouring with many men spreading the cement smooth. It was quite a sight, day and night, day after day, for a week or so. Yes, it was something to watch. My father would shake his head seeing the work on the road and say, 'It won't work.' I did not understand what Father was talking about; it looked great to me."

Grandfather continued with his story. "They finished pouring the cement in April. The cars and trucks were on the road by June. My father kept shaking his head, then came July. It was a ridiculously hot July. This brand-new cement road started to buckle. From Fort Henry to Route 32 the cement buckled. It was a mess and father stopped shaking his head and started smiling and he said, 'I told them so.' I asked my Father what he had told them, and my Father said. 'They needed expansion joints.' This was more than I could understand, so my Father explained to me that when cement gets hot it will expand. It is necessary to have an expansion joint every so many feet for the cement to expand in the hot weather. My father, your great-grandfather, laughed and said, 'The fools.'

Grandfather continued, "It took the next three months to cut up the cement road, re-pour portions of the road, and insert expansion joints into the highway from Fort Henry to Route 32."

My Grandfather's favorite saying was "Make sure you put the P in and not the S." The meaning of my grandfather's saying is put progress in your effort and not stupidity." My Grandfather taught me many lessons with his stories; his stories were alive with me that day as I worked on his truck.

Late in the day Lady and I were to eat a late lunch and traveled to Weston to an Auto parts store and a box-store. The items I purchased were parts to finish working on the pickup, a bed for Lady and a metal detector. We returned home and I continued working on the pickup.

It was a good day. At bedtime Lady was happy with her new bed and I was happy with my tiredness from a day of working with my hands on the old Ford pickup. The truck was running and tomorrow we would take it for a drive.

CHAPTER FIFTEEN

WEDNESDAY

The Truth Comes Out

I awoke and, there was no Lady beside my bed. I showered, shaved, dressed and was ready to go downstairs, as Lady ran up the stairs blocking my path down the stairs. She looked up at me and stopped. Lady was almost saying, "You don't want to go down there," but I did. At the bottom of the stairs again the wonderful morning aroma of bacon and coffee. Who was it this time? I was thinking to myself. *Who else could it be?* The only way to answer my questions was to head to the kitchen. I entered the kitchen and stopped; Lady was right: I really did not want to come downstairs today. There was no way of preparing myself for this. Busy in the kitchen was Sandra Martin, my long-term friend and mayor of Fort Henry, Susan Bradford Huff, assistant mayor, and my unofficial sister, CherylAnn Swift, my first wife, and Mary Campbell, my first love. Lady looked up at me as if to say, "I told you so."

Sandra Martin said, "Sit, we'll serve you your breakfast." I sat with a little hesitation and definite apprehension. What was it they wanted? Mary Campbell placed a culinary delight before me, and Susan Bradford Huff poured a cup of coffee. I was a kept man. CherylAnn Swift said, "Eat, enjoy." *Should I take a bite, or should I run?* I looked at Lady; she was offering no help. I took a small bite of eggs and a small sip of coffee. All four of them were sitting across from me at my Granny Ruth's white oak kitchen table, all with Cheshire-cat smiles.

"I will not be able to eat this breakfast without knowing," I said, viewing the four ladies, whose conspicuous appearances were overwhelming. This situation was dragging up way too many memories from my past.

"What?" Sandra Martin said as I did gesture to the room and the four of them in a questioning fashion.

"It's not going to work," CherylAnn Swift stated desperately.

"It has to," Sandra Martin said with determination.

Sandra Martin paused then said, "It will work. We are out of options." Mary Campbell sat quietly.

Susan Bradford Huff: "You tell him Sandy; he needs to know."

Sandra Martin, "OK, John we need your help. In fact, this is also your problem. You inherited the 320-acre farm northwest of town, right?"

"320 acres, yes," I said cautiously.

"Do you know who your neighbors are?" Sandra Martin said in a profoundly serious tenor.

"I'm not sure," I said still, cautious. *Where was this leading?* I asked myself.

"Look around; I'm your neighbor on the south with 340 acres." Sandra Martin said.

"I'm your neighbor on the west with 220 acres," Susan Bradford Huff said.

"I'm on the north with 280 acres." CherylAnn Swift said.

"Yes, I'm on your east with 360," Mary Campbell said.

"We four surround your farm." Sandra Martin provided this information which was awesome and troubling.

"This was more than I was prepared for, I hope to be a good neighbor."

"Neighbor, we need help," Susan Bradford Huff said as Sandra waved her off and continued, "Help is the name of the game and it maybe more than even you can help."

"OK, just what is it you all need help with?" I said, still not understanding their problem.

"You saved us once; we need you to save us again," Mary Campbell said in a state of anxiety.

"Remember I'm not what I used to be," I replied hoping not to offend.

"From what I hear you are twice what you used to be. Remember, I was married to you for seven years," CherylAnn Swift said with hope in her voice.

"That maybe__ but the last two years have aged me. I'm not the same," I said.

"We know about your wife's death and your falling off the face of the earth. We would have contacted you sooner, but we could not find you," Sandra Martin said in a tone of compassion.

"I had to take some time and put everything back in place, for my world fell apart," I said, remembering the last two difficult years.

"Do you have everything back in place?" Mary Campbell asked with concern.

"No, but I'm working on it," I said, looking Mary in the eye.

"You must have really loved your wife, deeply. I mean, ah...no offense, CherylAnn," Sandra Martin said, knowing she probably placed her foot in her mouth.

"None taken," CherylAnn Swift said defensively.

"Yes, what's more, she loved me. She made me a better person, a person who was enjoying life. One thing I learned from Jacquelyn that was, love never fades, only people." I said this with deep sadness.

"Sorry, we are not trying to put pressure on you, but we are out of options," Sandra Martin said, placing her hand on mine.

"So... what am I supposed to do? Just what is the problem?" I replied, questioning what this was all about.

"They're chasing us off our land." Mary Campbell said as she rose from her seat.

"They're what?" I said with some indignation.

"They want our land for pennies on the dollar," CherylAnn Swift chimed in.

"Who wants your land?" My voice raised as I questioned them.

"We think some big conglomerate fronted by the Grimm brothers," Sandra Martin said with force.

"So, that is why they made their visit to me yesterday," I said talking to myself out loud.

"They came here?" Susan Bradford Huff demanded.

"Yes, offering twenty cents on the dollar." I was starting to understand why the Grimms had visited me and what their offer really meant.

"I hope you didn't take their offer," CherylAnn Swift said sounding like the wife I remembered.

"No, but I did make them a little unhappy." I chuckled as I said it.

"Good. You're not planning to sell...are you?" Sandra Martin was genuinely concerned.

"No, I'm home and I'm here to stay," I replied.

Sandra Martin: "Great. Now there are five of us plus another seven or eight who have not sold out. Most of the others sold for fear or greed, even Sam Hills's children sold after Sam committed suicide. He was all dressed up, ready to go see his grandchild in a church play, and instead he committed suicide.... sure," Sandra said in an acidic tone.

"After Sam committed suicide five farmers sold out to the Grimms in a week," Susan Bradford Huff said.

Mary Campbell added, "The Grimm brothers, their sons and their friends have been threatening us and other owners who have not sold. There have been barn and out-building burnings and, animals killed, including Nancy Blacklow's pet dog and Nancy is only six. Bullets through windshields, it is a nightmare."

Sandra Martin responded, "The only good thing since this all started is that on your arrival home a couple of days ago, the price offered for our farms has doubled. I guess they are worried about you."

Susan Bradford Huff: "We have no choice, and we are out of options, for we owe a lot of money, and the bank is calling in on our loans, in two weeks."

"We all owe money...we cannot pay it now." CherylAnn Swift said, sounding like my wife again.

"How much?" I was questioning. How deep were they in debt?

CherylAnn Swift said, "What?"

"How much do you owe, what is the total?"

CherylAnn Swift had played this word game with me when we were married. I was losing my patience.

CherylAnn Swift: "About $124,000"

"Mary and Sandra, do you owe money?"

"I owe about $212,000," Mary Campbell said.

"About $76,000," Sandra Martin said.

Susan Bradford Huff said, "Bill and I owe $164,000."

"The total owed for all of us is about $576,000 plus what some other farmers owe," Sandra Martin stated. She is a very sharp business lady.

"Which means you probably owe some on your farm" Mary Campbell said.

Sandra Martin calculated, "We are reaching a million dollars in debt."

"Only one million dollars," I said with a smile.

"You were always good at defining problems. There is no way to raise that amount of money in less than two weeks. We are in trouble," CherylAnn Swift said with sarcasm.

"Now you know why we need your help, but it is more like we need a miracle," Sandra Martin responded.

"You sure know how to ruin a guy's breakfast," I said as I placed my knife and fork on the plate.

"Yes, we are all behind the eight ball and a hard place again, including CherylAnn. Tell him Sandy." Mary Campbell was almost pleading.

Sandra Martin: "About two years ago, unbeknownst to each other, the local bank offered loans at an incredibly low interest rate. We all fell for it. We were such fools. In the small print of the loan was a call back provision after two years. The provision of the loan stated we were to pay back in twenty days the full amount owed. This provision was to take effect after two years when the bank had the right to call in the loan. The bank is calling in our loans. We have less than ten days to pay up or lose our farms and property."

Susan Bradford Huff: "We thought the local bank was our friend, not an agent for the Grimms."

"You can see the mess we are in and unless you have a million dollars in your back pocket, we are out of luck," CherylAnn Swift continued with her sarcasm.

Lady she was eating her breakfast in pure contentment without a care in the world. I got up and started to leave the room. There were no smiling faces as I started to leave the room.

"You're walking out on us?" CherylAnn Swift said in a remarkably familiar acid tongue.

"Just hold your horses," I said was leaving the room. They looked at each other in bewilderment as I left the room. I was gone for an incredibly short period, just long enough to retrieve the phone upstairs in the bedroom and make a short call.

After dialing the number, I said, "Is Bruce in? I know, tell him John Henry is calling and it is important__ Bruce, John, yes nice to hear you too. Yes, there is something. I need one million dollars. No one million is enough. By Saturday. That will be great. Just some dirt bags trying to put some pressure on some of my friends. You will get it back as soon as I deal with this slight problem. No this is a loan, not a gift. Thanks Bruce. Bruce your assistant should fly into Carrollton… Yes, I am back home. Yes, I will meet your assistant on Friday. I will be in touch. No this should do, if I need any more help, I will call you. Thanks again… Yes, Bye." Bruce is an old friend from Vietnam. I knew I could count on Bruce, not because I saved his life, but because we were friends, incredibly good friends.

I returned to the kitchen and all four were down in the mouth, looking at each other but not at me. Lady had stayed to keep them company, and more importantly, finish her breakfast. I said, "What is the next problem?"

"But…" Susan Bradford Huff said with her mouth wide open.

"I will have one million dollars by Saturday. What's next?"

"You three said he could do anything, but this…," CherylAnn Swift said. Her tone had changed.

"How?" Susan Bradford Huff said in astonishment.

I said, "A friend."

"That is more than a friend," Mary Campbell said smiling.

"It is a long story, but the money problem has been taken care of. Let's see, what's the next dilemma on the list?"

Sandra Martin: "Next is dealing with the Grimms."

"This is too big for the Grimms to be buying farms. We need to find out what is behind all of this. Any ideas?" I said knowing the Grimms were small-time crooks. This sounded too big for them.

Susan Bradford Huff: "All I know is they want land badly. It is way too much land for them to farm if they ever farmed. Why do they need so much land, and where are they getting all the money to buy the land?"

"Something smells," Sandra Martin stated with certainty.

Mary Campbell shared, "They tried to run me off the road last week, if it hadn't been for a semi-truck blocking their path. I'm not sure what would have happened, and they said, 'We will be back.' It scared me."

Susan Bradford Huff added, "Someone started a fire behind the hardware store and if Bill hadn't seen it in time the whole place would have burned down."

CherylAnn Swift: "See what we are up against?"

"I'm only one person, what am I supposed to do?" I said bewildered.

CherylAnn Swift with firmness, "From what these three have told me, six to one is workable."

"I was much younger."

CherylAnn Swift and Mary Campbell, both teachers at the high school said they had to get to school, and they left. Susan Bradford Huff asked Sandra Martin for a ride into town, and they left soon after cleaning up the kitchen. I thanked them all as they were leaving. Again, I sat staring at the door for about ten minutes until Lady placed her paw on my lap and awoke me from my deep concentration.

I said, "Yes, Lady we have some work to do." I started by calling Chad Bradford the Pike County Sheriff and asked for a meeting the next day. He said 10:00 a.m. would be good but not at the Henry house. The Fort Henry cemetery was an excellent meeting place just north of town on the Tallman Road.

I spent the remainder of the day working on the pickup truck, garage, yard, and garden. It was a pleasure working with my hands. Byron Keats and Sally Kasey came over later in the afternoon. They were an immense help as we worked in the yard and garden. Byron invited Sally, Lady, and I for supper. This was welcomed. In the farm country, you have breakfast, dinner, and supper. Breakfast and dinner are the largest full meals of the day, with supper a smaller meal at the end of the workday. After supper you are to relax from a day of work and get ready for bed.

Byron was full of information and opinions on what was going on in Fort Henry and the surrounding area. Byron was of an opinion that the Grimms were the root of all the problems in Fort Henry and Pike County. He believed the Grimms were responsible for Granny's death.

I said to Byron Keats, "We have already talked about this and if I find out it is true. I will take care of it."

Sally Kasey: "It better not be true; your Granny was the nicest person on the face of the earth, and I will take revenge."

I said, "Sally I will take care of it, if it is true. Byron and Sally, how are you set financially?"

Byron Keats: "Your grandmother was able to get Sally and I positions with all three churches, the city hall and the fire station in town. We cleaned, ran errands and we were a jack-of-all trades. We are paid enough to make life comfortable and Social Security is taken out for our future retirement. Your grandmother was always taking care of people. She was the salt of the earth."

"This is nice to hear." I was happy to hear Byron say this about Granny.

It was an enjoyable evening. And we did not allow the discussion about the Grimms to ruin our evening, at about nine Sally and I left Byron's. Lady was happy to get home and to bed.

CHAPTER SIXTEEN

THURSDAY

I Found It

By 8:00 a.m. I was at the Henry farm and planning to find it. Taking my newly purchased equipment, Lady and I set out to search, knowing that approximately where I had been standing would be the starting point. Developing a line of direction from where the pickup truck was and where I was standing and figuring in my height and the distance of the shot, I was calculating where the bullet would have hit the ground; somewhere about two hundred meters from where I was now. With my new metal detector, I began searching. This was more than a needle in a haystack. This was a piece of lead the size of a dime in a field of twenty acres of hay. Lady did not question me; she started searching as I was searching. It was about nine-twenty when Lady who was about twenty yards ahead of me, stopped and barked. *Could it be?* I asked myself. With the metal detector I swept the area Lady had identified, and sure enough the metal detector's alarm went off. In a few moments I had in my hand a piece of lead, almost in perfect shape. I said, "Thank you Lady" and gave her a treat and petted her. She is amazing.

After finding the bullet, I headed to the Fort Henry cemetery, to meet with Chad Bradford the Pike County Sheriff. I was a few minutes late. The Fort Henry cemetery is a little over a mile north of town on Tallman Road on the north side of the Tallman River. Tallman River is more like a creek, but the people in the Fort Henry area have always called it a river. During the rainy season, the Tallman River was almost filled with fast-flowing water. Lady and I were exiting the car as I said, "Here is a present for you" and I handed Sheriff Chad Bradford the lead from the bullet.

"Where did you find this?" Chad said with a surprise look on his face.

"In the field where I was shot. It was about three hundred meters from where the bullet hit me."

"How did you find it?" Sheriff Chad Bradford questioned.

"A metal detector and Lady."

"This is magnificent work. Now maybe we will be able to find out who fired the shot. I will send it to the lab to check on the caliber and possible weapon," Sheriff Chad Bradford said with excitement.

"It's possible." My experience with forensics made me doubtful. The chances of finding the weapon or shooter from a piece of lead was slim.

"This could be the first mistake the person gunning for you has made, for they do not know you as I know you. Luck is your middle name."

"Let's hope so," I said hoping luck was still with me.

"You are sure, you don't know who or why someone would take a shot at you?" Sheriff Chad Bradford said putting on his professional hat for he was challenging me for more information.

"I had a dispute with the bully in Sandy's Café, but I don't think he is the one, for the man in the truck seemed smaller. One of the three, I had a disagreement with on the street outside of Sandy's Café is more likely. The one called Scott was wearing a similar colored shirt to the one I saw driving away."

"Could be, he is a bad one. But killing you over a little conflict just doesn't make sense."

"I seem to have made a few enemies in the brief time that I have been here or maybe they were already here just waiting for me to arrive."

"What makes you say that?" Sheriff Chad Bradford said questioning my statement.

"I do not know; it just doesn't make sense, none of them knew me, I was just a new guy in town. As far as they knew I was just passing through."

"Maybe you are right. Someone was waiting for you to appear when you returned to town. They were ready."

"It is a possibility, but why? I'm not rich, and except for the two difficulties in town the other day, I've not caused anyone problems in the Fort Henry area."

"It is something to keep in mind and you should be cautious."

"A shot in the arm is compelling me to be cautious."

"If we are right, they will probably try again."

"Chad let it be known that we have the partial pickup license number, type of truck, a description of the shooter, the bullet, and the casing. This information should force whoever is behind the shooting to lay low and hide the truck."

"I like the way you think. I will pass the word to the department and local news this afternoon."

Sheriff Chad Bradford and I continued our conversation. Chad Bradford asked for my help. He was concerned about the increased appearance of drugs in Pike County. He believed the town of Fort Henry and its high school were the center of the increase in drug trafficking. His plan was to send someone undercover into the high school and scout out the high school for drug trafficking and possible drug dealers.

Sheriff Chad Bradford asked, "Would you be willing to meet with me in my office tomorrow, about the high school and county drug problem? I have another concerned individual interested in talking with you."

"Why not talk about it now...here?"

"I do not have time to talk about it in length now, plus this other person may have pertinent information which you may find interesting."

"OK...what time?"

"Eight-thirty in my office."

"OK, see you then."

It was about noon when Lady and I returned to town. Lady's growl was telling me she was hungry. We stopped at Sally's Cafe' for lunch. Sandra was working, it was nice to see her smiling face. She was wearing a light blue dress with a full white chef's apron. She looked a little frazzled from the morning rush. There were about nine people in the restaurant sitting in small groups. A man and a woman were sitting in the back right enjoying their lunch. A group of four men were drinking coffee on the front left side, they looked like regulars. Two men and a woman were eating lunch toward the front right of the restaurant.

I sat at a table in the rear right of Sandy's Cafe'. Sandra seemed remarkably busy, so when she gave me a menu, she told me the specials. I ordered the special of the day, Swiss steak with mashed potatoes and gravy and a side dish of corn, plus of course coffee. This was more than I normally eat for lunch, but I was exceptionally hungry. Lady was given some lightly cooked hamburger.

We were both well satisfied. After we finished lunch, Sandra sat down across from me and said, "How did you ever come up with a million dollars?"

"A good friend," I said without commitment.

Sandra Martin: "Are we going to have to pay it back?"

"Yes, it will be paid back, but don't you worry about it."

Sandra Martin: "But___" I motioned to her to say no more.

"Sandra, my friend is not asking for repayment, now or ever, but I will repay the money somehow in the future."

"If you say so. All we can do is trust you."

"Sandra it will be taken care of in its own time."

"John we are in your hands for the repayment of our debts. It is wonderful."

"I see Lady is ready to head for home."

Sandra Martin: "It was nice talking with you. You will have to come by when we are not so busy."

I said, "Take care, see you soon."

Lady and I left the restaurant; we were on our way home hopefully for some peace and quiet. First it was necessary for me to make two stops.

My first stop was the Fort Henry cemetery located north of town off Tallman Road. Tallman Road runs from Route 17 to Fuller Road. It follows Tallman River east for about two miles then angles north to Fuller Road. Pulling into the cemetery I followed the stone drive until I was at the family grave site. My last time at this cemetery was for my wife's burial. Lady was by my side as I kneeled at my little sister's grave. Granny's and Grandfather's grave sites were to the right of my little sister and my parents were to the left. Lady laid beside me as I said a prayer. After a long moment I moved to my wife's grave, to the left of my parents. I stood there thanking her for being my wife and sharing her love with me. I was sad. Next to my wife was an empty grave site with "John Anthony Henry born July 18, 1949", on the headstone. It was an eerie feeling, as chill ran up my spine as I looked down at my own grave site.

My next stop was to the John Anthony Henry Memorial Park of Fort Henry. This is the official title of the Memorial Park; everyone calls it Fort Henry Memorial Park. The park honors more than Major John Anthony Henry. It honors veterans from the American Revolutionary War, the War of 1812, the Civil War, the Mexican War, the Spanish War, World War I, World War II, the Korea war, the Vietnam War and the Middle East war men and women who valiantly gave their lives for their country. It was honoring America.

At the front of the John Anthony Henry Memorial Park was a statue of Major John Anthony Henry, my great many times grandfather, who settled this land and named this place Fort Henry. There was a large pavilion standing at the bottom of the earth mount with an accessible area for picnicking and gathering between the entrance and the earth mount. The area was well kept. The earth mount was the original site of Fort Henry. I stood at the entrance of the Fort Henry Memorial Park lost in memories of my youth. There were so many fond memories.

After returning to the Henry house, I worked on my grandfather's Ford pickup in the barn. Later Lady and I relaxed, and I read until bed. It was a very fulfilling day.

CHAPTER SEVENTEEN

FRIDAY

Superintendent's Deal

L ady and I awoke six fifteen and readied ourselves for the day. We were to meet with Sheriff Chad Bradford and a secret guest at eight thirty. The meeting took place in Sheriff Chad Bradford's office. As far as everyone knew, the meeting was about the shooting at the Henry farm. Chad Bradford was making a major secret of who we were meeting with and the mysterious adventure we were to undertake. The secret guest was Fort Henry school system superintendent Harold Thomson.

Sheriff Chad Bradford the Sheriff of Pike County was a good friend of Superintendent Harold Thomson. The superintendent was just as worried about drugs in his school system as Chad Bradford was worried about the drugs in Pike County. Sheriff Chad Bradford was working with Superintendent Thomson. They had devised a plan to have me become a substitute teacher at the high school, so I could as a county deputy check out the high school for drug involvement and the drug environment.

Sheriff Chad Bradford was thinking I would be interested in doing this for many reasons: one, the problems at the high school could be related to the whole community; two, I had teaching experience in a high school; three, I would be able to look out for CherylAnn Swift and Mary Campbell; four, I had worked with drug enforcement in the past at my former county; five, I love Fort Henry and I was planning to put down roots, making me a concerned citizen; and six, they needed my help.

Sheriff Chad Bradford was explaining to me that I would not be alone and that there would be backup. The Pike County Sheriff's Department and the state drug enforcement unit would be ready to move in a moment's notice. I was not to make any arrest, only observe, gather information, and report. No one would know outside the superintendent, the sheriff, and me, what I was doing at the high school. As far as everyone else was concerned, I was just a substitute teacher making some extra money. The school year was almost over, with just two weeks left of school. I was to have double duty: first to observe, gather information, and report on drugs, drug traffic and drug pushers; and second, to observe the educational structure of the high school and report to the superintendent of any problems and suggestions for improvements.

I was not to make any arrest, or make it known my true reason for being at the high school. Under the cover of a substitute teacher, I was to go unnoticed, as I conducted my observations and evaluations. The superintendent was interested in two fronts: one, determining the scale of the drug involvement and environment and two, assessing the educational structure of the high school. Since part of my experience was teaching classroom management at a local university, I had the necessary background to observe and evaluate the educational composition of the school.

I said, "Yes, on one condition Lady is to be sworn in as a deputy too." Sheriff Chad Bradford quickly swore Lady and me in as Pike County deputies. After filling out some necessary paperwork, Sheriff Chad Bradford activated the badge and pistol he had given me earlier. A letter was given to me, which Chad had prepared ahead of time, stating I was officially employed as a Pike County Deputy and that my assignment was an official investigation at the Fort Henry High School. The three who were to have knowledge of this plan were Chad Bradford the Pike County Sheriff, Harold Thomson the Fort Henry School System Superintendent, and myself. I was to start Monday.

I was given no extensive training, for Sheriff Chad Bradford had talked to Tom Cotton my former sheriff who I had worked part-time for many years. After Sheriff Chad Bradford talked with Tom Cotton, Chad was comfortable with my being able to handle the situation. I was experienced in drug enforcement working with Tom Cotton and I assured both Chad and Harold that I had the knowledge, experience, and where with all to perform the necessary functions. The school phone and my cell phone would be my contact source with Chad Bradford. Chad's deputies and the state drug enforcement officials would observe from a reasonable distance. If I found myself in any difficult problems or if I gained any useful information on the drug environment at the high school, I was to call Sheriff Chad Bradford.

I received a call from Bruce's assistant, telling me he was arriving in town Saturday and that he had a million dollars ready to transfer to a bank of my choice. I told him I was able to meet him at the Carrollton Bank either Monday or Tuesday if he was available. He stayed in town until the completion of this business.

CHAPTER EIGHTEEN

The Bank

Saturday morning, I rolled to the side of the bed and watched Lady sleeping peacefully on her new bed. It was six-thirty and time to get up. Moving to the edge of the bed awakened Lady and she quickly stood up. She was ready for the day. I showered, shaved, dressed, and descended the stairs. At the bottom of the stairs there was no bacon and coffee aroma, the kitchen was empty. We were on our own, so I fixed breakfast for Lady and myself. After breakfast we walked the grounds checking the work that needed to be done. This is what my grandfather would do, each day, he had taught me well.

The memories of my youth kept appearing in my mind as I walked the land of my great-grandmother's grounds. I was lost in my memories of the scorching summer days long ago, the excitement of my visits to this wondrous place.

This was my Great-grandmother's house and grounds, her kingdom. Our farm, the farm Granny and Grandfather raised me on, was called the Henry farm which was about two miles outside of Fort Henry. The Henry farm was where I grew up.

The Henry farm, the house, barn, and most outbuildings were leveled during the tornado about sixteen years ago. My grandparents picked up what was left and moved into great-grandmother Henry's house in town. When I visited my grandparents after the tornado, I would stay in the Henry house, but this house was not home. The home giving me shelter and warmth was gone, gone like my parents, little sister, and now my grandparents. My grandparents were living in my great-grandmother's house after the tornado, even though my grandparents were living in this house. The Henry house was not providing me with warmth, only shelter. My emotions were torn as I looked around the house and property. There were so many memories. I was deeply missing the Henry farm, my grandparents, and the love and warmth my grandparents provided.

I was exceptionally aware that; I now owned the Henry house. I was going to live in this house, but I still felt like a visitor. The home I grew up in was gone forever along with my parents, sister, grandparents, and wife. Maybe this was the reason I did not return to Fort Henry until now. This was not the home where I grew up, the home that gave me comfort, and love. It was more than my first wife

CherylAnn's lack of willingness to move to this town. It was the loss I felt in my heart because so much had been taken away. Now after all these years with Granny gone, the only thing I had to hold on to were, my memories. My memories were here. My memories are alive here in Fort Henry, and in this house and the Henry farm. My memories are alive. This house was filled with memories and moments. I was here to stay.

Our children were remarkably busy with their lives. They will probably never have the love of Fort Henry, as I, and it now seemed CherylAnn have. She has found similar love as I. It was too bad CherylAnn, and I had not moved here after I got out of the service, but at that time she detested Fort Henry and everything it represented. Oh well! Could of, should of, would of... The reason our children would never know the magic and charm of Fort Henry, Granny was gone. She was the thread of love; she had sewn so well keeping the fabric of Fort Henry and our family together.

At eight o'clock Lady and I walked downtown; it was a brisk morning. The air was fresh, just as I remembered from many years ago. The slow walk placed us in front of the Fort Henry Bank at opening time. Lady and I entered. I asked to see the manager. After a few minutes of waiting, a well-dressed man in his late forties in a three-piece gray suit came out to greet us. "Wilton Graff bank manager" he said as he reached out his hand, just before our hands shook, Wilton stopped as if frozen by fear.

"Yes, Wilton, it is John Henry. Remember we went to school together. I think we should go to your office. What we have to discuss is not for public consumption."

The reason for my coming to the bank and talking to Wilton Graff was for information. Why were my friends tricked into taking out deceptive loans? I knew the bank and Wilton was the center of everything going on in Fort Henry. Wilton moved toward his office like a man inflicted with vertigo. He was acting as a man on his way to the hangman. In Graff's office Wilton sat in his chair heavily, sinking low in his chair. He had aged in the brief time of our entering his office. He was aging with guilt.

"Wilton, I'm not here to cause trouble, I'm only here seeking information." I said smiling.

"I can't tell you anything," Wilton said with anxiety and fear.

Firmly I said, "Wilton don't go there."

Wilton Graff: "But__."

"Wilton I will have a million dollars today to pay off most of the deceptive outstanding loans that you have used to ensnare my friends. I am here to ask how much I owe on my farm. I am here to get all the paperwork the bank may have on my properties." This was said with an air of confidence.

"I'm not sure I can provide you that information__ for I'm not sure you own the farm," Wilton said, trying to ignore the issue.

"Wilton here are the documents showing I am the sole owner of the farm and properties. As such I am entitled to all information the bank may have pertaining to my farm and properties." Despite the presentation to Wilton of the documents, he was showing little interest on his part, as if he knew that I owned the property already.

Wilton Graff: "But __."

"But nothing, get the information, NOW." I demanded.

Wilton Graff: "If you wait in the outer office for a few minutes, I will gather the information." Wilton again was trying to sidestep the issue.

"Wilton, you mean enough time for you to call the Grimms and ask them what to do." This was said looking straight in Wilton's eyes, desiring his reaction.

"I don't have the information at my fingertips. It will take time." Wilton was still trying to stall.

"Wilton you still have your fingertips to get me the information. You should ask yourself one little question, who do you fear more, the Grimms or me?" I said this in a threatening voice.

Wilton was sweating in this nice, air-conditioned office as he said, "They will kill me."

"Not without my permission. Do you remember who saved you from the Grimms in high school?" My statement was not reassuring Wilton.

Wilton Graff: "Yes."

"Then get me the information...now," I demanded.

Wilton started to get up and I said, "Have them bring you the information." I was not about to let Wilton out of my sight.

Wilton picked up the phone and asked for the information pertaining to my properties to be brought to him. The information about the Henry estate came far too quickly for it to be in a filing cabinet. It had to be on someone's desk already as if it were being reviewed. All the Henry properties had a clear title which I already knew and there were no loans outstanding.

After checking the information of the Henry estate, I looked up at Wilton and said, "You knew all about this, so why all the fuss?"

Wilton Graff: "I'm between a rock and a hard place the Grimms on one side and you on the other."

"Let us talk about which side you are on now." I was going to start a conversation with Wilton Graff that was not only going to make him uncomfortable but place him in danger for Wilton Graff had placed my friends in jeopardy. It was time to move the target off my friends and place it on Wilton Graff's back.

CHAPTER NINETEEN

SATURDAY

The Banker Talks

"OK, Wilton" I said, "Out with it or I'm going to call the Grimm brothers and tell them that you have been giving me all kinds of useful information."

Wilton Graff the bank manager, said, "Please, they will kill me."

"Wilton, it is your choice, I can tell when a person is lying. You're lying."

"I have not lied." Wilton did not want to make eye contact and he was displaying a high level of anxiety.

"Wilton, then why are you sweating profusely in this nice, air-conditioned office?"

Wilton tried to regain his composure, "I I I."

"Wilton, you are holding out on me. It is the same thing as a lie."

"I'm not holding out on you," Wilton said as I reached across his desk and took hold of his phone. H reaction was swift.

"John, wait...I just can't tell you."

"Wilton, you'll tell me, or I will make a phone call."

"You don't understand" Wilton Graff was starting to understand, he had nowhere to turn.

"Wilton, I understand...you are holding out on me, so give."

"My life will not be worth a plug nickel in this town if I tell you." What Wilton said made sense.

I reached into my pocket and found a nickel among the change in my hand. I flipped the nickel about his desk in front of him. His eyes widened as he stared at the nickel.

"Wilton, here's a nickel. This is the worth of your life. If you do not give me all the information about what is going on... it is your choice."

"I can't," Wilton Graff said I cannot, but he was realizing he had no choice.

"OK," As I got up and headed for the door, I turned slowly at the door, Wilton was frantic. I said to Wilton, "Spend the nickel quickly for it will lose value within the hour." I started to open the door slowly in a tormenting fashion. I was making Wilton squirm.

Wilton said, "Sit down. You must protect me. They will kill me and my family. You don't know them...they're evil."

"Wilton, I know them." I said with confidence for I knew the Grimm brothers far better than Wilton realized.

Wilton Graff was talking so fast that I had a tough time keeping up with him. He said, "The Grimm brothers were behind everything. They had brought in Jake Morrow and Scott Keener to help them with their evil plans. Their sons Bud and Roy are also a part of the whole conspiracy."

"Interesting," I added.

Wilton said, "It all started with a land grab, for the purpose of oil. Yes, oil, that is oil fracking. The Grimms were making a deal with an oil company to excavate oil from the county. It was worth billions, but the Grimm brothers only had a few hundred acres. A sheer drop in the bucket. To gain the billions they needed land and/or mineral rights, thousands of acres of land or mineral rights. They had little or no money, so they made a deal with an oil company...The oil company would front them $34 million to purchase land and gain mineral, oil, and gas rights on the sly, so no other oil company would know about the oil until most of the land and mineral rights were in the hands of the Grimms. It was an easy enough plan... but the Grimm brothers could not make anything easy. They were not about to share with anyone."

"Continue," I said.

Wilton: "You figure it out, there are about twelve thousand acres of valuable oil land and mineral rights in the county and the Grimm brothers wanted it all. At five hundred dollars per acre the total investment would be about $60 million. The Grimm brothers had scratch and instead of the Grimm brothers being up front with all the landowners, they were trying to steal the land, oil, gas and mineral rights for pennies on the dollar."

"Why was it necessary for the Grimms to buy land? Why not just purchase the mineral rights?" I said, because this did not make sense to me.

"The laws have changed recently dealing with mineral rights. Too many outsiders were purchasing mineral rights then coming onto people's land and destroying the land to take advantage of their mineral rights. The law dealing with mineral rights was changed to protect the landowners. The new law states the landowner has the right to refuse the owners of mineral rights from coming on the landowner's land without the consent of the landowner. Mineral rights are almost useless and worthless unless the landowner has the mineral rights or gives permission."

"So, the Grimms needed to own the land and the mineral rights to pursue their desire to benefit from their oil scheme?" This was complicated.

"That is correct," Wilton Graff said.

"Why would a landowner sell their land for pennies on the dollar?"

Wilton Graff: "Fear, intimidation and any other device the Grimm brothers could muster."

I said, "But wouldn't the owners complain to the authorities of what the Grimm brothers were doing?"

Wilton Graff: "Some did, but there was little or no proof of anything wrong happening."

I asked, "So how much land have the Grimm brothers accumulated?"

Wilton: "Almost two thousand acres and it's becoming more and more difficult to gain any more land. The pressure was turned up, buildings were burned to the ground, suicides, beatings, threats and on and on."

Confused I asked, "Again, what about the authorities?"

Wilton Graff: "The Grimm brothers had six working together on this scheme: their two boys, Jake Morrow, Scott Keener and themselves, plus the oil company pumping $34 million into this venture. Local farmers just wanted out."

"This has to stop," I stated with determination.

Wilton: "This is only half of it."

"Only half?"

Wilton Graff: "Jake Morrow's contribution to this evil enterprise was his contact with federal government agencies dealing with energy and the conservation of energy. Jake was setting up a solar and wind farms conspiracy. From my understanding Jake raised $14 million from government agencies to set up and manage a five-hundred-acre solar farm and a five-hundred-acre windmill farm. Of course, Jake and the Grimm brothers did not let the oil company know anything about this deal with the government agencies."

"How could Jake swindle the government?" This was all overwhelming.

Wilton Graff: "Jake had worked for one of these government agencies and he had an extraordinarily good contact with someone at another government agency."

I said, "But still, there are people in these agencies that supervise expenditures."

Wilton Graff: "I was told Jake paid off key people within these agencies."

"Someone should have been suspicious when there was no five-hundred-acre solar farm or five-hundred-acre windmill farm." I said questioning.

Wilton Graff: "You remember the Thornton farm in the bottom lands? It has three or four large buildings on it. Jake, and the Grimm brothers used the building facing the Sunnybrook Road to set up a solar panel and windmill distribution center with all the trimmings, including a half an acre of solar panels and a half an acre of windmills."

"How long did they think they could get away with this?" I asked as my annoyance was getting the best of me.

Wilton Graff: "You do not understand because Scott Keener's part in this whole scheme was to set up a drug factory and to distribute drugs throughout the county and state. The drug factory and distribution center were set up in a back building on the Thornton farm. They were growing pot there. This was a huge marijuana growing complex, and guess what? They were using the solar panels and windmills at the front of the property to power the electricity for the growing lights...can you beat that?"

"Do they know you know all of this?" I questioned.

Wilton Graff: "They know I know some of it."

"You're a dead man walking, and you don't even know it. You need to get out of town now, this minute. I think, I know how you can do it."

I used his phone and called Chad Bradford the Pike County Sheriff. I was giving Chad enough information to get the wheels in motion, but not enough information to get me in trouble. I did not want my fingerprints on any of this. My desire was to use this information from a distance with no interference from the law.

I told Wilton, "You are to pick up your family take only your necessities and drive to a location Sheriff Chad Bradford has given me."

I gave Wilton the meeting place Sheriff Chad Bradford had set up; Wilton Graff was trying to assimilate all of this.

I continued, "Wilton you are not to include me in any of this. You are to meet with the county, state and federal officials and give them bits and pieces of this information. This is most important. You are only to give them all the information after you and your family are safe and will stay safe. This will mean a new identity and location. You are to keep me out of this whole mess." Wilton Graff agreed.

Wilton Graff: "I have one last piece of business to attend; paying the taxes for the Grimm brothers."

"What?" I was amazed at the stupidity of Wilton Graff.

Wilton Graff: "Yes, the county and state real estate taxes, the state income and federal income estimated taxes… they need to be paid now or they will be in delinquency."

"I thought taxes needed to be paid in April. How much are we talking?"

Wilton Graff: "About six-hundred and forty-six thousand dollars. The Grimms received an extension."

"And if these are not paid, what would happen?"

Wilton Graff: "The Grimm brothers could lose everything."

"Do you have control of this money?"

Wilton Graff: "Yes, but…" I was thinking. *What is wrong with Wilton.*

"But what? You need traveling funds for your new life, right?"

Wilton Graff: "Yes, but they will kill me."

"They are going to kill you anyways if they find out what you are doing, right?"

Wilton Graff: "Yes, but…" How was I going to get through to this guy?

I said, "Are you able to get your hands on this money quickly?"

Wilton Graff: "It will take an hour or so to transfer the funds to an account that I set up for myself in Panama."

"Do it, then get your wife and children and tell everyone here you just received word of a death in the family in some other state. You are leaving this afternoon and you will be back by Thursday, then get out of town. It is all set up with Sheriff Chad Bradford, the state and the feds."

Wilton Graff: "But... there is one other thing. The Grimm brothers keep a couple million in their house safe and a hiding place in the barn, just in case they need to get out of town."

"Thanks for the information... here is your hat and what is your hurry?"

All this time Lady was lying next to me with total patience.

"I want a copy of all these documents, so there are no changes, in the future." The copies were made in a hurry and with the copies under my arm, I left the office.

I said, "Wilton, enjoy your permanent vacation, someplace far away where no one knows you. Sheriff Chad Bradford, the state, and the feds will help you stay safe until I straighten all of this out. Remember you are part of the cause of all this. I am letting you off easy__, that is if you are gone and say nothing to the Grimms. If you do, they will probably kill you. Remember you are never, ever to come back to Fort Henry." Lady and I left Wilton's office and the bank with a smile on my face. It was still a beautiful day.

Hopefully, I would be able to use the information Wilton Graff provided me, to my advantage.

CHAPTER TWENTY

SATURDAY

Poke Sally Appears Again

L ady and I walked down to Sandy's Café, and we took a seat on the right back side of the restaurant. Sandra came out of the back, greeted Lady and I, and said, "So what will you have?"

"Just coffee" Sandra came back with a coffee mug, a coffee pot and a couple of treats and water for Lady.

"Enjoy, I'm busy in the back." After pouring the coffee, Sandra headed to the kitchen.

I was sitting enjoying my coffee and Lady was enjoying the water and treats when. The door opened and the Grimm brothers walked in. They looked deflated and they seemed to have aged in the last two days. Lady growled and stood up and I said, "Lady lay down." She did.

Darrel walked over to me and said, "You are messing with something you do not understand, and I'm warning you."

"Hold on. Relax. Your face is turning red. Sit and have some coffee." I had a hatred for the Grimms, and my desire was to get under their skin. I had learned over time the best way to deal with a person causing a problem was to be nice, extremely, and genuinely nice.

"This is bigger than you and I." Darrel said in a demanded voice.

"Darrel calm down, sit. I am not here to cause trouble. I've come home to relax and enjoy my retirement." I was pouring sugar on my being nice.

Darrel Grimm: "But you"

"But nothing, I'm here to stay and run my farm with no outside interference." Looking Darrel and his brother Groch in the eye, I was being so nice.

"You don't understand there are forces greater than you, your farm and this whole town," Darrel said as he elbowed his brother.

"I guess, I do not understand. All I want to do is get up in the morning, get dressed, have some coffee and enjoy the day and my retirement." I knew I was getting Darrel's goat.

Darrel raised his voice and said, "You don't understand. We will double the offer, which is one million four hundred thousand."

"The answer is the same: I do not want to sell." I placed a great big smile on my face as I answered.

"You are going to be sorry," Darrel Grimm blistered.

"Sorry, like the time you killed my dog?" Darrel and his brother stormed out of the restaurant.

Sandra Martin came out of the kitchen and said, "That was interesting."

"You can say that." I enjoyed upsetting the Grimms.

"You are really getting under their skin," Sandra Martin said with a big smile.

"How about some more coffee? I missed my culinary chefs for breakfast this morning," I said with a smile.

"Sure. There is something I have wanted to tell you for years. Remember, you had a crush on me in the third grade?" Sandra said this as she was standing across the table.

"If I remember it right, I had a crush on you from the third grade into high school. All you wanted was friendship," I said, looking up at Sandra. She was as beautiful today as the first day I really noticed her when I was about eight.

"Yes, I was young, but that evening, you know, I saw you totally different. That evening I realized I wanted you more than just a friend. It was too late. You fell for Mary Campbell; I did not stand a chance. The world turned, Mary ran off to wherever and married whoever. It was my big chance. You did not come home from college after hearing about Mary, and you found another, CherylAnn to be exact. Well, I am telling you now I fell in love with you that evening in May. There, I said it."

"Sandra, I do not know what to say, I have given up on you and me over the years. By the time we reached high school, I had quit hoping, so when Mary Campbell came along, she needed me; I fell for her." I was flabbergasted by what Sandra Martin had just said.

"Friends," Sandra said as she reached out her hand.

"Yes, always," I said as I reached out my hand.

"Friend, get out of here, before I cry." Sandra Martin turned and headed back to the kitchen.

Lady and I left Sandy's Café and headed back to the Henry house. It was still early; the Ford pickup truck was working, so I would have to find a new project.

Arriving back at the house, I started looking around for another project, the garage. Yes, it needed work. The garage it would be. I busied myself taking measurements and making notes of the materials I would need. My arm was almost healed, so working on the garage would be a worthy project. The foundation and basic structure of the garage were sound. All the garage needed was some pieces of siding, a new roof, a new door, painting, and a good cleaning. I finished the necessary inventory of the materials needed to complete the work on the garage. With the list in hand, Lady and I were off to the lumber yard and hardware store in Carrollton. Whatever else I would need would be available at the Fort Henry hardware store.

My grandfather's pickup truck was humming and so was I. We were heading down the road. Lady was seated beside me. I still was not sure if I was taking care of Lady or Lady was taking care of me. The lumber yard and hardware store in Carrollton had all the materials I needed and soon the truck was loaded, and we were headed home. Within an hour Lady and I were back at the house ready to work on the garage. I spent the next couple of hours working on the garage as Lady supervised. The garage was taking shape and the only thing left to do was the roof and new door. The roof and door could wait until later in the week.

On finishing the work on the garage Lady and I were headed toward the house when Poke Sally Kasey appeared out of nowhere. Sally Kasey, as long as I had known her, could appear and disappear like magic. Her hair was short and well kept. Her skin was bronze, almost leather-like. Sally looked like what I believed Anne Oakley would have looked like in a Buffalo Bill Wild West Show. She was dressed in leather, well-worn leather, leather pants, leather shirt and leather vest, with a leather strapped necklace which disappeared into her leather shirt. The leather strap was attached to her Poke, the reason for her name, Poke Sally.

Poke Sally chewed tobacco. Yes, she chewed tobacco. Sally Kasey was a lady, and she would never spit her tobacco on the sidewalk, street, or ground. She spit her tobacco into her poke. When she thought no one was looking, she would pull her poke from her shirt and carefully spit into her poke. Her poke was a leather pouch.

Poke Sally was an especially important influence on my life. We built a remarkable bond early in my childhood somewhere around my seventh year on this planet. It was a simple gesture, a moment that would seemingly go unnoticed in time or space. We, my father, mother, and little sister were visiting the Henry farm one sunny hot July week. My father loved the Henry farm where he grew up as a boy and young man. His roots were on this farm. He was excited, comforted, and relaxed each time he returned to the farm.

My father was a teacher in a town three hours away from the farm; my father loved teaching. He loved the school and town where he taught. His family, Granny and Grandfather were a part of his heart along with the Henry farm, and Fort Henry. My father would make several short trips to the Henry farm during the year. I believe looking back, that he was re-energizing himself. I remember, on his return from the Henry farm and Fort Henry he was happy with a heightened spirit. I genuinely believe that had my father lived on to retirement, he would have moved back to the Henry farm and Fort Henry. He would have taken over farming from his father. Because of my father's love of the Henry farm and Fort Henry, I too grew a love of the Henry farm. The Henry farm was more than land to roam and buildings to investigate. It was the home of my Granny and Grandfather.

My father loved the Henry farm and on his frequent trips to the Henry farm, I would tag along as often as possible to visit my Granny, Grandfather, and the Henry farm. The Henry farm was my Disney World, my world of fantasy. There was excitement and adventure everywhere. There were buildings to explore, wild animals to tame, clouds to create visions, and hours of pure pleasure for a boy of seven to discover.

I loved the Henry farm and my grandparents; I was always looking forward to my next trip to the Henry farm with my father, visiting this wondrous euphoric exhilarating inspiring place where my dreams would come alive. Granny Ruth would encourage my fantasies by adding a story or two to open new adventures for a boy of seven to see into the unknown world of dreams. It was an enjoyable time, a time I have tried to return to often, in my dreams both awake and asleep. Reality is a demon that steals from us the dreams and visions of what once was, if once in dreams was ever to come again.

One dream filled afternoon on a sweltering summer day I was with my sidekick a lame goose who adopted me as its parent since I saved this wobbling fowl from a flock of domestic geese on the farm. The geese were in the process of killing this lame goose when I intervened. It's an animal thing. Once the lame goose was saved, I explained to the flock of geese to leave the wobbling lame goose alone. The lame goose followed me everywhere each time I visited the farm. I believe the attachment was more for safety than my parenting skills.

Anyways my sidekick Wobble and I entered the barn to find a girl crying in the second stall. This is where the horses used to be kept. The girl's crying was alarming. I stood at the entrance to the stall in silence for a few minutes. My sidekick could no longer hold his honk. The lame goose let out a rendition of "Johnny Comes Marching Home" a little off key. This was enough to turn the head of the crying girl. She looked at us with tears in her eyes. Seeing such a peculiar sight she half smiled and almost laughed. She wiped the tears from her eyes, turned and sat up. She was going to say something, but it was a long moment before either of us spoke.

"My name is John. This is Wobble. Why are you crying?"

"My name is Sally and I'm sad and alone."

"You don't have to be alone. I'm here and my friend Wobble is here."

"You're Ruth Henry's grandson."

"No Granny is my Granny. Why are you here?"

"Ruth Granny said I could stay here as long as I wanted to."

"Good I need a friend; Wobble doesn't talk much. Will you be my friend?"

"Yes." And she started to cry again.

"I'm seven and I don't cry at least much, and you should not cry. I will protect you. I protect my sister. Come on I have something to show you."

With that she stood up, wiped the tears from her eyes and followed me. It was a wonderful day because she followed me everywhere and I showed her all my secrets. We were friends.

She met me every time I visited the Henry farm with my father. Sally and I would play and talk for hours. It was grand. Sally did not cry anymore; she was happy. She was my friend. I stayed with my Granny, grandfather, and Sally for a week because I was a big boy. I was eight. This one day, a beautiful summer day, everyone was crying. My Granny with tears in her eyes came to me and said she wanted to talk with me. She asked me if I would like to come and live with her and Grandfather here on the farm.

"I love staying here, but I would have to ask my mother and father if I could stay longer. Is it alright if Alice could stay too?" With this my Granny started to cry, she said she needed to go into the house. My Granny never cried. Why was she crying now?

Wobble and I went for a walk. I was confused. What was going on? Granny never cried, even when she cut her finger and had to go to the doctor. Oh well. In the barn Wobble and I found Sally in the second stall. She was crying. *Why is everyone crying?* I asked myself. I was silent standing at the entrance of the stall watching Sally cry.

Sally was happy. She was my friend. She no longer cried, but she was crying. Did I do something wrong? Wobble started honking "Johnny Comes Marching Home" and Sally turned, for the longest time, sat there looking at me. Sally came over to me and took me in her arms. She never before took me in her arms. She was still crying, and she said, "I will always be your friend and watch over you."

"Yes, I am your friend too," I replied.

"Yes, you need to be a very big and brave boy, I have something to tell you that breaks my heart to tell you," Sally said with sadness and tears.

"Yes," I stood there confused.

"You know I am your friend and I love you," Sally wiped the tears from her eyes.

"Yes, I know, but..." I was thinking to myself that I had done something bad to get everyone crying and, it must have been something really bad.

Sally Kasey said, "There was a car accident, and your mother, father and little sister were killed."

My little ears were hearing this, but my mind was not absorbing what Sally was telling me.

"Mommy and Daddy with Alice are coming to pick me up this afternoon, they told me." I pulled back. What Sally was telling me was not true.

"Your mother, father and Alice are not coming; they were killed this morning on their way here in an automobile accident."

Once this information reached my eight-year-old brain, lacking total understanding, I ran, I ran, and ran. This was not true. I ran until I could not run any more, I was at the edge of the farmland where the large trees grew near the road. The largest tree was in front of me. I climbed and climbed to the very top. The branches were thin at the top of the tree. I swayed with the branches as I pushed my head out above the branches looking down the road for my mother, father, and sister. I knew they were coming.

Where were they? I held on to these branches for what seemed to be an eternity, looking down the road for the car to bring my mother, father, and sister to the farm. After hours of looking down the road, my grip was loosening as my hands tired. I fell from the top of the tree down into the grasp of the tree, into a bed of branches. After some time, I looked up through the branches and the sky was alive with the brightness of stars. I felt as if I could reach out and touch the stars if I just had the strength. These branches provided both security and a degree of comfort as I fell asleep. I was sure my mother, father and sister would be there when I awoke.

A soft rain awakened me; I was high up in this exceptionally large tree. I was awkwardly hidden among some large branches that had broken my fall. This was to provide an impractical bed for the night. It was daylight. My parents were not at the base of the tree. I asked myself. *Are they coming?* It was an effort to unhinge myself from my bed of uneasiness. I climbed down from the tree. I was bruised, scraped and sore. I sat at the base of the tree for some time; I was trying to figure out my next move.

Brilliance was flickering in my mind. If my parents and sister could not come to meet me then I would go and meet them. I started walking. I knew where they were coming from on the highway to the left. I started walking. I was going to find my mother, father, and sister no matter how far I had to walk.

My walk ended about a mile or two up the road as my grandfather's car was pulling up behind me. My Granny ran to me. She was crying and laughing at the same time as she embraced me with arms of love saying over and over "I know, I know."

I said to Granny, "They're not coming."

Granny: "No, dear, I'm sorry." Together we returned to the farm. Sally was waiting with tears and smiles. She took me in her arms and said, "I'm sorry, I didn't want to tell you."

I said, "Friends tell friends." I ran into the house, to my room and cried all morning. It was hard. At lunch time I came out of my room and said to Granny "Are they in heaven?"

"Yes, they are in heaven. They are happy. They will always watch over you and be with you," I said nothing. Granny cleaned me up, and I took a bath, it was an incredibly sad day.

Wobble was waiting for me when I went outside. Wobble followed me to the barn. Sally was in the second stall crying. Wobble and I waited in silence for a few moments. Sally was crying.

"Sally do not cry. They are in heaven and happy."

Sally turned and with a smile and tears said, "Yes, you are right, they are in heaven and happy."

The funeral was two days later. I did not understand all that was happening, I knew one thing. I was not going to the funeral without my friend Sally. Remember I was only eight years old, so I must have placed Sally in an uncomfortable situation.

Sally had set up her living place in the barn and she was comfy. She was not about to live in our house or any house. She had once lived in a grand house and the thought of the grand house, or any house, brought her a memory of hurt and anguish. Sally only trusted two people, my Granny Ruth and me, and Grandfather was tolerated. Going to church full of people was not high on Sally's list. There were too many bad memories lurking in Sally's mind. Asking Sally to attend the funeral with me was a problem. I lacked understanding when Sally said she was not going to the funeral.

I said to Sally, "Why are you not going to the funeral? Don't you want to help them get to heaven?" Sally was just looking at me with a blank stare.

Sally said, "There are too many people."

I said, "Am I too many? I need you. You are my friend and Granny Ruth said I cannot take Wobble. I will have no friends." There was a long pause. "I need a friend." Pause. "I need you."

Sally said, "For you, I will come."

Sally and I attended the funeral, and I held her hand because I knew she was nervous. This helped mother, father and Alice go to heaven. I was sad, and I missed them. Looking back into my memories, I now know how difficult it was for Sally to attend the funeral with me. She was my friend on that day when I needed her most.

The first time I saw Poke Sally spit into her poke, I was about eight and it made me both afraid and sick. During that year, our friendship grew. Sally had not only attended the funeral with me but saved my life. As a boy, I was very adventurous; one day climbing out the top window of the barn to have a better look at a bird's nest, I slipped. I was hanging by my fingertips from the window edge. I looked down and the ground seemed a mile away. My fingers were starting to hurt.

I did not yell because I was too busy trying to figure out how I was going to get back in the window. It was remarkably high and letting go was not an option. There was not enough strength in my arms to pull myself back into the barn. What a dilemma. I should have been scared but something then and now, deep inside of me always had faith. A guardian angel was and is watching over me, but that day the guardian angel was Poke Sally. Just as my fingers were about to give out, someone grasped my right arm and pulled me back into the barn. It was Poke Sally. She was my guardian angel.

Years later when I was about fourteen, Grandfather was going to cut down the trees on the northeast corner of the farm. This was very troubling to me, and I said to my grandfather, "Grandfather please do not cut down the trees. This tree saved me." I was pointing to the largest tree.

He looked at me questioningly and said, "What are you talking about?"

I said, "This tree kept me from going to heaven."

Grandfather said, "How did the tree keep you from going to heaven?"

"It caught me." No more was said. The trees remain standing to this day.

I did not know Sally's last name when I was young. My Granny Ruth told me a story about Sally when I was a little older. Sally had become pregnant as a young girl by a traveling salesman, not by choice. When Sally's parents found out she was pregnant, her father threw her out. She was pregnant, no matter how it happened. Her mother gave her twelve dollars, some clothes and food. Sally was on her own, alone. She hopped a train and traveled for a day and night until she became deathly sick and fell off the train. Sally lost her baby, and she was found by Granny. Granny nursed Sally back to health and told Sally she had a home here with the Henry family as long as she wanted. Sally was an especially important part of my life. Sally was probably eight to ten years older than me. Finding Sally again has made homecoming even sweeter. This home is as much of Sally's as it is mine. After the tornado, Sally moved into town with my Granny and Grandfather. She would not live in the house. Where Sally lived was a mystery to all but Granny and me.

Sally Kasey said, "It is looking good. Your Granny would be proud of the work you are doing around the place. You had better be careful; I have heard some dreadful things concerning you. The Grimms are not happy you are back, and they never will forget what you did to them."

"Thanks. With you by my side who can harm me. You were always there when I needed you. You are my best friend in this town, in fact, the entire world. You are my family. You remember the time I was swimming in the Tallman River and a moccasin was swimming toward me/ You shot the snake at over one hundred feet right between the eyes with your pistol. Do you still have your pistol?"

"Yes, I still have it."

"You taught me how to shoot a pistol, rifle and shotgun and the knowledge of how to handle weapons has come in handy." I looked around and Sally was gone.

Sally was lacking trust in men, so she armed herself. She was always armed. It was known throughout the county that she could shoot like Anne Oakley. Sally tolerated my grandfather because Granny Ruth explained to Sally that Jason was a good man. Granny told me my father was like a big brother to Sally. He would not let anything happen to Sally. Dad was more than willing to provide a talking to anyone making fun of Sally. After a while no one did. Sally would not attend school, even though she was school aged at the time Granny found her.

Sally would not go to church or hang around when there was a group of people. Sally has lived a very lonely life. She found her gift in fixing anything and everything, but only for women. Granny said, "Sally loves you, probably because you were broken like her." I lost my parents and little sister when I was eight to a car accident. I never got over it. It hurts today as much as the day Sally told me. Granny said she never had to worry about me because Sally was always watching out for me. Sally was my guardian angel. Life was becoming complete, I now had Sally and Lady in my life.

CHAPTER – TWENTY-ONE

SATURDAY

An Invitation

I t was a little after five-thirty when I received a phone call from Sandra Martin, inviting Lady and me to dinner at seven o'clock. I said, yes, because I was hungry and did not want to cook. I fed Lady because I was not sure what food was available for Lady at Sandra's. I showered and dressed, and Lady and I were ready by six-thirty.

Sandra Martin had not informed me of the guest list for dinner. In attendance was Sandra Martin, of course, Jean Jefferson Sandra's niece, Mary Campbell and CherylAnn Swift. I once again was the odd man out. It was a delightful meal and fun company, with my ex-wife, two girlfriends and Sandra's niece. Jean Jefferson and I went out to the front porch as Sandra, Mary and CherylAnn cleaned up the kitchen. Jean was quite a conversationalist, informing me of many of the happenings at the high school. This was valuable information, because I was going to the high school in an undercover role on Monday.

Jean Jefferson told of the in-crowd, the jocks, the losers, the drugs, the good teachers (including Mary Campbell and CherylAnn Swift), the bad teachers and on and on. Jean stated a remarkably interesting and extremely important fact: there was a party center north of town. It was to the rear of the Mills farm. About half a mile up an old dirt road off Route 17 was an abandoned shed and open area used for partying. This was just past the Mills farm. I asked Jean about what went on at this party center, and she was quick to answer: yes, drugs, buzzes, sex, and the like. This was all I needed. Perfect.

It was quite an education. I was being provided with all the background information about the high school in preparation for Monday. When Sandra, Mary and CherylAnn came out on the front porch, Jean Jefferson went to bed.

Mary and CherylAnn were also helpful and informative about the high school. They knew of the drug problem at the high school, and they had suspicions about who was behind the drugs. They gave me a few names of those who they believed were the problems at the high school. They gave me information about the staff, the good, the bad and the indifferent. I was careful not to tip my hand about my arrangement with the sheriff and the superintendent. It was important no one related to the high school should have the slightest idea of my mission.

The dinner party was breaking up around nine and it was time for Lady and me to head for home, because I needed to pick up a few items at the house. We were headed to Mills' farm. The Mills house was empty because no one had lived there for years. I drove my grandfather's pickup truck to the back of the house, so the truck would be out of sight. Lady and I walked across the field toward where I believed the abandoned shed stood. There was almost a full moon making it easy to see the party center.

We moved in close to the shed and heard party noise. I told Lady to stay as I moved very close to the on-going party. A bonfire was burning bright, so it was easy to identify the party goers. I took many photos without the flash. The party goers included the three guys I had a conflict in town with; I found out later, they were Scott Keener, Bud Grimm, and Roy Grimm. Most of the other guests looked like high school students. They were having an incredibly good time.

Most interesting. I backed off, gathered Lady and we headed home for the night. At home I called Chad Bradford the Pike County Sheriff and arranged to meet him, so I could give him the film for developing. I was well prepared for Monday.

CHAPTER TWENTY-TWO

SUNDAY

The Four of Us Together in Church

Sunday started as usual, Lady was waiting for me to get up and get ready. When I finished all the necessaries of showering, shaving, and dressing, Lady led the way down the stairs, for she knew something. What was it? In the kitchen were five smiling faces: Sandra Martin, Mary Campbell, CherylAnn Swift, Susan Bradford Huff and Jean Jefferson. They had fixed a breakfast fit for a king. My apprehension was shown by my shock of this gathering. The door to the Henry house was going to remain open to the citizens and friends of Fort Henry. Being welcoming was more important than the sense of security of a locked door. Plus, there was Sally Kasey, Byron Shelley Keats, and Lady to protect the Henry house.

We all took our seats at Granny's white oak table after a few moments of prayer and socializing. We sat and enjoyed a marvelous breakfast, including Lady, who was delighted with the bacon mixed into her dog food.

"I want to thank all of you for your very warm welcoming home," I said waiting for the other shoe to drop.

"It is the least we could do for all you have done and are doing," Sandra Martin said a little tentatively.

Jean Jefferson said, questioning her aunt, "Aunt, what are you talking about? Done what? It is like a big secret. No one will talk about the secret."

"Yes, Sandy, Mary, and Susan, what is this secret? Why do you have such deep reverent feeling for John?" CherylAnn Swift was wondering what this big secret was.

"Should I?" stated Mary Campbell not as a question, but something she had to get off her chest.

Sandra Martin: "Yes, they should know."

"It was an evening in May in my junior year of high school. You must remember we were small-town girls, a little wet behind the ears," Mary Campbell paused.

"A whole river could flow behind our ears. We were very innocent," Sandra Martin added.

Susan Bradford Huff said, "Stupid."

"Stupid is a better word." Mary Campbell paused again not really wanting to talk about the secret.

Sandra Martin: "Jean, do you hear what we are saying? Young and stupid. The three of us... safety in numbers, right? We went with the Grimm brothers to a party. The rich wild Grimm brothers were taking us to a party. We were big-time."

"My parents did not have the slightest idea where I was. Where I was going. Come to find out, neither did I," Susan Bradford Huff chimed in.

"We arrived at the party and the first thing I asked myself, 'where is everyone?' Mary Campbell paused again.

"Who was there?" Jean Jefferson questioned.

"There were four guys and the Grimm brothers. The Grimm brothers said more people were coming and they should be here soon. They offered us some beer. We were big girls; I took a few sips. It was awful." Mary Campbell made a face, then stopped.

Susan Bradford Huff continued, "There were six boys, the Grimm brothers and four others standing around the fire. They started playing, 'who got the girl.' Susan Bradford Huff was getting embarrassed.

"It was at this point, we__ the three of us knew, we were the party," Sandra Martin said as she lowered her head.

Susan Bradford Huff: "We tried to leave, but there were too many of them. One boy said "Relax, you're going to enjoy it." Susan Bradford Huff continued, "I started crying and I asked for my mother."

Mary Campbell: "I knew what was going to happen and I said to the boys, 'She is only fourteen leave her alone.'"

One boy, laughing, said "She looks sixteen to me," as two boys started ripping off her clothes."

"I begged for them to take us home and they just laughed." Susan Bradford Huff was becoming emotional.

"We had one or two boys on us, and their hands were everywhere as they were ripping our clothes off," Sandra Martin said with a cold chill.

Susan Bradford Huff: "There was no hope. I was crying. Most of my clothes were off. I was terrified."

Sandra Martin spoke up: "Out of nowhere, we heard a voice, loud, so loud that everything stopped. The voice said 'STOP,' and from the darkness a boy stepped out, a boy we knew from school. He seemed so much bigger. The look on his face. It scared me...that look. I have never seen such a look before or since. I was the closest to this boy we knew as John Henry. He entered the party area and the two boys who were planning to have their way with me stopped. They looked at John Henry as he approached." Sandra Martin paused.

"John said in a voice that terrified even me, "Let her go." One boy let go of me and the other did not, John stepped forward to the boy who still had a hold of me. John said nothing as he grabbed the boy, pulling him off me. John hit the boy so hard, with such force, that he sent the boy flying. He was not going to get up and John turned to the other boy, who was frozen in place, and said, 'Get out of here or I will kill you,' Sandra Martin said reliving the moment.

"The boy ran as if the demons from hell were chasing him. Next, John, without a word, moved to Susan who had one boy on top of her. John seized him, pulling him off Susan. John started pulverizing him as Susan kept saying over and over, 'Hit him again.' Finally, John stopped. The boy was just a bloody piece of meat." Again, Sandra Martin paused.

"The Grimm brothers and one other guy were about to have their way with Mary Campbell. They did not notice a storm heading their way. Mary was nude. The Grimm brothers were on each side, holding her down. Mary was kicking, screaming, and doing everything in her power to free herself. The third boy had his pants off and was hovering over Mary. He was readying himself for the penetration of Mary." Mary Campbell squirmed hearing her story told.

"Mary was no longer begging, but she was still screaming obscenities. Mary's face told of the anger and disdain she was experiencing. From the rear of the boy hovering over Mary, a boot caught the boy in the balls. The powerful kick continued driving the boy off and over Mary into the bonfire three feet from Mary's head. The boy landed in the fire. He was yelling and rolling trying to get out of the fire. It seemed to take an hour for the boy to get out of the fire, even though it was just a few seconds. He was burnt pretty bad, as he continued to roll around wailing and crying."

Sandra Martin continued, "John stood over Mary with the Grimm brothers still holding her down. He said in a voice that shook the earth 'Let her go.' They let her go and she stumbled to her feet. John said, 'Sandra take them, get them out of here and go home.' We grabbed our clothes and ran. We were dressing as we headed toward the pickup truck. I look back, the Grimm brothers were standing with John facing them. The fire was blazing with John facing the fire, the Grimm brothers standing with John on one side and the fire on the other side." Everyone took a deep breath.

Sandra Martin: "The Grimm brothers were standing with slumped bodies as if all life and desire were drained out of them. I will remember that sight; for as long as I live. I can only imagine the punishment the Grimms were facing. We drove off toward town. We stopped at my house putting ourselves back together, the best we could. We went to school Monday, and we never spoke of that evening again, until now."

"Thank you, John. You saved me… and Sandy, and Mary," Susan Bradford Huff's face showed her true thankfulness.

Mary Campbell: "We were going to be raped and possibly killed. Thank you for giving our lives back. I will always love you. Jean and CherylAnn, one more thing, John and I dated for almost two years, and he never put any pressure on me…he knew."

Sandra Martin: "I knew John had a thing for me since third grade. I never really noticed him in that way, until that night, when it was too late. I want to thank you for that night and for being our guardian angel. John, you have always been there for us, though you did intimidate everyone who wanted to date us."

Susan Bradford Huff: "Thank you John, I have two lovely boys, a daughter and a great husband, because of you. I'm happy."

CherylAnn Swift: "John, I am sorry...I always thought you were jealous, overbearing, and overprotective. I am starting to understand. I am sorry."

"What did you do to the Grimm brothers?" Sandra Martin questioned me.

I said, "I talked to them."

Mary Campbell: "I hope it was a nice long talk you had with them."

"Yes," I said.

Sandra Martin: "If we are going to church, we better get going." We left for church and never more was this to be talked about. Susan's husband Bill and their two sons and daughter joined us as we entered the church. We sat together, for we would always from this day forth be together, at least in our hearts and minds. We each said our prayers and counted our blessing. Our one big blessing was that we were bound together for life.

We were at the Methodist church, though not all of us were Methodist. Someone was playing the organ before, during, and after the service. It was magnificent. I have heard organ music played at this level only a couple of times in my life; it was a real treat. On the way out of the church I said, "Mary who was playing the organ?"

Mary Campbell smiled and said, "Adele Muti Waserman is the organist. She is a world-famous pianist."

"Here in Fort Henry?" I said with great interest for my late wife Jacquelyn was a pianist and piano teacher. Adele playing brought back cherished memories.

Mary Campbell said, "Adele teaches math at the high school."

"She is a math teacher?" It was the end of the conversation, but not the end of my wondering.

After church we gathered outside of church. It was a bright sunny and warm day. Lady who had waited at the church door was playing with Susan's two boys. Mary Campbell and CherylAnn Swift introduced me to a well-dressed man. They were unaware that I already knew this stately man.

Mary Campbell: "John Henry, I would like to introduce you to our superintendent Harold Thomson." CherylAnn Swift explained to the superintendent I was a retired teacher and a surprisingly good teacher. Superintendent Thomson asked if I would be interested in substituting for the high school.

Superintendent Thomson said, "We could sure use some help finishing up the school year."

"Yes, I would be interested in substituting."

CherylAnn Swift and Mary Campbell were surprised at my response.

The superintendent said, "Good, you may start tomorrow. The high school is wrapping up the year. Tomorrow morning all you will have to do is show up early and fill out the necessary paperwork."

"I will be there with bells on." CherylAnn Swift and Mary Campbell were delighted. Sandra Martin glared over at me with a questioning look on her face; her face was saying, "What are you up to? All I could think of was tomorrow.

Sunday afternoon the three churches in town, the United Methodist church, the Fort Henry Church of Hope and St. Peter and St. Paul Catholic church were having an annual welcoming to Fort Henry picnic in honor of Major John Anthony Henry founder of the town. This took place from one to five at the John Anthony Henry Memorial Park of Fort Henry. It was a potluck picnic. The churches supplied soft drinks, hot dogs, and burgers. This picnic gave me the opportunity to meet many members of Fort Henry's community and refresh old friendships with people I knew when I was young. It was startling to see how people aged, but they were the same in my memories. They lived in the same houses, they wore similar clothes, they told the same stories. They were the same, only twenty or thirty years older.

Major John Anthony Henry settled in Pike County and renamed Fort Hutchins to Fort Henry. This was where the history of the John Anthony Henry Memorial Park of Fort Henry started. I was standing in the middle of the John Anthony Henry Memorial Park of Fort Henry remembering what my Granny had said about the mounted fort now called Fort Henry. She said this mounted fort had been here for at least two thousand years. This small earthwork on this gently sloping hillside was not established by the French, English, Americans nor even the Shawnee Indians. The Muskogee Creek Indians lived in this area from 1,600 to 1,800. They were mainly agriculturalist. From 1,000 to 1,750 various Indian tribes lived in this area. They were descendants of the Hopewell culture who lived in this area from about 100 BC to 500 AD. The history of the earthwork mount now called Fort Henry is a little vague. It was believed the mount was not established for defensive purpose, but for agricultural purposes.

Granny said a group from the university in the late 1930's studied the site and they found stone tools, bone tools, horns, shells, antlers, flint arrowheads and flint knives linking this site back to over 2,000 years ago. Somewhere in the 1,600 to 1,800 diseases, because of trade between the eastern Indians and white men devastated the Indian population in this area of the country. The Indian population in this area was never to recover. The Shawnee Indians during this time diseases broke from smaller groups and moved from agriculture society to a warrior society. This was as devastating to them as the disease had been to the earlier Indian tribes.

The true history of the earthwork mount has been rewritten over time with many distortions. The true and correct history of Fort Henry and the earthwork mound is something I am going to try to rectify in the future.

After the picnic Lady and I returned home in the evening to gather the necessary items for our next adventure. It was time to head to the Bottoms.

I was waiting for darkness, so I could move without being seen. Lady and I drove my grandfather's truck to the southern section of the county, called the Bottoms; it was so named because about three thousand acres were hundred to two hundred feet below the rest of the land in the county. During heavy rains, the Bottoms would often flood, making the land less desirable than the higher areas of the county.

Jim Thornton owned 420 acres of bottom land and he always had trouble making ends meet because of the continued flooding. Every two or three years, his crops would be flooded out. He decided to find another way of making a living off the land. He borrowed every cent he could get his hands on and built four large warehouse buildings. He was going to go into the storage and warehousing business. The problem was what was he going to store and warehouse? He was not the greatest businessperson in the world. His total enterprise went belly-up. He was devastated. There was nothing he could do. He gave up and moved out of state looking for new opportunities. He was gone, but his buildings remained.

Lady and I were heading for the Thornton farm and the buildings Jim Thornton had left behind. I was not familiar with the Bottoms or the Thornton farm. I had only been to this part of the county a few times when I was a kid. After driving around in the Bottoms for about a half an hour, I located the Thornton farm and the buildings Jim Thornton had left behind. I parked the truck on a cow path well covered from the road by trees and brush. It was just as Wilton Graff had said. There were about two windmills and several solar panels with a building at the front of the property. This all faced the road; I was not interested in this part of the property. I was interested in the building which sat back away from the road.

Lady and I moved carefully through the brush to the rear of the property. There was a large building sitting about five hundred feet from the road. No one was around, so we moved up to investigate by looking in a window. The windows were darkened. The doors were locked. I moved to the rear of the building, and I found a door in the back hidden in a thick brush. The door was unlocked. With some effort, it opened. Inside was a huge pot growing factory. It was ready to start growing pot, growing tables after growing tables, row after row. It was big. Big enough to supply the county, the state, even other states. It was mind boggling.

My first desire was to burn it, burn it to the ground. There was a large diesel tanker truck in front of this building. It would be extremely easy to open the valve and flood the building and surrounding area with diesel fuel. This would make quite a fire. This was not the answer, there had to be a better way. Time was what I needed. Another day or two to come up with a better way of destroying this facility and the people behind this evil enterprise. I was sure that I could come up with something remarkably interesting.

CHAPTER TWENTY-THREE

$$\boxed{\text{MONDAY}}$$

To School We Go

It was early Monday morning as Lady, and I pulled into the high school parking lot and parked in a spot labeled "Visitors." Only a couple of cars were in the lot. Since school did not start until 8:00 a.m. Lady and I walked the grounds and the halls of the high school looking for any signs of drugs and/or remnants of drug use. We found a few leftover pot butts, just enough for Lady to identify the smell. Inside the high school Lady identified seven possible lockers. I wrote down the locker numbers, to be checked later. The school had not changed much, a new gym, career center and library, but mostly it was the way I remembered the old place. It was an eerie feeling walking the halls again. I could feel someone watching me as I was checking out the school. The hairs on the back of my neck were standing up.

As I walked the empty halls of the high school, I heard a door open, I was not alone. After thirty minutes of roaming around the school, I felt someone behind me, I turned and looked. Who was it? Was I seeing another vision? It could not be after all these years. I called out "Uncle Douglas?"

"Yes," was returned from a voice down the hall. Was it…? Yes, it was…but was, but how? My mind was spinning. Was this town getting the best of me? As I moved closer, I could see it was Uncle Douglas. I said, "You don't recognize me?"

"John, John Henry?" Uncle Douglas said without surprise.

"Yes," as I closed the gap.

He said as we were shaking hands, "What are you doing here?"

"I'm substituting at the high school. Do you believe it?"

"Some teachers are turning over in their graves" Uncle Douglas said with a smile.

"Come on Uncle Douglas, I wasn't that bad…was I?"

Uncle Douglas said touching his chin with his thumb and fore finger in a doubtful striking motion said, "A substitute, hum?"

"Yes," I said reassuringly.

"You sure that is all you are doing?" Uncle Douglas said with a suspicious tone.

"Just a substitute," I said looking Uncle Douglas in the eye.

Uncle Douglas: "The way you were roaming around this place I was wondering."

"Uncle Douglas just substituting, I was roaming the school remembering of days gone by."

Uncle Douglas: "If you need any help, let me know. I must get the school ready, have a good day."

"Good to see you." I was not sure that I was fooling Uncle Douglas.

I am not sure how Uncle Douglas is related to me. He was not my father or grandfather's brother, but everyone in the family called him Uncle Douglas. My Granny Ruth once told me Uncle Douglas was not related to us. My grandfather adopted Douglas into the family after Douglas saved my father's life. Granny said my father was about to drown in the Tallman River when Douglas jumped in and saved him.

My father was young at the time when this happened, and my grandfather unofficially adopted Douglas as part of the family. From that day forward I believe Douglas Digger was called Uncle Douglas. Uncle Douglas it is. Uncle Douglas was, and it seems still is, the custodian of the high school. Uncle Douglas was a young man when he started work at the high school some fifty years ago. The high school position was made available by my grandfather because grandfather was on the school board at the time. Uncle Douglas it is.

He was my scholarly angel, for any problem I had with my studies, Uncle Douglas could and would explain it in a way I could even understand. He was the most brilliant man I have ever known. He was smarter than any teacher at the high school or professor at the university. He was not even a high school graduate, but he read everything, and he knew everything. He would help befogged confused high school students with their studies. He was the go-to guy. He was always there. This was his life. He would work with students on the weekends, before and after school. He would never turn down a student asking for help. I know for I needed a lot of help. I was going to be a scholar like it or not, thanks to Granny's with after school studies and Uncle Douglas's encouragement during school. It was easier to give in and learn.

It was about seven as I passed the auditorium, I heard someone playing a piano, so I opened the door. On stage was an unbelievably beautiful, composed pianist playing a movement from Mozart. My wife Jennifer was a pianist who loved Mozart, which was the reason I recognized the piece being played. It was breathtaking. This incredibly beautiful woman was playing on a Steinway piano. Was this woman practicing for a major concert at some extravagant venue? Why with her enormous talent was she here at Fort Henry High School? The woman was exceptionally talented. I had only heard this quality of play a few times in my life. I was blessed to listen to this exceptional pianist. I was grateful, thankful, appreciative, and overwhelmed. I applauded when she finished the movement. She looked at me for a second as I was still applauding, and she left the stage. I realize this must be the math teacher Mary Campbell was talking about.

At about seven-twenty the school office opened, and I made a beeline to the office. This was my first day of school. It was ten minutes until eight when I finished all the paperwork and Mr. Durkins, the principal, completed his conversation with the superintendent. Mr. Durkins was not happy when he was told Lady and I were to be given free range of the school, no questions asked. Mr. Durkins was not happy that I had some secret connection with Superintendent Thomson.

Mr. Durkins had a smile on his face as he assigned me to Mr. Stalnaker's World History class. Being a teacher for many years, I knew this must be a challenging class. Mr. Durkins thought he was getting even with me for his being left out of the circle. I was an old hand at handling difficult classes and problem students. Once I opened the classroom door, I knew why the regular teacher was out. The teacher was out because he was another deficient teacher.

I stood at the entrance of the door waiting for the devilment behavior to subside. A few students were seated, but most were wandering around the room. I walked to the teacher's desk and quietly said my name. There was excitement of being in front of a classroom again. It sent chills up and down my spine. I loved teaching; I was in my comfort zone.

Only two girls in the front paid any attention. The two girls were Terri Trenton and Jean Jefferson. I was appreciative of their behavior. Lady stayed at the door, looking at me, as if to say. You got to be kidding. I picked up a large paperback textbook and proceeded to rip it in half. More students were starting to notice me. By the time I ripped up the second textbook, most of the class stopped in place and looked at me. "Please take your seats," I said in a soft smooth voice. With this most of the students sat. I had a third book in my hands as they all sat. "My name is John Henry, and it is my pleasure to be your instructor today."

From the back of the room, "Yea, right."

I said, "No, I am John Henry. I am a little rusty, but my analyst told me I should be able to teach again, if I just take it easy. Most of my anger issues are behind me. That student from two years ago is almost back to normal. Just a little limp." I stopped and looked at the book in my hands and said, "I better not. We may need this book, just like we may need most of you." Lady entered the room and went to the back of the room. She was carefully watching all the students, readying herself to attack. A hand raised in the back row, as if he wanted to and not want to ask a question. I said, "Yes, you have a question?" From the back of the room "Aren't you the one who flattened Butts and stood up to the Grimm brothers?"

"I didn't mean to hurt him, but sometimes my anger gets the best of me." There was silence. The first period proceeded with little difficulty and a reasonable amount of productive education. My classroom management skills were useful. Lady singled out two of the students as possible users. I praised Lady after class.

After first period, Uncle Douglas handed me a slip of paper when no one was around. I was not fooling Uncle Douglas, for he knew everything. I read the slip of paper after he left. It was a list of the drug dealers, drug users, problem students and problems at the high school, including the staff. This was extremely helpful.

The word had passed so in the next class, the students were on time, in their seats and ready to start class. Lady picked out one student in this class as a possible user and it checked out. His locker was one of the suspicious lockers. During my free period, I located the lockers of the students on Uncle Douglas's list and who Lady had picked out in class. I kept an eye out for students who were at the party center at the Mills farm.

I observed three boys from the party last night. They joined with two others. Together, they left the building at lunch. I followed. I kept my distance, but I could see through my binoculars they met up with a guy at the back of the Mills farm, the same guy who was with the Grimm boys. They were smoking and doing drugs. The five students came back to school with ten minutes left in the lunch period. It was just enough time to sell their wares. Yes, the high school has a drug problem, right here in River City. I discouraged their enterprise by taking my lunch duty seriously, and supervising lunch with dedication. No sales were made during lunch.

At the end of lunch, I called Sheriff Chad Bradford and informed him of my progress. There were five definite drug abusers and they had drugs on them for sale. Chad said he and seven deputies would be at the school in a half an hour. I told Chad; they were to park away from the school. Come to the back of the school, so no one will spot you. Within thirty minutes Sheriff Chad Bradford and his deputies were in the building.

During this time, I had CherylAnn Swift cover my class, so I could meet Sheriff Chad Bradford and his deputies. With Sheriff Chad Bradford and deputies in place we had the five students, one by one come to the office. Once each suspect arrived at the office they were handcuffed, separated, and moved to an isolated location with a deputy supervising. It took twenty-five minutes to complete the arrest of all five suspects. Once the arrests were completed, Mr. Durkins was instructed to call a school assembly. The students were moved to the gym and the teachers were guarding all the doors.

Now it was sweat time. Sheriff Chad Bradford and his deputies did an excellent job of sweating the five. Within ten minutes four of the five were spilling their guts. The fifth was like a clam. We had the drugs, the money, the location, the dealers, the users__, we had everything. The fifth boy, name Rod Ginnger was new to the school, a real hard case. The five were taken to the Carrollton Sheriff's Department. Three deputies remained to deal with the students who were identified by the four students cooperating. A total of twenty-six students were ushered out of the assembly, separated, and confined.

Crying, shouting, foul language, sweating and vomiting was the behavior of the twenty-six students as they sat in separate rooms with deputies, teachers, staff members, and whoever was available. Fourteen were sent home with their parents for discipline which would occur later. The lockers of eight were searched and with the help of Lady, drugs were found in five lockers. Four students were allowed to return to the assembly. Six cars were searched with the permission of the students. Three cars were found containing drugs. Of the eight remaining four were sent home with their parents for future discipline. The last four were taken to the Carrollton Sheriff's Department. It took until four o'clock to finish the interrogation. School was let out and a buzz could be heard throughout the community.

One particularly important note: I was known only as a substitute teacher helping the high school for the day. My fingerprints were not on any of the repercussions of the day. I was not linked to the drug bust, the interrogations, and/or disciplines of the day. I was under the radar. No one was aware of my involvement except Chad Bradford the Pike County Sheriff and Harold Thomson, the school superintendent.

CHAPTER TWENTY-FOUR

MONDAY

Scott is On the Go

From the information I gained from the interrogation of the high school students, it seems Scott Keener was the key to the whole drug program at the high school, Fort Henry, and Pike County. I had the approximate location of Scott Keener in Carrollton; Lady and I drove to Carrollton to see if we could find the exact location of Scott Keener. I parked on the block identified and went into a coffee shop and sat next to the window, so I could observe the block. A little after six Scott exited a two-story apartment building.

Now I had two choices: to follow Scott Keener or to enter his apartment. Scott Keener was surely paranoid, and his apartment was probably booby-trapped. Following him seemed to be the better of the two choices.

I said to Lady, "Lady, what do you think about searching the apartment?" Nothing. "Follow him?" Lady barked.
Quickly we got in grandfather's truck and headed the same
direction as Scott. We caught up with him a few miles
outside of town.

He headed west. I was not sure where he was going,
so I laid way back. Scott Keener was headed toward Fort
Henry, but east of Fort Henry he turned off, cutting up to
Fuller Road and then drove on Route 17 toward Weston.
The road was straight and flat, I could see for miles. The dot
of his car was in sight. His car turned off where I expected,
and I pulled grandfather's truck into the Mills' drive to the
back of the abandoned house. No one would see my pickup.
It was still light. I carefully crossed the field to a vantage
point where I could observe what Scott Keener was up too.

He took a cloth bag from his car and walked toward
me. Lady and I sunk down behind a bush. We could see
Scott Keener hiding the bag in a tree stump. He went back
to his car and took some boxes out of the trunk and moved
the boxes to the shed. It looked like Scott was preparing for
another party or to leave town. It was getting dark as Lady
and I sat, waiting. Our wait was not long. Scott Keener left
the shed, got in his car, and drove off.

Lady and I waited a few minutes, then we circled
around to come into the party center from the opposite
direction. I was hoping the circuitous route would make it
difficult to identify my trail and my being here. Lady stood

near a large tree where Scott Keener had hidden something. Lady was making a low growl, as I joined her at the tree and noticed some fresh branches and leaves covering something. I removed the branches and found a hole in the bottom of the tree; a bag was in the hole.

I pulled out the bag and opened it. It was full of money and papers. I took my jacket off and filled my jacket with the money and papers. I filled the bag up with leaves and twigs and replaced it in the tree trunk. I was careful to replace the branches and leaves covering the hole in the tree as I had found it. On my way back to the truck I stopped at the shed Scott was using and found a stash of drugs.

Scott Keener's apartment was not too far out of my way. I stopped at Scott's apartment and placed the bag of drugs I'd found in the shed at the party center in his car. The next item on my agenda was to call Sheriff Chad Bradford and give him the location of Scott's apartment. Scott Keener had a front and rear entrance for his possible escape. This was information I passed on to Chad. It was only a brief time later that, Sheriff Chad Bradford and four deputies surrounded Scott Keener's apartment.

I had successfully kept my hands off everything that happened today, even though I was at the center of everything. Scott Keener was arrested once they searched his car and found the drugs. Scott Keener went crazy. Scott Keener thought he was home free, for he had made sure there was nothing incriminating around his apartment or car. How could the deputies find drugs in his car? Scott Keener was beside himself. How could this be happening? Someone was setting him up. Who?

Once I was home, I opened my jacket and counted the money. There was over 2.8 million dollars. In checking the papers there was an identification of a bank account number owned by the Grimms for a bank in Panama. This number could only be reached and identified by phone, so with my trusted phone, I followed the instructions on the paper. In ten minutes, I had transferred all but $32.68 in this account number to a new account I had established. The amount I transferred was over $32,680,000.

Next, I was surprised to find a slip of paper with the directions and combination to the safe at the Grimms house and the secret hiding place in the Grimms barn. There was further information identifying the drug operation in the county and state, Scott kept an incredibly detailed notebook of all the drug enterprises in the county and state including names, dates, and places. Was he in it alone? All this information told me one thing Scott Keener was planning to steal all the money from the Grimm brothers and whoever else participated in the drug operation. I believed Scott was planning to skip town.

I hid the money and the papers in the secret place in the semi-circle fruit cellar that only my Granny and I knew of. I was tired from this day's effort. Lady and I ate a late supper and went to bed.

CHAPTER TWENTY-FIVE

TUESDAY

The Transfer

Lady and I went downtown for breakfast, because no one was in the Henry house kitchen to fix us our morning meal. We walked up town for breakfast to Sandy's Café. It was busy. Lady and I found a place in the back of the restaurant to the right. Sandra Martin was too busy for conversation this morning, so Lady and I ate and moved along.

There was too much to do today to linger at Sandy's Cafe'. Lady and I stopped at the local bank to be informed that Mr. Graff had been called away on family business. They were not sure when Mr. Graff was returning. I was talking to Bobbie Smith the assistant bank manager, to gain information about the pay offs of Sandra Martin, Susan Bradford Huff, CherylAnn Swift, Mary Campbell and other farmers' debts. All these debts orchestrated by the Grimm brothers to swindle Pike County residents out of their land, were to be paid today by me.

I arranged for my friend Bruce's assistant to meet me at the Carrollton Bank at 10:00 a.m. this morning, to turn over the million dollars. It was to be deposited in my name.

At 10:00 a.m. my friend's assistant was waiting for me outside the Carrollton Bank. We entered the bank and together we made all the necessary arrangements to transfer the funds to my name. It was about 11:00 a.m. when all the paperwork was filled out, signed, and filed. I thanked the bank officials and my friend's assistant, and, with the deposit and a certified check, Lady and I were on our way back to Fort Henry. I had a certified check for $600,000 made out to the Fort Henry Bank.

This was more than what Fort Henry Bank was showing in their books for the outstanding loans. Wilton Graff was a part of this whole mess and he had better never show his face in town again. Once Lady and I arrived at the Fort Henry Bank, Bobbie Smith, the assistant manager of the bank, was delighted. She was a good friend of Sandra Martin and Mary Campbell. Bobbie Smith finalized all the necessary paperwork, and she provided me with all the receipts of payment. The loans were paid in full for Sandra Martin, Susan Bradford Huff, CherylAnn Swift, Mary Campbell and seven other farmers. Their farms were now free of debt.

At one o'clock Lady and I were in Sandy's Cafe' for a late lunch. Sandra Martin was still terribly busy. After lunch, she and I only had a couple of minutes to talk. I told her she was to contact Susan Bradford Huff, CherylAnn Swift and Mary Campbell and have them meet here at three-thirty. There was something especially important I wanted to tell them.

Sandra Martin: "I will contact all three, but what is it about?"

"Something important to all of us...I want to tell all of you at the same time." I reassured Sandra.

"Three-thirty will work because Jean will be here from school to work the restaurant."

It was time for Lady and me to head for home.

After returning home, Lady and I were walking around the Henry house property when I spotted Anna Walker, the across-the-street neighbor. Anna Walker was on her porch, and she waived at me, I stopped for a moment to chat. Anna was one of my many guardian angels when I was young. I did not know she was still alive, or I would have visited her sooner.

Anna said, "Have a seat," and we moved into her living room or today, we would call it the great room. We were making ourselves comfortable as Anna asked, "Would you like something to drink, maybe some cold water?"

"That sounds great." Anna Walker went to the kitchen and busied herself preparing chilled water from her kitchen sink faucet for all three of us. It was refreshing. When I was a boy, I would visit Anna on many sweltering summer days. The pick-me-up of the day was always chilled water from the tap. Anna's water, like most people's water in Fort Henry, was well water. It was cool and very refreshing. Two glasses, one for Anna, one for me and a bowl for Lady. We enjoyed this delight. Cool clean well water is very invigorating, City processed water does not compare.

Anna Walker: "I knew you were coming home when your Granny died, I just knew it. I would have come over sooner, but I've been out of town visiting my sister." When Anna said this about my Granny's death, it tugged at my heart, for I should have been here.

"It feels good to be home, but I'm sorry I missed my Granny's funeral."

Anna Walker: "Her death was sudden. I was talking to her that morning, and she was in fine health. I saw the Grimms pickup parked next to her house and that afternoon, she was dead." The tone in Anna Walker's voice indicated there were doubts in her mind about how and why my Granny had died.

I said, "Everyone says she was in good health, and then she was dead. Very concerning."

Anna Walker: "I believe the Grimms had something to do with your grandmother's death."

"We probably will never know for sure."

Anna Walker: "I still believe it."

"Anna how have you been?" I asked, trying to change the subject.

Anna Walker: "Just getting old, older. You know I'm in my late 80's."

"You don't look a day over 50, you have not changed in all the years I'm known you."

Anna Walker: "You're saying that to be nice, you always were nice, nice to me."

I said, "You are my friend and you always kept me out of trouble."

Anna Walker, "You helped me out of trouble many a time. You remember the time my fan was broke? It was so hot. I think it was over a hundred in the shade. You stopped by that afternoon. You took one look at me. I was so hot, and you took that fan and walked in that heat back to your farm. You returned later that extremely hot afternoon with my fan you had repaired. It was a lifesaver."

"Yes, I remember." It was the least I could do for a friend, plus I believed she was going to have a heat stroke if the fan were not fixed.

Anna Walker continued. "And remember the time that orange and black cat got stuck up in my tree? You climbed up the tree and rescued the cat. I think that was Mrs. Dibbert's cat. She never thanked you. You would come by and cut my grass, do yard work…, yes you have always been nice to me."

"You were always nice to me." I enjoyed Anna Walker's company and our many conversations.

Anna Walker: "How many afternoons you would come by and visit this old woman when you had kids to play with."

"Yes, we would talk. You would tell me about the history of Fort Henry. It was fascinating."

Anna Walker: "You would bring me things, things I needed. You sent me money over the years; it really helped."

"You remember when I was eight on my birthday you sent me a birthday card with a quarter in it. It was shortly after my mother, father and sister were killed. Inside the card you wrote, 'I will always be your friend no matter what. Love Anna' I still have that card and we are still friends. Now I know a quarter to you was a fortune. The real fortune to me was your friendship."

Anna Walker: "Yes, we have good memories, friends always do. Being alone for these many years has given me time to think. I was so happy when your grandparents moved into the Henry house about sixteen years ago. Your grandmother became a close friend. She was such a comfort. Sally Kasey has been here for me with anything I needed to be fixed. Sally could fix and repair anything. Bryon Keats has become an incredibly good friend in the last few years. He would drive your grandmother and me to the store, doctor and even the county fair. Life has been good, but I missed you."

"I missed you too and now I am back." I was thinking to myself. *Why did I leave Fort Henry?*

Anna Walker was small with a small body frame. She was thin, thin from missing too many meals. She ate almost no meat, not that she was a vegetarian. The choice was not hers to make. She gardened and canned; she was proud. She would not ask for help. Once my Granny moved to the Henry house across the street from Anna, Granny realized how much help Anna needed. Anna's husband had died about two years before my parents and sister died. He was a good man but earned little as a clerk for the local dry goods store. There was little in savings and no insurance. Anna's house of little value was paid for; she had a roof over her head, but little else. I was too young to understand. Poverty was a word I heard in school, but it had little meaning.

Shortly after my mother, father and sister died in an auto accident I received a birthday card from Anna Walker. Anna Walker was a part of my life from that point forward. In the birthday card Anna wrote in a shaky script, 'I will always be your friend no matter what.' The card stirred my curiosity. This was a woman I needed to meet. One afternoon while my Granny was taking a nap, I walked to town. I knew Anna Walker lived across from my great-grandmother's house. This was my destination. I approached Anna's house, softly stepped up her steps and looked in her house. She was playing with a gun. I knocked on the door. This startled Anna. Anna Walker came to the door, and she said, "Yes, what can I do for you?" This was said in an almost angry tone.

"I'm John Henry and I want to thank you for my birthday card."

Anna said, "Come in," and I did.

Inside all was quiet with a dusty smell. She still had the pistol in her hand as

I said, "My mother doesn't allow me to play with guns."

She knew my mother was gone and my saying this astonished her. Anna said, "Your mother is right you should not play with guns. You may get hurt."

"You should put the gun away; you don't want to hurt yourself."

Anna Walker: "You are right I will put the gun away, so I will not get hurt. Do you want some water? It is cool and refreshing."

"Yes." Anna went to the kitchen and in a few moments, returned with two glasses of water and no gun. She was not going to hurt herself.

Anna Walker: "You were only a little boy, and you came and saved me."

"I had to save you; I needed a friend." Looking back, I now realized what had transpired that day.

Anna Walker: "You said something very strange that day; you said a tree caught you and saved you, so you must save me. What did you mean?"

"I climbed to the top of a big oak tree trying to see my parents and sister coming back to the farm. I stuck my head above the tree looking down the road, I was up in the tree for a long time. I must have fallen asleep. I fell; when I awoke the tree had caught me and kept me from falling to the ground."

Anna Walker: "The tree is very special."

"Yes, it is my special tree. My great, great, Grandfather John Anthony Henry planted it, so it could save me."

The expression on Anna's face was glowing and she asked, "Do you want some more water?" After an enjoyable conversation with Anna Walker, it was time for me to head up to town, to Sandy's Café.

At twenty after three Lady and I entered Sandy's Cafe', Susan Bradford Huff and Sandra Martin were seated at the right front of the restaurant.

Sandra Martin said, "Mary Campbell and CherylAnn Swift are on their way. At three thirty we were all gathered.

Sandra Martin looked at me and said "So."

"I have some good news all of the debts for all of our farms are paid off." I said with a smile.

CherylAnn Swift: "That is great news. Not that I doubted you, but that is great news."

Susan Bradford Huff: "Thank you John. Again, you came through and saved the day. You are my superhero."

"No, Susan you are my sister, my adopted sister and I will do the best to watch out for my little sister." I was remembering my sister Alice who'd died, and I was not able to protect her.

Mary Campbell: "There is so much I want to say, but if it is alright, I will just say thank you."

"Mary and all of you, you are welcome. You are my friends, and it is the least I could have done."

Sandra Martin: "I guess we are out of trouble."

"No, we all need to watch our backs and each other's back. I believe this is going to get nastier before it is over. We are to check in with one another throughout the day to make sure we are all safe," I said, trying not to be an alarmist.

"You think we are still in danger?" Sandra Martin said with hesitation.

"Yes, this is not over. The Grimms are not going to lie down and do nothing. Now go home and keep a low profile. Lock all doors and windows, be extremely cautious."

The joy at the beginning of our meeting turned into concern and fear. With heavy hearts the meeting broke up. Sandra Martin and CherylAnn Swift stayed in the restaurant. Susan Bradford Huff went across the street to her hardware store. What was going to happen next?

Mary Campbell and I walked out together, and I asked Mary "How is our math teacher pianist doing?"

Mary Campbell: "Adele is a wonderful addition to our community. She plays most mornings at the high school, she has quite a following."

"Was that a Steinway she was playing on?" Why was there a Steinway at the high school or as a matter of fact in Fort Henry? This is not Steinway country.

Mary Campbell: "Yes, how do you know it's a Steinway?"

"Jacquelyn my wife used to play piano, of course not on a Steinway. When we would go to a concert, Jacquelyn would rave about Steinway pianos, the quality of sound a Steinway could produce." Sweetness entered my mind as I remembered Jacquelyn playing the piano, even if the memory of Jacquelyn was only for a second.

Mary Campbell: "Adele when she first came to the high school, she was playing on an old school piano. The piano was in miserable condition, out of tune, beat up. Somehow Adele made beautiful music come out of that miserable instrument. Her playing was magnificent, but the piano was terrible. Mr. Digger purchased a Steinway for Adele to play on. She was delighted."

"You mean Uncle Douglas? Where did he get the money?"

Mary Campbell: "Mr. Digger is loaded, he has been purchasing items for students at the high school for years. Books, clothes, you name it. He also bought Adele a Steinway piano for her home." I whistled and said good afternoon, and Lady and I continued home.

CHAPTER TWENTY-SIX

TUESDAY:

Susan's Hero

I t was 6:05 p.m., Susan Bradford Huff was in a hurry to close the hardware store. She closed the back door and locked it. Before she could pull the key from the lock, she grasped. It was from behind and she did not have a chance. Her assailant wore gloves. He covered her mouth, so she could not scream. The other hand was around her waist pulling her away from the backdoor. Susan fought with all the force in her, but a second assailant was holding her arms. She was still kicking when the second assailant punched her hard in the face and she went limp. She was unconscious.

Susan awoke finding her head covered with a cloth bag and her hands tied. She could tell she was in the bed of a truck. The truck finally stopped; Susan knew this was not good. She was pulled out of the bed of the truck, then

Susan Bradford Huff landed hard on to the ground. All seemed to be lost; Susan believed she was going to die. After all her dignity was taken away. Susan decided she was not going to die so easily.

Susan decided she would make them pay no matter how little or how much, She was going to make them pay somehow. The anger grew in Susan as the fear diminished. Hope was in limbo. She was blinded by this bag over her head and restricted by her hands being tied behind her. Think, think. What could she do?

Susan heard at a distance the faint sound of a vehicle. A flicker of hope was starting to grow as the vehicle noise was approaching. The vehicle noise faded; there was no noise. The hope slipped away. Where was the vehicle she heard? Was the vehicle on a nearby road? Where was she?

"Go get some beer from the shed" Bud Grimm said to Roy Grimm, for it was time to start the party. Hearing the voice telling the other villain to get the beer, Susan knew there were at least two scoundrels. Susan knew the villains. This was not good.

"Why?" Roy questioned Bud, Roy was a little slower and a follower. Roy was accustomed to taking orders from Bud. Susan, hearing the second voice, confirmed there were at least two villains.

"We are going to have a nice little part.," Bud Grimm was looking forward with excitement to get the party started.

"Yes, I will get the beer then can we deal with the girl," Roy said with anticipation.

"She is no girl; she is old enough to be your mother," Bud said.

"But you said__," Roy replied.

"I said they all give pleasure alike, young or old. Go get the beer," Bud ordered.

Susan said from under the cloth bag, "You better let me go, if you know what is good for you." Susan was still holding out hope that this was just a bad dream. Susan was terrified, but she knew if she was going to get out of this mess, she had to keep her cool. Susan's hands were tied behind her back, but her legs were free. She could run if only she could get the bag off her head. Susan said to herself, *Keep your cool, think.*

"We will let you go when we are done with you," Bud answered Susan.

"You are going to be sorry; I know he is coming" She was thinking to herself, *John, Chad, where are you?*

"Who is coming?" Bud Grimm demanded.

"Your worst nightmare." Susan was hoping it would be their nightmare and not hers.

"Just listen to her, we're her worst nightmare." Roy laughs.

"Roy get the beer from the shed, it's time to get started," Bud ordered.

Roy was gone for a brief time when there was a small thud noise. Bud said, "Roy are you OK?... Roy? Roy?"

All was quiet, Susan laid still listening. *What was happening?*

* * *

Sandra Martin called when I was fixing dinner for Lady and me. "Susan is missing" Sandra Martin sounded tormented. "I don't know what to do...she was supposed to meet me at six and we were going to church."

"Where was she?" I was trying to understand what Sandra was talking about.

Sandra Martin: "At her hardware store, she was going to close up and come right over to the cafe'. She called ten minutes to six from the hardware. The lights are out, and the door is locked. Susan is not answering."

"I will be there in a couple of minutes." I was hoping to myself this was not the work of the Grimms.

Lady and I jumped in the truck and headed to the hardware store; I made sure I had the 9 mm Chad Bradford the Pike County Sheriff had given me. At the back of the hardware store, I noticed the keys were still in the door's lock and Susan's car was still there. Susan would not have left the keys in the door; something was terribly wrong. I bet it was the Grimms, but where would they have taken her? A couple of days ago I'd found a party center behind the Mills farm. This location was hidden from the main road. It was a perfect place to take someone and do whatever. This was not the work of the Grimm brothers. It was too messy. It had to be Darrel's sons or their friend Jake, since Scott was in jail. Hopefully the party center was the right place.

Lady and I were back in the truck and before I headed north, I stopped at the back of Sandy's Café and told Sandra Martin I was going to search for Susan. I told Sandra she should get in touch with CherylAnn Swift and Mary Campbell and that all three of them should hold up someplace safe. I told her to call Sheriff Chad Bradford and tell him what was going on with Susan.

I was driving at a high rate of speed when I closed in on the party center. I pulled into the back of the Mills house and quickly Lady and I ran across the field to the party center. There was no sound. Then I heard voices. The voice was saying "Roy get the beer from the shed, it's time to get started." With this I moved slowly and quietly to the shed. I was positioning myself near the shed.

Someone was approaching the shed. I moved to the side of the shed and picked up a short log and waited. The guy was standing about six feet from the shed. He entered the shed; I was ready for his exit, as if were coached and rehearsed. Lady growled in a low soft growl from the front left of the shed. The guy turned toward the front left of the shed. I attacked, striking him with the log, hard. He went down and I took his weapon in time to hear "Roy, are you

OK? Roy? Roy?" I did not have time to tie up Roy; I had to move on to the next guy, quickly. I moved to the back of the shed to the tree line. I was moving toward the next guy.

I was just about within striking distance when I was spotted. I pulled my pistol into a shooting position as the guy pulled up his rifle, aiming at me. It seemed like minutes all of this was taking place, but I knew it was seconds. Then out of nowhere a flash of an animal was upon the assailant. It was Lady. Lady hit the assailant chest-high; Bud was driven backwards. The force of the attack moved the rifle up toward the sky as it fired into the air. The assailant was hurt as he'd landed on his back hard and his head hit a rock. He was down, and Lady had found a new chewing toy.

I moved from the tree line and headed to Susan as the assailant yelled "Get imam off, get imam off," over and over. I almost was feeling sorry for the new chew toy, almost, but first I needed to help Susan. I pulled the feed bag off her head and started to untie her; she was laughing, crying, and trying to catch her breath all at the same time. Susan lunged into my arms knocking me down. On the ground I'd finished freeing Susan. There was a smile on her face that I will always remember.

I said, "Wait, I have to take care of these two characters." Susan was understanding and moved to the side. Back on my feet, I went over to Lady and her chew toy and said "Lady, OK."

Lady stopped playing with her chew toy and stood over this bloody mess that once was a man. I said, "Good girl, good girl, watch him" I picked up the rifle and found some rope in the bed of their truck. I turned him over and tied his hands; he was growling in pain. Next, I moved to the guy called Roy. He was still unconscious. I tied him up, then pulled him to Susan and his brother's location.

CHAPTER TWENTY-SEVEN

TUESDAY:

The Grimms Are Secure

I took out my phone and gave it to Susan Bradford Huff. Susan called Chad Bradford her brother and the Pike County Sheriff and gave him details of what had happened. He and every deputy in the county were on their way. Susan called Sandra Martin and told Sandra that she was OK, and Susan gave Sandra some of the details. Susan told Sandra to call her husband Bill and let him know she was OK.

I turned to Susan Bradford Huff, and said, "Are you OK."

"Yes. As little shaken, but I am OK, thanks to you. This is the fourth time you have saved me. I will never be able to thank you enough." Susan Bradford Huff said, with appreciation in her voice.

I told Susan to watch the two while I started a signal fire for her brother Sheriff Chad Bradford and his deputies. I gathered up wood, branches, paper and of course the cloth bag now filled with leaves and twigs. I collected gasoline I had found in the shed and poured it on the wood and branches. I placed a few twenty-dollar bills near the fire once I lit the fire. I made sure drugs from the shed were in the Grimm boys' truck. I wanted as many offences against the Grimm boys as possible. I wanted them to serve as much time for this and any other crimes that could be manufactured.

I returned to Susan Bradford Huff. She was smiling and said, "This one tried to get away."

She was pointing to one of the Grimm boys with his face bashed in, Susan was holding the log as she said, "I had to use it." *I thought, Good for her.*

Sheriff Chad Bradford Susan's brother arrived alone and took over. He was planning to send Susan, his sister, to the first emergency vehicle when it arrived, and Roy and Bud could wait.

"I have never seen such brutality in my life and these two are really having a dreadful day." Sheriff Chad Bradford was smiling as he said this.

I said, "Those who play with fire are likely to get burnt."

"This was my sister, and I could not have beaten them better if I wanted; you do magnificent work." Sheriff Chad Bradford said thankfully.

"Remember Susan is my sister too. By the way thank Lady, she used Bud as a chew toy."

"Remind me to buy Lady a steak. I will talk to you tomorrow. Again thanks," Sheriff Chad Bradford said wondering where his deputies were.

I said to Chad and Susan, "I was never here. Is that good with you?"

Sheriff Chad Bradford: "If that's what you want, it is OK with us." I disappeared before Chad's deputies arrived. I was not interested in being connected to any of this. The Grimm brothers did not need to know I was responsible for destroying Darrel's beloved sons. It was not time to have it out with the Grimm brothers.

Lady and I returned to the Henry house to clean up and contact Sandra Martin telling her Susan was OK and not to mention my name in any of this. I explained to Sandra Martin of my desire that the Grimm brothers not know my involvement. It was not time to have it out with the Grimms. Sandra understood, and she told CherylAnn Swift and Mary Campbell. They agreed with the story, Sandra Martin would say Chad Bradford the Pike County Sheriff and, Susan's brother found and rescued Susan. It was a perfect story.

Everyone was at the hospital when Lady and I arrived, Mary Campbell, CherylAnn Swift, Bill Huff Susan's husband, and Sandra Martin and her niece Jean Jefferson. Susan had told her story, minus my involvement to all of them as they gathered around her bed. Susan winked at me as she told everyone she had freed herself and called her brother then fought Bud and Roy with a log until her brother appeared.

Sheriff Chad Bradford stopped by and brought us news about the two Grimm boys. They were being treated two floors down and then they'd be transferred to jail. Sheriff Chad Bradford placed a guard on Susan Bradford Huff's hospital room door. This was a precaution.

Susan Bradford Huff was very sleepy as she looked up at me and said very quietly so no one else could hear, "Thanks again. I knew you would come. I have two brothers to look after me." After an hour of sharing our stories and concerns, we headed home, except for Bill Huff, Susan's husband, who was staying with Susan for the night. Sandra Martin and her niece Jean took Susan's children home with them.

I said to Susan Bradford Huff before I left, "Susan you are my friend and little sister. You know this is what friends do." With that I left Susan to rest.

On the way out of the hospital Sheriff Chad Bradford stopped me and asked, "How did you know?"

I said, "Sandra Martin called me and said something was wrong."

Sheriff Chad Bradford: "I know Sandy called you, but how did you know...cancel that, just thank you for saving my sister again."

"Our sister. it was a lucky guess."

"Whatever it was; luck, guess, knowledge… thank you," Sheriff Chad Bradford said.

I got Chad aside away from the others into a small private room and said, "Chad you are against drugs in your county, and you want to see the Grimm boys pay dearly for what they try to do to our sister, am I right?"

"Yes. What are you getting at?" Sheriff Chad Bradford replied questioning.

"You have Scott Keener in jail and now you have the Grimm boys under arrest. What if I told you they were linked to a drug enterprise that is going statewide? They are part of a pot growing operation that is going to supply the county, the state and probably other states."

"I would be very interested in any information about this," Sheriff Chad Bradford said.

"You did not hear this from me."

"Hear what?"

I responded, "Where did you hear this?"

"Let us say Scott, Bud and Roy. One of them spilled the beans." Sheriff Chad Bradford replied with a smile.

"I could live with that," Yes, this was what I wanted to hear.

"Ok, give," Sheriff Chad Bradford demanded.

"You know the Thornton farm at the south end of the county?"

"Yes, what about it?" Chad was still puzzling over what I was about to tell him.

"The building in the back has been turned into a pot growing factory, just about ready to start production."

Sheriff Chad Bradford questioned, "Who says?"

"These two eyes." I pointed to my eyes.

"You don't say…" Sheriff Chad Bradford made a whistling sound.

"Chad, I do say, and this is bigger than the county. You will need state and federal help. Do not only shut it down, but also catch the people behind this enterprise in the act."

Sheriff Chad Bradford: "I'm glad you are on our side. You know the Grimm boys' and Scott's lives will not be worth ten cents once this information hits the streets. Thanks."

"I will give you five cents," I said. With this information Sheriff Chad Bradford was out the door.

Lady was happy to get home. She and I finished our dinner, and we went upstairs. Lady thought we were going to bed. I changed my clothes into dark clothes to blend in with the night. I said, "Sorry Lady. We have one more task." There was something else I needed to do before bed. We headed downstairs and out to the car. I opened the car door; Lady was standing next to me, and she jumped in the front seat. I said, "Were you afraid you were going to miss out?" She cocked her head and looked at me, as if to say, "I am here to protect you."

I said, "Thank you Lady. You seem to know what I'm thinking."

Our destination was the Grimms farm. We drove about a half mile past the Grimm brothers' farm. Noticing the farmhouse was dark. I parked the car about a half mile from the house; it was out of view. Lady and I were incredibly quiet as we moved toward the Grimm brothers' house. I told Lady she was to stay on guard just outside the house and to bark if anyone came around.

Finding a window unlocked, I was careful to slip into the house without making any noise. I was making sure that I did not leave a trace of my being there. I moved to the wall safe. The wall safe was concealed behind a large photo of their father. With the combination in hand, thanks to Scott Keener, it took me only moments to open the safe. It was full of money and papers. There was not enough time to read all the documents, so I emptied the safe.

This time I was prepared, placing the money and papers from the safe into a sack that I had brought. Silence was the order of the night as I slipped through the house to the open window. Outside, Lady greeted me with excitement. She had become a wonderful friend. Next was a visit to their barn and the hiding place Scott Keener had written down. Scott's information was most helpful. The hiding spot was in the second stall. The money and papers were hidden under two boards toward the rear of the stall. More money and papers were secured from the hiding place in the barn. I placed all the money and papers in the sack. I was done. Lady and I left the same way we had entered the farm. It was time to head home.

Once I was home, I checked on the contents I had secured from the Grimm brothers' safe and barn. There was a little over three million dollars, deeds, titles, and evidence of every underhanded scheme that the Grimm brothers had been involved in. This evidence was enough to bring them down. All I had to do was get this evidence into the right hands. The money would be used to buy back the farms the Grimm brothers had swindled from their rightful owners.

The money and paper were placed in a very secure place in the fruit cellar and tornado shelter located in the inside of the semi-circle drive area on the south side of the house.

After completing the task of securing the valuable documents and money, Lady and I were ready for bed.

CHAPTER TWENTY-EIGHT

An Angel Appears

I awoke, Lady was looking up at me as if to say, "What do you have planned for today? Why not stay home?" I shaved, showered, and readied myself for the day; I was excited for everything which was unfolding nicely. Downstairs I was entertained by an empty kitchen, no ex-wife, ex-girlfriends, or friends. The kitchen was all mine. Lady and I fixed and ate a very leisurely breakfast. It was comforting sitting at Granny's white oak kitchen table finishing my second cup of coffee. My memories were visualizing my Granny Ruth standing at the stove humming as she often did as she prepared a delicious meal.

Before I finished my breakfast, I called the hospital to find out how Susan Bradford Huff was doing. Susan's husband Bill answered the phone and informed me Susan was feeling great and she would probably be going home this afternoon. I told Bill it was not safe for Susan to be left alone for any reason. Susan needed to be guarded until this whole mess was over. Bill assured me that Chad Bradford, Susan's brother, and the Pike County Sheriff's Department was assigning female deputies around the clock for security for Susan. I told Bill I would stop by later to see Susan. I was comforted by the conversation, so I went back to my coffee.

After breakfast Lady and I went out to the garage and checked on my grandfather's pickup truck. My grandfather's truck was in good mechanical shape after working on the engine and brakes, but the truck needed something. Being in good mechanical order was not enough. The truck needed to look as good as it ran. Bodywork and painting were necessary to bring the truck back to life, as it was when I was young.

Yes, bodywork and painting were the order of the day, to make the truck look like new, so I called the auto parts store and ordered all the materials I would need, including auto paint and spraying equipment. There was a five-horse air compressor in the barn and the air compressor would be adequate to power a good paint spray gun. After ordering the necessary supplies, equipment, and materials from the auto parts store, I had everything I needed to complete the job.

This was an excellent hands-on project for the next couple of weeks sanding, priming, taping, and painting my grandfather's pickup truck. This project was a brilliant way of using my rusty bodywork and auto painting skills. This skill I had acquired some years ago when I used to recondition cars. It was a useful skill, one that was going to come in handy with this truck. I loved restoring old cars and restoring my grandfather's truck was going to be an exciting project.

Projects were starting to line up, the pickup truck, the garage, the barn, the garden, and the farm. Lady was enjoying my many activities. She was always with me, but never in the way. She was always willing to help, like chasing rabbits out of the garden or supplying moral support when the project I was working on had a setback. Which project would I start first? It was going to be the garage roof. Luckily, I had purchased the shingles and needed materials for roofing and brought them home a couple of days ago, so I could start roofing the garage tomorrow.

I looked around and Lady was gone. She had been with me day and night and now she was gone. Gone where? Maybe she was bored with my hours of working on my grandfather's pickup truck. She was gone. I felt a tinge of loss, more than just her being gone. Where was she? We had been joined at the hip for days and Lady's closeness gave me a feeling of comfort. Lady had edged her way into my life and not seeing her, I was lost. Where could she be? She appeared in the doorway of the barn and barked softly. She was trying to tell me something. Lady came over to me and pulled at my pant leg. She was saying "Come on, follow me." I followed. Lady led me pass all the outbuildings toward the back field that had not been tilled in years, another project. She stopped near a red oak tree and began to bark softly.

She was looking down into some weeds; with her right paw she scratched the ground. I came closer and saw a black cat shivering in the weeds. The cat looked in miserable shape. It was ill, uncomfortably ill. The cat was caught, tangled in the weeds, branches, and what looked like twine. I reached down, untangled the cat, and lifted this limp cat with care. The cat was on the edge of expiring. I cradled the cat in my arms, holding it close to my body. This was to provide warmth for the shivering cat.

I said to Lady, "Good girl." Lady and I returned quickly to the house with an extremely sick passenger on board.

At the house I took a clean piece of cloth and dipped it in warn water. I opened the cat's mouth and dripped a few drops of water into the mouth of this almost lifeless cat. Lady and I worked on the cat for about twenty minutes before signs of life started to appear. I knew there had to be an eye dropper somewhere, for this was farm country, so I started searching. Yes, in the right top drawer next to the stove, I found three eye droppers. We were in luck. I warmed some water with sugar and with the eye dropper gave sustenance to the cat.

Within the hour the cat was showing signs of life. There were some eggs and bacon from breakfast which I warmed up and the cat ate. I fixed a box for the cat with a blanket. I placed the cat in the box and the cat was asleep in a moment.

My project today was paying off the loan of one million dollars, plus a reasonable amount of interest, which I had borrowed from my friend Bruce. While the cat was sleeping and recovering, I went to the fruit cellar and filled a travel bag with one million sixty thousand dollars. I took an extra ten thousand dollars for travel expenses for Bruce's assistant, and I called the assistant, who was staying in Carrollton waiting to hear from me about the repayment procedure.

"I have the funds to repay the loan plus interest. Where and when should we meet?"

The assistant said, "If you can make it, in thirty minutes at the Carrollton Airport, I have a plane ready to take off at a moment's notice. The airport is just north of town."

"Yes, I know where the Carrollton Airport is located, and I should be there within thirty minutes." We headed for the Carrollton airfield, just north of Carrollton. Lady, the cat in a small box on the pickup truck floor and me. The family was growing.

Lady was enjoying the scenery, for she rode in the passenger seat. She was seated as if she was on a throne; with great dignity she held her head high. Looking at me

I believe she was almost saying. "'Drive on my good man.'" At the airfield, a plane stood on the runway readying for takeoff. I drove to the plane and my friend's assistant was outside of the plane. The assistant was waiting as I drove up. I got out of the pickup and handed the assistant the travel bag with the money.

I said, "Tell Bruce thanks." I handed the assistant ten thousand dollars and I said, "This is for your travel expenses."

Bruce's assistant entered the plane, and the plane was off in ten minutes. I had paid my friend back the money I had borrowed from him plus interest. Now our farms were safe. Lady sat on her throne as we watched the jet take off and fly. It seemed to go straight up; it was a wondrous sight.

I felt relieved; a major speed bump was overcome thanks to Scott Keener. He probably would never know the tremendous help he had supplied single-handedly. He was providing the funding to pay off the debts for so many people. Their gratitude and felicitations would surely never be bestowed on Scott. His loss was our gain, and life goes on.

Since I was in Carrollton, I stopped by to see Susan Bradford Huff. There was a house full of guest, including her brother Sheriff Chad Bradford, Sandra Martin the mayor of Fort Henry, friends Mary Campbell, CherylAnn Swift, Adele Muti Waserman and a sheriff's deputy. Susan was resting in her room, so I only popped my head in to say hello.

A very tired Susan whispered, "I knew you would come."

Susan Bradford Huff was to be released later that afternoon, with the deputy sheriffs around the clock protection.

Before I left town, I was to stop at the Pike County Sheriff's Department and give Sheriff Chad Bradford all the information I had found at the party center. This information minus the money and the combination to the Grimms safe and the location of their stash in the barn was most helpful to Chad Bradford. This information was from Scott Keener's stash found in the tree at the party center. It was a detailed record of all criminal drug activities in Pike County and the state including all the necessary documentation of everything that had happened in the county and state. It was detailed information of what was going to happen pertaining to drugs in the state. Sheriff Chad Bradford was most pleased.

CHAPTER TWENTY-NINE

WEDNESDAY

Sheriff's Plan

I decided not to tell Sandra Martin, Mary Campbell, Susan Bradford Huff and CherylAnn Swift where I accumulated the funds to pay off all the debts. This information was not necessary for them to know. Our farms were now free and clear of debt. It was time to learn how to farm and enjoy farming like my grandfather. Grandfather was one who had a deep appreciation and love of the land and farming, which he did well. The five of us Sandra Martin, Susan Bradford Huff, Mary Campbell, CherylAnn Swift, and I had a total of about 1,200 acres and none of us were farmers. It would be wise to hire someone who knows how to farm and have them farm all our farms.

Ben Steward was currently farming the Henry farm and Sandra Martin's farm. Ben was in his early thirties, and he loved to farm. Ben had been farming the Henry farm for over ten years. He was given the position when my grandfather decided he was too old to continue farming. Ben was my first choice to Ben continue farming the Henry farm and maybe with help he could farm for Mary, Susan and CherylAnn as well. The five of us would need to have a meeting to discuss the possibility of a joint venture; a joint venture was in all of our best interest. Since none of us were adequately knowledgeable about farming.

There was no school for me because Sheriff Chad Bradford and Superintendent Thomson felt all was accomplished and they did not want to push their luck. Besides, there were only a few days of school till the end of the year. The drug bust had changed the school schedule and I was no longer needed. There was assembly today dealing with the drug problem at the high school and the school district's new no tolerance policy concerning drugs and drug use. The assembly was to cover saying no-to-drugs, drug users and drug pushers. Parents, guardians, and the community were invited to the assembly. This was a total community effort, to stamp out drugs. The school administration with the help of local and state law enforcement was enacting this stringent no drug policy.

The only remaining major school activity for this year was the end-of-the year exams. The preparations for the exams were starting to take place. In less than two weeks there will be an end of the year school picnic for the whole community. It would be held at the John Anthony Henry Memorial Park of Fort Henry from 9:00 a.m. to 3:00 p.m., on the last day of school. The school administration, the community leaders, parents, guardians, alumni, guest, and this year's graduates were to be welcomed and honored. The school administration and community leaders would provide hamburgers, hot dogs, and soft drinks. It was requested that all attendees bring a food item to share. The purpose of the picnic was to take our community back.

The end-of-the school year celebration was an annual event, and the students, staff, parents, and community enjoyed this festivity. This was a reward for many hours of study and a time to acknowledge the seniors who were graduating. The senior graduation commencement address and recognition would be held the following Friday evening at the high school.

Lady, the cat, and I returned to town in the afternoon. We stopped at Sandy's Café, and were greeted by Sandra saying, "You're not at school."

"I've been laid-off."

Sandra Martin: "Too bad," as if she knew something. She asked, "Coffee?"

"Yes" Coffee was a delicious idea.

Sandra Martin said looking in the small box, "Where did you get the cat?"

"This is Lady's friend. Lady found this poor cat in a field behind the house."

Sandra Martin: "It is so sweet, but it looks sick."

"Yes, Lady and I rescued her from dying and I believe the cat is going to be OK."

Sandra and I made some small talk about the upcoming Fort Henry Fourth of July celebration. She asked me to help with the celebration because a Henry has always been involved ever since Major John Anthony Henry, the founder of our community. We talked about how the loans and taxes were paid off and what the future would hold for all our farms. This conversation made her incredibly happy. She was anxious to talk to Susan Bradford Huff, CherylAnn Swift and Mary Campbell and include them in our vision for the future.

It was necessary for me to stop at Ted's Grocery Store a few doors down from Sandy's Cafe'. The needed supplies were cat food; a litter box; litter box liners; a scooper; treats (for both Lady and the cat) bowls, flea, lice and tick collars, and a cat bed. Lady, the cat in a box and I with a handful of pet goodies were on our way back to the Henry house.

Sheriff Chad Bradford was at the Henry house when Lady, the cat and I pulled in the drive. He was desiring a meeting with me on how to deal with the Grimms, Scott Keener, and Jake Morrow. He was working on a plan, and he wanted my input. While Chad Bradford waited, I placed the cat in the box and all the newly purchased pet supplies on the side porch. Lady was staying on the porch to watch over the cat and our bags of treasures.

Sheriff Chad Bradford explained his plan. Chad's plan seemed workable; first the Grimm boys Bud and Roy were to be placed in jail without bail after they recovered. Their trial was to come up in a month or two.

Sheriff Chad Bradford said, "I'm greatly confident the boys would be going away for an awfully long, long time. Kidnapping, assault, attempted rape, attempted murder; drug possession, resisting arrest... whatever else can be thrown at them. These are some of the charges. The judge overseeing the case is Susan Bradford Huff's godfather. Case closed."

Sheriff Chad Bradford continued, "I heard rumors that the organized crime element of this part of the state was very unhappy with the Grimm brothers and Scott Keener because of the recent arrests and the money owed to the crime organization. After the arrest of Scott Keener and now the arrest of Roy and Bud Grimm the drug operational portion of the Grimm brothers' enterprise is in peril. The crime boss is concerned Scott, Roy and Bud will make a deal to save their skins. The crime syndicate wanted assurance from the Grimm brothers that Scott Keener, Roy Grimm, and Bud Grimm will not be a problem."

Sheriff Chad Bradford was planning to use Roy and Bud as puppets. They were to be played to disrupt the whole drug movement problem in the area.

Scott was a whole different problem. He was very slippery. It had always been hard to make any criminal connection stick to him. The best arrest was for the drugs found in his car, but a good lawyer could plead this down to a petty offence. Chad Bradford was not as confident of sending Scott away; Chad had a plan. The plan was in two parts. The first was based on greed and the second was to divide and conquer. Sheriff Chad Bradford believed Scott had a great deal of money stashed and with the heat turned up he will just as soon get out of town, until things cooled down. The word on the street was that Scott owed local drug dealers an excessive amount of money and that the drug dealers were extremely nervous about their money and since Scott had been arrested.

I said, "Interesting" Sheriff Chad Bradford was positive the drug dealers had contacted Scott and demanded their money immediately. Chad Bradford was unaware of my knowledge that I had found Scott's stash and that Scott was broke. This was going to make Scott Keener desperate. Scott owed the drug bosses a large amount of money, plus he had no money to get out of town.

Sheriff Chad Bradford's plan was simple: put the word out on the street that Scott was about to skip town as soon as he could make bail. This would make the crime bosses even more nervous. A prisoner was willing to do a favor for Chad Bradford and pass the word about Scott Keener's skipping town. The crime bosses would be unhappy with this news; they wanted their money, yesterday. They were going to get their money from Scott one way or another.

Scott Keener was no longer an easy-going prisoner. He was extremely aggressive, almost frantic. He wanted to see his lawyer immediately. He was anxious to have bail set. Before bail could or would be set Chad Bradford was working behind the scenes, to have a bug placed in Scott's apartment, a GPS unit attached to his car and his best deputy tracker assigned to follow him.

CHAPTER THIRTY

Scott's Stash

After my meeting with Sheriff Chad Bradford, Lady, the cat, and I occupied ourselves with setting up the litter box and cat bed. I placed, the collars on both Lady and the cat and feeding both. The cat ate all the canned food I prepared and went over to her bed near the stove and fell asleep. My desire was to work on the garage today, but this would have to wait. Instead, Lady and I busied ourselves with work outside. The garden needed tending, the yard needed mowing, branches needed to be picked up. There was a lot of work the homestead needed.

We were working until after 1:00 p.m. when I called Sheriff Chad Bradford and said "Yes." This was a signal that Sheriff Chad Bradford was to let Scott Keener out on bail. Sheriff Chad Bradford believed that as soon as Scott found his stash, he would be gone. Chad Bradford did not have my inside information; the stash was really gone. Before Sheriff Chad Bradford released Scott Keener, Chad Bradford and his deputies searched Scott Keener's apartment, his car, and his place of work. There was no stash to be found. On the release of Scott Keener, Sheriff Chad Bradford's best tracker was assigned to follow Scott Keener.

Scott Keener moved around town until he felt it was safe to go for his stash. All Scott Keener wanted was to get his stash and get out of town. Scott Keener figured someone was two-timing him. He was not trusting anyone. Scott Keener owed his drug partners over one million dollars. Scott was going to pay off his drug partners as soon as he secured his stash. He just wanted out of this whole mess. It was going south, and he did not want to go down.

He knew his stash was worth two plus million and minus the million that he owed his drug partners, it would leave him over a million dollars. He would get lost and spend a few years living off this money. He was going to live well. The deputies had taken most of his money when they arrested him as evidence; Scott only had about one hundred dollars in his pocket. The stash was especially important.

After Lady and I finished our chores, we entered the house to find the cat awake and well. Lady went over to the cat and sniffed it well. The cat came to me, smoothing and rubbing itself against my legs, going around and around as it purred. Looking down at the cat I said, "I guess we have another member of the family. What is your name?" The cat sat in front of me looking up. Looking deep into my soul, the cat purred. "Angel it is," I said.

Scott Keener showed up at the party center about 4:10 p.m. and he found his stash missing. The only remnant of his stash was a staged area around the bonfire with a few scorched twenty-dollar bills. He was furious, kicking and stamping all over the place. The deputy kept his distance; he was not sure what was going on, only that it seemed Scott Keener was losing his mind. Scott Keener kept searching running from one area to another turning everything over, looking, looking. Scott was like a wild animal.

Scott Keener looked so fierce and confrontational like a tiger on a hunt that the deputy had a thought of throwing Scott Keener some fresh meat. Scott Keener was not aware of being observed or followed. He was aware of extraordinarily little, for his world was closing in on him. His stash was gone. His chance of getting out of town was disappearing, plus the million dollars he owed his drug partners. In Scott Keener's stash was incriminating information about the drug operations in Pike County and the state, including names and dates. Scott knew he was in serious trouble, __ jail, death or even worse.

Scott located his 9 mm pistol hid under the shed; this was a starting point. Pistol in hand he was ready for action. He did not believe for a minute someone had burnt his stash. Who had it? Who was double timing him? The

Grimm boys were in jail. Had they had time to take the money? He was not sure they knew where the money was hidden. There was one person who possibly knew the hiding place of the money, Jake, Jake Morrow. Jake Morrow and Scott Keener were ready to double cross the Grimms. Scott Keener was thinking to himself. *Is Jake double-crossing me?* Scott Keener was in such a hurry when he left the party center; he did not notice a tail following him about a half mile back.

Scott Keener was tormented. What was he going to do? All his money was gone, and he owed the criminal associates a million dollars. He needed to hide for a day or so until he could figure this all out, but hiding was not an option, Scott Keener needed to act and act now.

CHAPTER THIRTY-ONE

THURSDAY

A Death Contract on John Henry

During the same day, Darrel Grimm was not happy that his sons Bud and Roy were in jail. He believed John Henry was responsible for putting his sons in jail. Bud and Roy were just gathering information from Susan Bradford Huff, as they were told. They were to gain all the information in any way necessary from Susan and after gaining the information they were to have some fun with her. She would disappear, never to be found. It was only right, for she got away from being a playmate many years ago. She was to receive her just rewards and the boys should not be in jail. It was all John Henry's fault; he kept screwing up everything.

Morning coffee was being shared by Darrel and Groch Grimm as they sat in their kitchen planning the downfall of John Henry. The Grimms had a history of hating the Henrys for many years, starting with John Henry's Grandfather Jason. Jason had stopped the Grimm brothers' grandfather from expanding the Grimm farm over sixty years ago. John Henry's father Joe had married the girl the Grimm brothers' father was in love with.

The Grimm brothers' father never forgave Joe Henry for marrying the woman he loved. The Grimm brothers father told his sons, after they had received the beating from John Henry that no man was going to steal from him. If he could not have the love of his life; no one was going to have her. The Grimm brothers' father alluded to having something to do with the deaths of John Henry's parents and their daughter.

This knowledge of the death of John Henry's parents and sister warmed the hearts of the Grimm brothers with satisfaction. John Henry's Grandfather Jason had again stopped the Grimm brothers from expanding the Grimm farm twelve years ago. John Henry's Grandmother Ruth had stopped the Grimm brothers from expanding their holdings three months ago. Now John Henry himself was going to stop the Grimm brothers from gaining over 1,200 acres.

The Grimm brothers hated the Henry family. Their hatred for John Henry was the deepest among all the Henry family. John Henry was the one who gave them a severe beating when they were in high school. John Henry had put the Grimm brothers in the hospital for a month. They were never going to forget what John Henry had done. They were just having some fun with a few local girls. Why was it he took it so personally? They asked themselves whether maybe John Henry was aware of the truth of how his parents and sister died. It could be the reason for his not wanting to sell the Henry farm. They were sure their father had told no one about the "accident" except them.

The Grimm brothers took over the farm after their father died. They felt their father died way too early and his early death was because of the stress of dealing with the Henry family. They were planning revenge on the last Henry to stand in their way, John Henry. Ruth Henry, John Henry's grandmother inherited the Henry farm after her husband Jason died. She was no easier to deal with than her husband. She was in good health a couple of years ago when the Grimms started gathering land. She died suddenly about two months ago, from a mysterious heart problem. The Grimms smile every time the death of Ruth Henry was mentioned. They were sure after her passing that her grandson John Henry would be easy to deal with. If not, there was a back-up plan: to eliminate John Henry.

The Grimm brothers' encounter with John Henry did not go well. He was not going to sell the farm. John Henry was here to stay. Selling the farm was not an option. The Grimm brothers could feel the hatred for them seeping out of every pore of John Henry. John Henry hated the Grimms as much as they hated him. It was a stand-off.

After coffee and planning the Grimm brothers contacted Jake Morrow to come over so the three of them could devise a workable plan to eliminate John Henry. Darrel's two sons and Scott Keener's efforts to kill John Henry had failed; it was now Jake Morrow's turn.

Jake Morrow's involvement with the Grimm brothers was his connection with government agencies promotion of green energy, both solar and wind energy. Jake Morrow had bilked the government out of millions and the money was being used in the scheme of buying oil rich land with the Grimm brothers.

When Jake Morrow arrived at the Grimm brothers house, they busied themselves with deep discussion on the need to eliminate John Henry. Jake was not anxious to kill John Henry. In fact, Jake wanted no part of killing. It was distasteful to him. The Grimms' were insistent. John Henry had to be killed and killed now. The Grimm brothers and Jake decided they would like to make it look like an accident, if possible, like his wife's accident.

"I'm up to the task and I will take care of John Henry," Jake said, knowing he was not up to the task. He was not going to kill John Henry, or anyone. Jake knew doing nothing was not an option: the Grimms would probably kill him.

Darrel Grimm: "Jake this would be the third attempt on John Henry's life. It had better work or else," Darrel said with blood in his eyes because he had wanted John

Henry dead for many years. It was going to happen now, today.

"Accident or not John Henry is going to die. It will be tonight," Jake said knowing he was between a rock and a hard place. He was out of options; he had better make the necessary arrangements or else.

Groch Grimm: "If only he had been driving the car instead of his wife; it would have been perfect." Jake was wondering what Groch was talking about, but he was not going to ask for clarification.

Darrel: "Let us not worry about history. She probably would have needed to be dealt with sooner or later, anyway. Let us get it done now and done right."

Jake: "It will cost about twelve thousand dollars." Jake knew someone in Carrollton who for a price would make all the necessary arrangements. Jake was going to farm the killing out. Jake was not going to kill John Henry himself. Jake was thinking to himself that it was time he gathered up all the funds he could get his hands on and get out of town. Jake no longer wanted anything to do with the Grimms. They were crazy.

Darrel Grimm: "Jake you put up the money and we will pay you when it is over."

"Ok, but…" Jake doubted he would ever see any money from the Grimms. They would stiff him or kill him. It was time to get out.

"No 'buts,' just do it," Darrel said. He was tired of dealing with John Henry.

Jake left the Grimm farm and found a pay phone outside of Carrollton. He made all the arrangements with someone at the other end of the line. The other end of the line had a throw-away phone. There was no one to trace. Jake was given instructions as to where to make the drop, not face-to-face. Jake dropped the twelve thousand dollars per the instructions. He felt comfortable everything would be taken care of tonight. The twelve thousand dollars was cash the Grimms did not have, for they were not aware their Panama account, house safe and their hiding placed in the barn were depleted.

* * *

Lady, Angel, and I had a most enjoyable dinner and after dinner the three of us continued working in the yard until dark. We went into the house, where treats were enjoyed by all. I positioned myself in an easy chair and began reading a Hamish Macbeth mystery. It was a comfortable evening me reading, Lady sleeping, and Angel curled up next to Lady. Where was Rockwell when you needed a painting? About ten o'clock we ventured up to bed. Looking down from my bed, Lady was asleep on her bed and Angel was asleep with her head on Lady's paw.

It was about 2:00 a.m. when a car with no lights drove slowly down Oak Street. The car pulled into the semi-circle drive of the Henry house silently and stopped. There were three passengers intending to do great harm. They were enjoying the thought of a cold bloody murder, as they re-checked their weapons. The driver remained behind as the other two with weapons in hand exited the car.

The two executioners were almost to the side porch when out of nowhere, two shots rang out. The two would-be murderers were on the ground screaming in pain. Both were shot in the right knees. The driver ran over to the two on the ground and helped them to the car. From the pool of blood near the side porch two trails of blood crossed the yard to the car. Once all three were in the car, they were off, tearing down Oak Street, waking up half of the households.

The foiler of this enterprising production of murder was Poke Sally Kasey. She was, as always, vigilant of everything happening in Fort Henry and to her unofficial adopted son John. She had protected John ever since his parents and sister had died, and he was a handful. He was always getting into trouble. Somehow, she was always there, as she was tonight.

A sixth sense awoke her. Something was wrong; what she did not know, but something. She was armed as usual. Was it a fox in the hen house? Coyotes? Something? Sally Kasey was walking around the grounds when she heard the car pull into the circle drive. They were up to no good. She saw they were armed and heading toward the house. From the shadows two shots rang out, Sally Kasey never misses. They were no longer going to be of harm to her John.

At the same time, Lady and Angel were aroused, for they could hear a car pulling into the driveway. Lady was trying to awaken me, with little success, for the exhaustion had seized me and all I wanted to do was sleep. The two shots were enough to spring me out of bed. I headed downstairs, opened the side door leading to the porch and turned on the lights. Standing in the drive was Sally Kasey with a pistol in hand.

"What's going on?" I said Sally would not fire her pistol in the middle of the night unless there was a definite reason.

"I had to shoot a couple of rats, no worries," Sally Kasey said. Her rats were two guys trying to get into the Henry house. This was not going to happen on her watch.

"In the middle of the night?" I said, trusting Sally, knowing she would always protect me.

"They were trying to get into the house. Everything is OK, now." Poke Sally was not going to let anyone unbeknownst to her into the house at this hour.

"Thanks, Lady was really upset, hearing the pistol shots," I said, knowing Sally Kasey knew what she was doing.

Sally Kasey: "It is all over now; you can go back to bed."

I thought to myself. *It was over, but what had just happened? Would Sally Kasey ever tell me what had transpired?*

After I reentered the house Sally Kasey took the garden hose and sprayed off the blood, so there would be no trace of what had happened.

Miles away in a car speeding with blood still pouring out of two of the passengers, one of the men who was shot said, "I am going to kill that Jake Morrow and all of his partners. It was a setup."

The other brother said, "Get me to a doctor fast before I bleed to death."

At the hospital in Carrollton after being admitted Chad Bradford the Pike County Sheriff was called. The brothers told Sheriff Chad Bradford it was a drive-by shooting and they did not know who had shot them or why. Sheriff Chad Bradford was not buying any of their stories; he put further investigation on hold because both shooting victims were going to be in the hospital for more than a week. The Grimms' and Jake Morrow were facing one more problem, that they were not even aware of. Everything was spinning out of control, almost as if John Henry was planning the downfall of the Grimms.

The crime boss Nick Martina who assigned his sons to this easy contract, just found out his sons had been shot. He was upset. The crime boss showed up to the hospital with his lieutenants to check on his boys. Sheriff Chad Bradford knew there was a whole lot more to the story. The boss told one of his lieutenants to put out a contract on Jake Morrow, but before Jake Morrow was killed to find out from him if anyone else was involved and kill them.

Sheriff Chad Bradford was thinking to himself. *This situation is growing by leaps and bounds. Somehow, this must lead back to the Grimm brothers.* Knowing the Grimms were in serious trouble placed a smile on Chad Bradford's face. Chad Bradford was anxious to pour gasoline on the fire the Grimms had started. It was time to rid the county of these vermin. Chad Bradford was sure Darrel and Groch Grimms were behind what happened to his sister Susan and bringing down the Grimms was going to happen if it was the last thing, he ever did.

CHAPTER THIRTY-TWO

FRIDAY

The Money is Gone

Money was needed by Darrel Grimm to hire a lawyer and pay for the bail of Darrel's sons. There was over three million dollars in the house safe for a rainy day and another couple hundred thousand hidden in the barn. On hand there was about four thousand. They owed Jake $12,000 for taking care of John Henry; it was time to check all their funds. The Grimms checked their house safe and the barn, but they were both empty. They checked their secret account in Panama there was only $32.68 in the account. What? Who? When? Why? How? Their heads were spinning. No one knew of their hidden funds. How was this possible?

It was money they had worked so hard for. Now it was gone. Who? It could only be one person; Jake Morrow. Jake Morrow was the only person who knew of the Panama account, but he did not know the account number. Only the Grimm brothers were privy to this information. The question the Grimm brothers were batting their heads over was how Jake Morrow could get the Panama account number and the combination to open the house safe. He had to be the villain who had taken their money, but how? The Grimm brothers set out with blood in their eyes and greed in their hearts. Jake Morrow was going to pay and pay dearly.

The Grimms were unaware of the double cross in progress, taking place between Scott Keener and Jake Morrow. Jake Morrow had raised millions from the government agencies as startup money for the solar panel and windmill farms. The Grimms had gained millions from the oil fracking companies for fracking on the twelve thousand acres the Grimms were promising. Scott was a little behind, for he only raised about four plus million from his drug enterprises. In total there was almost $48 million that the six had pulled together for their evil ventures.

Most of the money Jake Morrow and Scott Keener had accumulated was used to purchase land and set up the shell game of solar panels and windmills. The Grimm brothers used extraordinarily little of the money they had personally ripped off from their devious ventures to buy land. The Grimm brothers' plan was to use all of Jake Morrow and Scott Keener's money to buy land, then squeeze them out or remove them altogether.

Jake Morrow and Scott Keener were aware that everything was about to come crashing down. It was time to get out. The Grimms were incredibly delusional. They believed they could control this mess and make it work. Darrel Grimms sons were in jail and even if he wanted to run, he could not leave his sons Bud and Roy. Jake Morrow and Scott Keener could care less about Bud and Roy; they were concerned about their own skin.

Jake Morrow and Scott Keener were unaware the money in Panama was gone. They had gained the account number of the Panama bank, the house safe combination and the hiding place in the barn from Roy Grimm. The Grimm brothers were unaware that Roy had given this precious information to Scott Keener and Jake Morrow. Jake and Scott were planning to drain the Panama account, empty the house safe and the hiding place in the barn and skip town.

This was going to happen in a couple of days, but Scott Keener was arrested, and this threw a wrench into their plans. It was important Jake Morrow and Scott Keener clear out the accounts and clear out of town now, not next week or even tomorrow. Jake Morrow and Scott Keener needed the Panama and house safe money because the Grimm brothers had used almost all their money to buy land. Jake Morrow and Scott Keener were greedy; they wanted all the Grimms money so they could skip town. Time was of the essence.

Unbeknownst to the Grimm brothers, Jake and Scott and Darrel's boys Bud and Roy were having their own trouble. After a couple days of stitching, bandaging, and processing Bud and Roy were transferred to the county jail in Carrollton. They sat in jail, waiting for their hearing on a whole assortment of charges. The ten years to life was not their concern today. Staying alive was their concern. The grapevine was saying one of them was going to die, because of some screw up their father had made. The word was being spread__ something about a how contracted killing the Grimm brothers had paid for had gone sour. A local crime boss was distraught because his sons were shot during this attempted contracted murder. The crime boss believed it was a double-cross. The cross hairs were on Jake Morrow and the Grimms, and someone was going to pay. The Grimm boys were the easiest target, sitting in jail with no place to hide.

It was at 12:35 p.m. when the prisoners were on their way back from lunch. A fight broke out off to one side; away from the fight a prison-made knife was being plunged into Bud Grimm. No one was around Bud Grimm as he fell hard to the floor. He groaned, jerked and was in a convulsive state for a moment, then he laid still. He was dead. Roy Grimm was seized with fear as he pushed himself against the wall. He was terrified. Roy wet himself as the other inmates laughed. The guards came within seconds, but for Roy it was like hours. The guards were moving the other prisoners to their cells leaving Roy standing against the wall in his self-produced puddle.

Roy was not able to speak or move. The guards had to escort him by force to the showers and spray him down. After the guard sprayed Roy down and redressed him in clean clothes, they moved him to a cell away from the other prisoners. He was in a daze. Sheriff Chad Bradford was called and informed of what had transpired.

Chad Bradford the Pike County Sheriff was to arrive to find Roy Grimm in a state of fear, in convulsions, almost foaming at the mouth. Roy was removing himself from this world. Chad Bradford acted quickly not in compassion, but with a desire for information, Roy was the key to the downfall of the Grimms.

Sheriff Chad Bradford said to Roy, "You better start talking, or I will have them put you back in with the other prisoners. You hear me, I will put you in with the other prisoners. They will do to you what they did to Bud. Talk! Talk!"

Roy Grimm with Sheriff Chad Bradford and three witnesses including a stenographer and the top drug enforcement official for the state was telling Chad Bradford and the witnesses anything Chad wanted to know. The questions went on for an hour. Roy Grimm covered all the Grimms criminal activities for the last fifty years including murders, rapes, drugs, land grabs, intimidations, blackmails, abuses, swindles, and on-and-on. Sheriff Chad Bradford came away from this interrogation of evil with a tear drop in his eye and anger in his heart. Sheriff Chad Bradford was going to act and act fast.

The reason for the presence of the top drug enforcement official from the state with Sheriff Chad Bradford was that the state drug enforcement drug task force and Chad Bradford were planning a raid on the Thornton farm. This was a combined effort to eliminate the Thornton farm drug complex this evening after dark. Sheriff Chad Bradford and the state drug officer had received an incredibly good tip that the Thornton farm and its buildings were being used for an extensive drug operation. The cultivation of marijuana and the distribution of a variety of drugs were going to be facilitated from the Thornton farm.

The information provided by an exceptionally good source stated the Thornton farm was not only a major drug enterprise but the center of drugs for the whole state. As luck would have it, Sheriff Chad Bradford, and the state drug official listened to Roy Grimm as he reaffirmed the Thornton farm was the center of all the drug activities in this part of the state.

Everything was in place with the direction of the state drug task force and the support of the county deputies. The raid on the Thornton farm was to take place at 9:45 p.m. that night.

After listening to Roy Grimm's confession Sheriff Chad Bradford was on information overload. Chad knew the Grimm family was despicable. Chad Bradford had not comprehended or understood how evil the Grimm family was until Roy Grimm spilled his guts. The words Roy Grimm spoke during the interrogation would stick in Chad Bradford's mind the rest of his life. It was a realm of evil Chad wished he never heard of. Chad asked himself how he could be so blind to the Grimms, and their wicked deeds which had covered over sixty years of vile acts against the human community. The Grimms actions were available for all to see if they would just open their eyes.

Listening to Roy Grimm mouth squeal such immoral, horrible, and disgusting wickedness including two times trying to kill his own sister, Susan, killing John Henry's wife Jacquelyn, killing Ruth, Henry John's grandmother, killing Patricia Henry, Joe Henry, and Alice Henry, John Henry's parents and little sister and an inventory of crimes against humanity was more than Chad could endure.

Sheriff Chad Bradford ordered all present at the interrogation of Roy Grimm to silence. They were never to repeat a word of what Roy Grimm had said. All present at the interrogation were in full agreement. Chad Bradford's duty was to remove this blight, the Grimms, and associates from the face of the earth. This was a duty Sheriff Chad Bradford assigned to himself and this duty would be conducted by him.

CHAPTER THIRTY-THREE

Jake's Very Popular

J ake Morrow was becoming immensely popular. Jake lived in the country about three miles from Fort Henry on the way to Carrollton in a small house. His nearest neighbor was about a half a mile away. Jake Morrow was a loner, he did not like the small-town life. He was only here to gain a fortune and return to his roots, a large metropolitan environment. Jake Morrow was disgruntled with his current situation and arrangement. Because of his government connections, Jake had raised millions. Much of his money was being used to seed a deceptive solar panel and windmill enterprise. Most of the funds Jake amassed were being used to finance Grimms evil schemes. Jake had raised millions; he was sitting on his front porch realizing he only had a few thousand in his pocket.

Jake Morrow was questioning himself. How did he let the Grimms bamboozle him out of the millions he had raised? How Grimms promises were as empty as his pockets. Jake's dilemma was clear. He had three choices: one, take the few thousands he had in his pocket and get out of town; two, play the rotten hand he held with the hope of gaining millions; and three, empty out all the Grimm brothers' holdings and skip town. Jake Morrow knew everything was falling apart. Scott, Bud, and Roy were in jail. The charges against the three were overwhelming. Jake Morrow knew one if not all three of these lowlifes would talk. Jake was concerned for they would take him down with them.

Jake Morrow was not cognizant that his anxieties were more than apprehensions, but reality was about to bite him. His haunting uncertainties were to become certainties and probably terminate him. The first to find Jake Morrow was Scott Keener at about 4:20 p.m. in the afternoon. Jake Morrow was working on his car in the yard. Scott Keener approached yelling and demanding money. This was totally confusing to Jake. Scott Keener was in jail; how did he get out? Why was Scott asking for money? Scott Keener was the one with money. Jake Morrow was almost broke. This confrontation made no sense to Jake. Jake was asking himself. *Why did I not get out of town yesterday.*

Jake Morrow was caught like the India monkey. In India, the inhabitants capture monkeys for food by placing a few morsels in a jar. The jar's opening is large enough for the monkey to reach its hand into the jar. The monkey grabs the morsels. The monkey clutching the morsels makes a fist. The monkey is unable to pull its fist out of the opening of the jar. The monkey will not let go of the morsels. The monkey is caught. Jake Morrow was now caught in a jar of greed.

"I need money now, so I can get out of town," Scott Keener said in a mental state of pure insanity.

Jake Morrow said, "I only have a few thousand dollars and you can have a thousand." Hearing this drove Scott over the edge and Scott Keener pulled out a pistol and continued demanding money, all the money. This confused Jake, and he was not going to have any part of it. Scott had obviously lost his mind. Scott Keener was becoming a liability and he had to be managed.

"What money are you talking about?" Jake Morrow said, knowing Scott was the one with millions from his drug operation.

"Jake, you know the money I hid at the party site," Scott Keener said believing Jake was the one who took his money from the hiding place at the party center. Jake Morrow had been to the party center only one-time last year, for Jake Morrow was not into drugs and wanted no part of Scott Keener's operation.

"Scott are you crazy? What money?" Jake asked himself. *What money was Scott talking about?*

"You know dam well the money, the money I hid," Scott Keener was convinced it had to be Jake Morrow for Bud and Roy were in jail, who else could it be?

Jake Morrow never was happy with the involvement with Scott Keener and his drug trafficking. The Grimm brothers said they needed the money Scott was making. The Grimms were confident that they could control Scott. The two sons of Darrel were working with Scott and the three of them had made millions in the drug trade. The Grimms were not going to give up this easy money.

Jake Morrow was facing a demented frantic Scott Keener with a pistol in his hand. Jake believed Scott was high on drugs; why else would Scott demand drug money? This did not make sense, for Jake Morrow had nothing to do with drugs or the drug money. Why was Scott demanding this money? Jake Morrow was sure that Scott Keener was crazy. The pistol pointed at Jake was a major problem. Jake Morrow surmised that Scott Keener was going to kill him no matter what, money or otherwise. It was kill or be killed. How was Jake going to get the upper hand? Jake Morrow, looking down at the barrel of Scott's pistol, knew he was dealt an awfully bad hand. Jake's mind was racing. He would have to distract Scott, so he could turn the situation in his favor.

The deputy was perplexed. He saw Scott pull into a driveway, about three quarters of a mile up the road. The deputy following Scott decided to stop about a half mile up the road. The deputy was making his way through a thick growth of trees to see what was happening. When the deputy saw what was going on, he called the Sheriff's Department and informed the office of what was happening. The Sheriff's Department told the deputy he was to stay out of sight for his own safety and that more deputies would be there soon.

Jake Morrow was getting nervous with Scott Keener holding the pistol on him and Scott making no sense. Just then the Grimm brothers pulled in Jake's drive blocking Scott's car. The Grimm's were out of their car quickly and walked over to this tense encounter.

"What is going on?" Darrel demanded as he and his brother observed Scott Keener holding a gun on Jake Morrow. This did not make sense. Why was this happening?

"This nut case wants money," Jake yelled to the Grimm brothers, hoping for some help.

"You shut up," Scott Keener said. He was too far gone, and the Grimms were only a small distraction. In Scott's mind he was fighting for his survival.

"What money?" Darrel was thinking the money was probably from their safe and barn. Darrel wanted his money, and he wanted it now.

Scott Keener: "You know all the money__" While Scott was distracted by the conversation with the Grimms Jake pulled his pistol and shot Scott. Scott Keener jumped up then dropped over dead.

"What did you do that for?" Darrel said as his confusion was growing. Darrel could care less about Scott or Jake; he only wanted his money. His mind was questioning. *Where is the money?*

"Survival," Jake Morrow said, taking a moment of relief. Scott was dead, and Jake was not going to be shot. Jake could now breathe easier.

"We are here about the money," Darrel said. He was sure Jake Morrow had their money; why else would Scott Keener demand the money from Jake?

"It sounds like a broken record," Jake's confusion was growing as the tension was escalating. What is this about money? Jake had no money, why was Scott and now the Grimms asking for money?

"Jake, where is the money?" Darrel was convinced Jake had their money and as soon as Jake Morrow returned their money, he was going to kill Jake. No one was going to steal from the Grimms and live.

"What money?" Jake Morrow could see death in Darrel's eyes. Like Scott, Darrel was going to kill him no matter what.

Groch Grimm from behind his brother Darrel got the drop on Jake. Jake Morrow looked like he was going to drop his weapon and surrender. Jake whirled around toward Darrel as if to shoot; Groch shot Jake three times. This all happened in seconds. Now Scott and Jake were dead. Darrel was deflated. His hope of recovering his hard-earned evil money was gone. Darrel stood looking at the two bodies in anger. He wanted to scream. He thought to himself. *Where is my money? Tell me, where is my money?* No one was answering Darrel; dead men do not talk.

Darrel Grimm sank to his knees and said to his brother in agony, "Why did you do that?"

"He was going to shoot us," Groch said as sirens could be heard in the distance.

Darrel Grimm wanted to search Jake's house. He believed all the ill-gotten money he and his brother had accumulated was hidden in the house. The money was ready to be retrieved. Groch, hearing sirens, found it necessary to grab Darrel by the arm and direct him toward the car. The Grimms, with hesitation jumped in the car and took off.

Darrel said in disbelief to his brother Groch as they raced down the country road, "Why did you shoot Jake? He has our money?"

"I had no choice; Jake was going to shoot us," Groch noted his brother's anguish, but he had to shoot. It was necessary that they get out of there. They were hearing sirens in the distance.

Darrel Grimm in total disillusionment, for all his dreams were vanishing, said, "Now what do we do?"

Groch Grimm: "We need to get to the house and check out our hiding place in the barn again. There must be money, there just must be. It is our only hope. We will have to wait until dark because the cops will be all over the property."

"I guess we have no other choice." The fight and anger were sucked out of Darrel. His only hope was that money was still hidden in the barn, but how could it be? They had checked the barn. The money was gone. In his deluded mind Darrel thought maybe the money was still in the barn. They just had to look again.

Groch Grimm knew the authorities would probably be after them. "Let's hide at the hunting shack in the Summerville woods until it is dark."

The deputy came running out of the woods just in time to see the Grimms driving away. The Grimms worst fear, seeing the deputy, was that now they knew there was a witness to the shooting. The deputy was shaken after witnessing all the shootings. It was five minutes later when the two deputy cars arrived. The deputy in hiding who witnessed the shooting scene quickly informed the other deputies of what had taken place. The officer in charge sent deputy cars to pursue the Grimms, but by that time the Grimms had a ten-minute head start. The officer in charge contacted his office sending an all-points bulletin on the Grimms, as armed and dangerous.

A little after seven the word had spread; the Grimms were wanted for murder. They were armed, dangerous and desperate. Chad Bradford returned to the Pike County Sheriff's Department after the interrogation with Roy. He learned about the shooting of Scott Keener and Jake Morrow and the Grimm brothers running. Sheriff Chad

Bradford was almost happy that Scott and Jake were dead. He wanted the Grimms. His desire to apprehend was forged in a deep hatred, deep into his soul. His hatred of the Grimms had always been present, even in high school, but now, his hatred plunged into the depths of hell. Chad Bradford wanted his hands on these two evil demons of murder and destruction; they should not live in his world.

Sheriff Chad Bradford and the state drug officials sent arrest warrants throughout the state for the many criminals and locations identified from the information provided by Roy Grimm and Scott Keener. The arrest warrants were to be served after 10:00 p.m. because the state drug official did not want any interference with the drug raid on the Thornton farm that was to take place at 9:45 p.m. The state and the county were to be a healthier place by morning.

Sheriff Chad Bradford set up roadblocks. He was slow to place deputies at the Grimms farm. Chad Bradford had his own plan in apprehending and dealing with the Grimms. Chad called me and explained some of what had transpired in the last seven hours. This was a warning. Chad Bradford was not about to tell me all of what Roy said in the interrogation. Chad Bradford was mentally and physically drained from the interview with Roy. I knew this was both good and unwelcome news from Chad's interview with Roy Grimm. I knew Chad was not telling me everything.

Sheriff Chad Bradford said, "Desperate men will do desperate things and the Grimms are desperate." This was a warning.

After Chad Bradford called me with this information. I knew the Grimm brothers were in frantic need of money. I had to stop the Grimm brothers from gaining the necessary funds to skip town. I knew, I had cleaned out their safe, their Panama account and the money in their barn but knowing the Grimms. There was more money hiding somewhere. The hidden money was probably in their house or barn__, at least somewhere on their property.

Sheriff Chad Bradford and I had the same idea; it was to burn them out. Chad Bradford was going to be a little late to the drug raid on the Thornton farm. He had some business to take care of first. Four cans of gasoline were enough to take care of a problem needing attending. Chad Bradford was driving fast to a desired destination and the solution to the problem.

By eight o'clock someone with a deep hatred for the Grimms was busy dousing the Grimm brothers' house, barn, garage, and all out-buildings with gasoline. Within minutes all the Grimm buildings were aflame. The power and force of the fire lit up the sky for ten miles. The Grimms who were making their way across the back fields towards their farm, they stopped in anguish and anger, for their last hope was gone. It was going up in flames. *Hope-*

fully, this will seal the Grimms fate thought Chad Bradford and I as we stood watching the flames.

Sheriff Chad Bradford was in place at 9:45 p.m. as the drug raid on the Thornton farm commenced. There were sixteen criminals caught in this vise of law enforcement. The criminals put up a fight to the pleasure of the law enforcement officers. The night was ablaze with gunfire. Six criminals were killed, four were wounded and six surrendered after a ten-minute gun battle. None of the law enforcement officers were injured. This was a phenomenally successful termination of evil. The drugs wars would continue, but tonight a major bite was taken out of the drug operations of Pike County and the state.

Sheriff Chad Bradford and the state officials were well pleased with the outcome of the Thornton farm raid.

CHAPTER THIRTY-FOUR

FRIDAY

From Bad to Worse

Everything had gone from bad to worse for the Grimm brothers. They were virtually broke, with no place to hide and were wanted by the authorities. The federal, state and county tax offices wanted them for back taxes, fines, and processing fees. The Tri-Oil Company wanted them for thirty-four million dollars forwarded to them for an oil venture. The law wanted them for the killing of Jake Morrow, witnessed by a deputy. The drug crime boss of Carrollton wanted them for the over one million dollars owed by Scott Keener or the Grimms, they did not care which.

There was another crime boss who wanted his pound of flesh because his sons were shot in carrying out a contract for the Grimms. The Grimm brothers had cancelled their insurance on the house, barn, and outbuildings, because they did not believe in insurance. This was not a good day for the Grimm brothers. They were wanted and there was no place to run. They knew their days were numbered, but they had one last thing to do, before they went down for good. It is amazing how in their paranoid psychotic state they visualized victory as an outcome during their downfall.

The Grimm brothers were unaware of the death of Darrel's son Bud or the confession by Roy Grimm. They were only concerned for themselves a way of life for them. They were first and no one else counted. Darrel's sons were of little concern. Now it was every man for themselves. Bud and Roy being in jail? It was their fault, for they screwed up and let the law catch them. The Grimm brothers were sure John Henry had something to do with the downfall of Bud and Roy Grimm.

In the minds of the Grimm brothers, one person was responsible for their downfall. It was John Henry. John was the cause of all their trouble. They did not know how John Henry was causing their downfall, but their lives were going down the tubes since John Henry returned. He had engineered their destruction, step by step. Many years ago, the Grimms had killed my dog Boso.

This act tore my heart out. My dog Boso would wait by the edge of the road in front of the Henry farmhouse on Route 17. Every time I left Boso to go to school, town, or wherever. Boso would lay next to the road for hours waiting for my return. Almost everyone in the Fort Henry area knew about my dog that waited by the road. The Henry farmhouse was two miles from Fort Henry on Route 17 on the way to Weston. Weston was fourteen miles from our farm. The Grimms were aware of this. On one sunny afternoon in May, the Grimms pulled off the road and ran over my dog. My Granny had witnessed this cowardly act; it was no accident.

It was the afternoon before the evening the Grimms had invited Sandra Martin, Mary Campbell, and Susan Bradford to a party. I had a deep loathing for the Grimms. My disgust was turning to anger and my anger was starting to fume. Boso was my friend. Boso was always there when I needed a friend. The dog was old and slow in movement, but his heart and loyalty were as young and vibrant as the day he was a puppy. The Grimms would have to pay; this was something I could and would not let lay.

I was not a person of violence or vengeance, but the Grimms had tipped the scale of my world. I was no longer vertically conscious as to right or wrong. My entire world was slanted. I was falling off my high and mighty moral perch from the teachings my Granny Ruth had instilled in me. I was consumed with a venomous deep darkness of passions that I had never known before. Only a faint glance of goodness flickered in me from the decency that my Granny Ruth had breathed in me. This was keeping me sane. I was no longer a boy. I was looking for the Grimms and they were going to pay, dearly.

I never told Susan, Sandra, or Mary that my showing up at the bonfire party was not to save them, because I did not know they would be there. I was there to take a pound of flesh from the Grimms because they killed my dog. Since Sandra Martin, Mary Campbell and Susan Bradford were there, my poisonous anger saved them. Saving the three of them was a bonus along with taking vengeance for my dog. That was then and this is now.

That evening I was in a state of consuming anger; the Grimms were going to pay, and they did.

Desperate men do desperate things, if they could not get to John Henry then anything related to him was fair game. Chad Bradford, the Pike County Sheriff, understood the mindset of the Grimms and placed deputies at John Henry's house and Mary Campbell's house. We all were congregated at Mary Campbell's house for the afternoon and night because we knew the seriousness of the situation. We were not cowering from the Grimm brothers, only waiting for them to stick up their demented heads. Chad Bradford made sure the deputies that had a negative experience with the Grimms were the ones protecting all the people the Grimms might go after.

Almost everyone in the county had problems with the Grimms; it was not hard to identify deputies who passionately disliked the Grimms. These deputies' purpose was to bring the Grimms to justice. It was believed by Chad Bradford, the Sheriff of Pike County, that the Grimms were responsible for the death of a Pike County deputy three years ago. At Mary's house, which was almost as big as mine, we were all comfortable Mary, Sandra, CherylAnn, Jean, Susan, her husband, her daughter, her two sons, Lady, Angel, and me.

We kept a vigil from the time we arrived, all day and into the evening. We were armed and prepared. We had slipped into Mary's house, so quietly, no one knew we were there. We were waiting. No one went out or to work, just waited, for we knew the Grimms and what they were capable of if they were given a chance. We were wondering where the Grimms were. Would they just take off or knowing there was no hope, would they come after all of us?

The Grimms parked about a mile outside of Fort Henry and slowly and methodically moved toward the Henry house at about 2:00 a.m. They came to the back of town through the farm fields. They were positioning themselves, so they could see the house. They were watching the Henry house from about a half mile away behind the barn and outbuildings. They saw no movement, so they made their move. They came from behind the barn and in front of the garage, slowly watching for any sign of life. They were well-armed, and they moved cautiously toward the house.

Their excitement was overwhelming as the Grimm brothers approached the Henry house with murder in their hearts. Their safety was not an issue. Their mission was all-consuming. The Grimms were spotted, and gun fire broke out. Two shots from the deep darkness next to the barn rang out and the Grimms were dead before they hit the ground. They were both shot between the eyes as fast as a pistol would fire. The two shots were a thousand-to-one chance, but the shooter did not need chance. It was all but humanly impossible that any one person could make those two shots, but both Grimm brothers fell to the ground at the same moment. They were dead, and she walked away.

Sheriff Chad Bradford knew in his heart his deputies were not capable of such shooting, though he allowed his deputies to take credit.

Chad Bradford called us at about 3:00 a.m. It was over.

CHAPTER THIRTY-FIVE

MONDAY

Meeting at Sheriff Chad Bradford's Office

Sheriff Chad Bradford called and asked me to meet him at eight in the morning at his office; he said, "There were some critical issues involving the whole case I want to discuss with you."

I was anxious to talk to Sheriff Chad Bradford so Lady, Angel and I drove to Carrollton to the Sheriff's Department. There were a few dots relating to the case that needed connecting. On entering Sheriff Chad Bradford's office, I said "Chad, what is this all about? It just doesn't all add up?"

Sheriff Chad Bradford asked me to have a seat and he began, "It has taken me a few days. I think that I have put enough pieces together to make some sense out of the deluded minds of the Grimm brothers, their sons, and associates. It was all greed, double crossing, triple crossing and every possible underhanded dealing a human could imagine. There were drugs, swindling, blackmailing, intimidation, threats, abuse, and even murder. For the Grimm brothers, Darrel Grimm and Groch Grimm, Darrel's sons Roy Grimm and Bud Grimm and the partners in crime Scott Keener and Jake Morrow, they were shafting everyone including each other. Everyone was shafting everyone. A lot of this information was gained from Roy Grimm after seeing his brother Bud killed in front of him."

I said, "Yes," agreeing with Chad Bradford.

"To start the Grimm brothers were acquiring land in a quest of greed. Their scheme was to buy land supposedly oil-rich. At the start they would make it seem there was oil on the land. They were in contact with an oil investment broker. This oil investment broker was just about as unscrupulous as the Grimms. Together their plan was to contact and hoodwink an oil company after they had salted the land to show it to be oil-rich."

Sheriff Chad Bradford paused, then continued, "To their surprise they found out the land was oil rich, at least some of the county. What a dilemma, their shady deal was now a real enterprise, a money-making enterprise. It was important, the oil investment broker suggested the three of them keep the information secret. The Grimms were owners of only one hundred and sixty acres, and they stood only to make a few thousands out of this fantastic opportunity. They believed the whole valley was rich in oil, which meant millions, possibly billions. Their plan changed instead of swindling an oil company, they were going to secure as much land as possible and make a killing in oil."

I said nothing as Chad Bradford continued, "First the oil company executive who thought the twelve thousand acres of land to be rich in oil was encouraged to joint this scheme and buy as much of the twelve thousand acres as possible before anyone found out of the land's oil riches. The oil company executive would have his company put up $34 million; this was seed money that would derive billions. This corrupt group estimated every one thousand acres they owned were worth a billion dollars. They wanted it all."

This was becoming a long story as Chad Bradford continued. "The Grimms did not have enough money to buy more than one hundred acres, but the county's oil rich land was over twelve thousand acres. This was a major dilemma they faced. At five thousand dollars an acre times twelve thousand acres of farmland equals $60 million. They knew the twelve thousand acres of oil producing land was worth at least twelve billion dollars, maybe more. They had real incentive to grab as much of the twelve thousand acres as possible and they did not care how they did it."

"Did they have the funds to buy land?" I said, trying to figure out how this whole scheme started.

Sheriff Chad Bradford: "No that was the main speed bump they faced. The Grimms had about one hundred and sixty thousand dollars in total worth__ this included their farm, equipment, house, buildings and borrowing power. Sixty thousand dollars was only a down payment on one hundred acres, another dilemma. There they were with their noses against the candy store window with extraordinarily little money to buy any candy. If you thought this was going to stop these two, you had another think coming. They put their heads together, working on how they were going to get hundreds of acres of land with little or no money?"

I said, "How did they raise the money."

Sheriff Chad Bradford: "The $34 million gained from the oil company would only be used as last alternative. The Grimms somehow were to befriend Jake Morrow. Jake Morrow was well connected with government agencies. Jake had a great idea on how to get money from the government. How? The Grimms asked. Jake said the government is made up of some jillion agencies with piles of money. Jake Morrow was an energy broker who had worked with many government agencies. His connections with government agencies were an open hunting season for fraud."

Sheriff Chad Bradford again said, "Jake Morrow told the Grimms that with the money they gained from the oil company, they would grease some government employee's palms. It would be easy since government workers were so stupid, and Jake knew the perfect fools. The Grimms did not buy into this notion wholeheartedly, but they were desperate."

After pausing Sheriff Chad Bradford said, "Jake convinced the Grimms the new fad was green. The current government would throw money at anything green. Wind power and solar power were the new snake oil medicine of today. All they had to do was bottle their own brand of snake oil medicine in the way of wind power and solar power, grease a few palms and they would secure millions. The money gained from government agencies would be used to buy land. This was a great plan."

I asked, "Is there more?"

"There was a division of tasks: Jake Morrow would work on the solar and wind power and the Grimm brothers would work on accumulating land. All were vigilant in carrying out their assigned tasks. The Grimm brothers brought in Scott Keener; Scott was a young successful up start in the drug industry. Their venture needed money, lots of money, and lots of quick money. The Grimm brothers knew drugs were the answer for quick money. They had worked with Scott Keener very successfully in the past. Scott Keener was in a position of drug resources and the Grimms had two high school boys, who could distribute the drugs in the high school and the county."

"Is this where I came in?"

Sheriff Chad Bradford continued, "Jake was working on his contacts with two government agencies, one for solar power and the other for wind power. Jake Morrow was promising the two government agencies five-hundred acres each to be used for solar and wind power. Jake and his partners would put up the land, equipment, materials, and inter-structure, and the government agencies would put up the cash for the development for the new Midwest Solar and Wind Company."

I was thinking to myself. *This falls in line with what Wilton Graff said.*

Sheriff Chad Bradford: "This new company was to be a conglomerate to serve the Midwest. Once the enterprise was up and running the government would be paid back the seed money the government was providing. It was too good to pass up, plus the agency's employees would receive kickbacks, a win, win situation. Within three months Jake Morrow had established a solar and wind pipeline and secured government investment funds of fourteen million dollars. Everything was rolling along beautifully."

"Very interesting" I said in a voice like an actor on an old TV program *Laugh In*.

Sheriff Chad Bradford continued, "Jake Morrow knew the government agency's employees were easy targets: wine, women, and song. Jake was moving the government money to the Grimm brothers, so they could purchase land. The devilish trio was figuring out using $14 million of the government money to purchase two to three thousand acres of land. Three thousand acres of land was worth three billion dollars. Their plan was working. Scott's drug enterprise was to bring in one, two or three million dollars or six hundred to one thousand acres. Their plan was working. The Grimms were not planning to use much of the $34 million gained from the oil company. This money was to be used only when necessary. The Grimm brothers were working with another oil company trying to gain another $12 million to $20 million for their evil scheme. Money was flowing in from everywhere. The Grimm brothers felt they were invincible."

I said, "You can say that again."

Sheriff Chad Bradford: "The Grimm brothers with this new open spout on funds from the solar and wind government investments and the drug enterprise with the help of Darrel's sons, were grabbing land. The land in the area was worth four to five thousand dollars an acre, but the Grimms were not planning to pay the full price. The Grimms knew if they paid full price for the land, it would cost $60 million, so they plan to pay twenty cents or less on the dollar. Another problem the Grimms faced was some of the people did not want to sell their land at any price. The Grimm brothers were confident these individuals not wanting to sell their land could be convinced otherwise. All they had to do was use the right incentives and all the landowners would fall in line."

"You mean threatening owners."

Sheriff Chad Bradford: "The Grimms started buying land once everything was in place. They used every means possible to gain the land. They coerced and threatened the local bank manager so the bank would foreclose on land, which the Grimms would then buy for pennies on the dollar. They had the bank make short term loans using the land as security. The loans were incredibly attractive, low interest, short term, but with a catch. The catch was how and when the loan would be paid off. The Grimms made sure that these loans were not paid off in a timely fashion and the land was taken from the owners. If these tricks did not work, burn a barn, crash a car, kill some livestock, kill a pet or two, threaten wives and children__ do whatever was necessary, but get the land. And they did."

Chad's exceptionally long story continued, "Everything was going splendidly. They had accumulated over two thousand and six hundred acres. It was getting harder to gain more acreage and they had to satisfy the government agencies about the progress of the solar and wind power ventures. Their original plan was to have everything completed in two to three years. It had been well over two years, and they'd only reached twenty percent of their goal. They put their heads together and came up with a new plan to gain all this land for the oil development venture."

I asked, "What was this new idea?"

Sheriff Chad Bradford: "They knew the government agencies were getting worried about the lack of progress for the solar and wind fields. They were to show progress, but how? The original plan was to pay back the seed money the government had provided within two years. Realizing it was economically impossible to make the venture work in a timely fashion, returning the funds to the government agencies currently was out of the question. They had already used the government money to buy land."

"Using government money?" I said, wondering how long this story was.

Sheriff Chad Bradford: "They needed one or two more years to gain as much land as possible and then pay off the government. Scott Keener came up with a plan which would give them one or two more years at the same time to show the government agencies that progress was being made. Jake Morrow, the Grimm brothers, and Darrel's sons all looked at Scott Keener. What was his solution? The solution to all their problems was pot and drugs. The only one excited about the idea was Scott Keener, so he explained."

I asked, "So, what was Scott's great idea?"

Sheriff Chad Bradford: "Scott Keener explained that the acreage they gained last month in the bottoms has five abandoned warehouse buildings on it; they could convert a building in the back into a pot-growing and drug distribution center. This land they were going to use was the Jim Thornton farm about 420 acres. They could use the building in the front to display the solar and wind power goodies and the building in the back could be used to grow pot and set up a drug distribution center. We could put in a few windmills and several solar panels in the front of the land, so it would look like they were in the solar and wind business."

"OK."

Sheriff Chad Bradford said, "Wait till you hear this, the electricity from the solar panels and windmills could be used to power the growing lights for the pot growing operation. The others were becoming more and more interested as Scott Keener presented his plan in detail. Scott explained that for less than a million dollars, they could have the pot factory up and running in three months. He would make a deal with some people he knew to finance, set up and operate the pot enterprise and drug distribution center."

"That is ingenious."

Sheriff Chad Bradford: "The Grimms and Jake Morrow were sure Scott Keener would take the fall if something went wrong with this enterprise, a win, win. They put Scott's plan into action: more money, insignificant risk and a front for the solar panels and windmills to keep the government off their backs for a year or two. Once there was no longer need for the pot factory and drug distribution center, they could sell it to a third party for good money."

"This is some story. I have one request that Pike County and the state donate the Thornton farm to Fort Henry."

"Why would Fort Henry want the Thornton farm?" Chad Bradford asked.

"The Thornton farm is not very good for farming because of the flooding and the buildings will start to deteriorate if they are not maintained. Fort Henry will maintain the buildings and find a productive use for the land," I said.

"If you and Fort Henry want the land, I will make sure Fort Henry gets the land," Sheriff Chad Bradford said.

Sheriff Chad Bradford continued, "Again, this sleazy group was up and running and they picked up another eight hundred acres. It was all going well. Another 1,200 acres was right under their noses and the key to getting this land was Ruth Henry. They made her a good offer, but no sale; she said she would not sell for any price, for the land had been in the family for generations. The gruesome group was not making any head way when Ruth Henry died suddenly. The person inheriting the land was none other than you, John Henry, of all the luck. The Grimms task was to find John Henry and convince him to sell the Henry farm."

"This is where I come in."

Sheriff Chad Bradford: "The Grimm brothers were planning, three years ago when they started this land grabbing venture. Their plan was to eliminate individuals and heirs connected with the land. The Henry farm was the center of the twelve thousand acres and if they could gain ownership of the Henry farm then the other landowners would follow suit. In considering the Henry farm they needed to remove the heir John Henry and then Ruth Henry, your grandmother. This would be easy, they thought.

"There was a hatred for you by the Grimm brothers, because of what had happened. John, this may be incredibly difficult to hear, but. I believe it is important for you to know this information. The plan was enacted to kill you and if possible, make it look like an accident, so no one would be suspicious. The Grimm brothers were so incompetent that they were like a mosquito in a nudist colony and were not able to find anyone to bite. They killed your wife in the staged automobile accident. Yes__ it was the Grimms. It was supposed to be you, but to my understanding, you traded cars with your wife that day. I am deeply sorry I am the one who must tell you this."

"Yes, this is hard to listen to."

Sheriff Chad Bradford continued, "John, you became the center of the whole enterprise; you were the new owner of the Henry farm. It was decided to either deal with you or kill you and deal with your heirs. At this point this unsavory group started coming apart. Scott Keener was becoming only interested in the drugs and building a pot production and distribution venture. Jake Morrow was interested in his government contacts and the money to be made from solar and wind power. Jake Morrow was starting to believe that there was real money to be made in the solar panel and windmills venture. The Grimm brothers were negotiating with another oil company for fracking. Darrel's boys were having fun selling drugs, assaulting, and threatening people. Each to their own, but they were no longer working together. Their single focus of evil was coming apart at the seams. Everything was getting confused and out of hand. Like a house of cards, it would soon fall apart, with the smallest amount of wind."

"OK."

Sheriff Chat Bradford: "This is where you, John Henry entered the picture and threw a monkey wrench into the works. Scott Keener was having trouble with the drug crime bosses about growing pot and distributing the pot and other drugs. His drug partners wanted a larger cut and the people distributing the drugs wanted a larger cut__ this was getting out of hand. This became a nightmare for Scott Keener. Moreover, the authorities were starting to nose around. Jake Morrow was having difficulty with the government agencies. The government agency with solar panels had a new chief, who wanted documented proofs of all the transactions since the start of this venture. The person in charge of the wind power venture was becoming concerned and wanted more detailed information."

So, I stated, "It was all falling apart."

Sheriff Chad Bradford: "Darrel's boys have been rousted by the local police because of many complaints from local citizens. The Grimm brothers' accumulation of the thirty-plus-million-dollar deal from an oil company was going sour. The oil company wanted their money back or for them to show proof of farmland purchases. You come along in the middle of all their problems. Your appearance and presence was making everything worse. Everybody was two timing each other. There was no trust. This was boiling over, and it came to a head. You can understand why all of this was blowing up and why they began shooting each other__ no trust, and a pound full of greed. It is going to take years to straighten all this out if we ever get to the bottom of this whole mess. The drug operation has been shut down. Twenty-four people are being charged, including Roy Grimm. The government agencies are not speaking, but we think they lost most of their money. The oil company is not speaking, but seven people were fired. The Grimm properties are being sold for back taxes. We are hoping everyone is now safe and the town will get back to normal."

"Let us hope everything will get back to normal," I added.

Sheriff Chad Bradford: "One last note to this evil unsavory barbarian episode was that there was no funeral for the Grimm brothers, Bud Grimm, Scott Keener and Jake Morrow. The State drug official as a favor to me had these extremely sick individuals buried in some other part of the state. The grave sites will not be marked. The state drug official is not aware of the burial location because he had someone from the state penal system to provide all the arrangements for these despicable individuals. This information is between you and me and it is to go no further."

When Chad had finished, I just sat there for a few moments, this was over whelming.

"Chad, I want to thank you for bringing me up to speed, I knew the Grimms were lowlifes, but in my wildest imagination, I would never have believed they were this despicable."

Sheriff Chad Bradford: "One irony: there is little oil in Pike County. The scheme was for not."

With a heavy heart I left Sheriff Chad Bradford's office and headed home. If it were not for Lady, Angel, and my tender memories of Fort Henry, I would have just kept driving.

CHAPTER THIRTY-SIX

The Sheriff Informs

We were all in Sandy's Café: Chad Bradford the Pike County Sheriff; Susan Bradford Huff my unofficial sister; Mary Campbell my first love; CherylAnn Swift my first wife; Sandra Martin my friend since the third grade; Lady my chocolate Labrador retriever; Angel my all-black cat; and me. The conversation was of course pertaining to the last couple of days. School was winding down and it was Saturday, so teachers like Mary Campbell and CherylAnn Swift were able to join us at nine in the morning. It was quiet at first, until Sheriff Chad Bradford broke the ice and started talking about the aftermath of the Grimms.

Sheriff Chad Bradford said, "All of the Grimms wealth__ what little there is left will be used to help cover the damages the Grimms had caused. The Grimm brothers' holdings gained from illegal despicable criminal behavior including the farms, land, equipment, and assets are what is in question. These illegal properties appropriated by the Grimms through their devilish greedy enterprise will be returned to the rightful owners, at no cost to the owners."

"That is very good news, it would be nice to erase the memories of the Grimms from the face of the earth," Susan Bradford Huff said, smiling.

"You can say that again," Mary Campbell interjected.

"Unfortunately, only twenty-three of the over forty families harmed by the Grimms were willing to return to their farms and start over. The other sixteen or so want no part of this town or this county. They are happy to be alive and away from this place." Chad Bradford stated this, as a sour note.

"I am sorry to hear that... any help we may offer in making the transition for our neighbors to get back to a normal life, let us know," I said reinforcing our compassion as a community to help one another.

"I will pass the word on, and I am sure any help will be much appreciated," Chad Bradford said in his hope and desire that everything would get back to normal.

Sandra Martin as Mayor of Fort Henry said, "An anonymous concerned citizen has donated $2 million to help all individuals injured by the Grimms. This money is to help all injured parties to get back on their feet and help the community heal."

"That sure is welcome news. Do you know who this concerned citizen is?" Susan Bradford Huff said thankfully but questioningly.

"No, the money is being funneled through the local bank from some unknown source," Sandra Martin said. The unknown source would remain unknown as she looked at me with a very suspicious glance.

Mary Campbell explained, "This is very interesting, because the school system has received grants and scholarships from anonymous benefactors."

"Someone cares about Fort Henry and us... I was wondering if your grandmother had something to do with this help. John, you know what this town of Fort Henry meant to her," Susan Bradford Huff said.

"I'm sure she is looking out for us," I said, knowing my Granny, was looking after us, one and all.

"Someone likes us, but who?" my ex-wife CherylAnn Swift questioned.

"Don't look a gift horse in the mouth," Sheriff Chad Bradford said with his own opinion of who was the benefactor.

"Chad what has happened to Roy Grimm?" Chad's sister Susan Bradford Huff asked concerned about her future, for she never wanted to see Roy ever again.

Sheriff Chad Bradford assured his sister, "Roy is under arrest by the state. He has so many charges against him by the local, state, and federal jurisdictions that he will never see the light of day. They are unable to prosecute him at this time, because Roy has had a complete mental breakdown."

"Poor Roy, they should feed him to a pack of wild dogs. How many girls has he and his brother kidnapped, assaulted, raped, and murdered; I will not be able to sleep at night knowing Roy Grimm is alive," Susan Bradford Huff said with bitterness.

"Don't worry Susan. If Roy ever gets into the general prison population, they will tear him to pieces," her brother Chad Bradford said assuring his sister. Chad knew the criminal world despised the Grimms more than the community of Fort Henry.

"It is not enough. I will not feel safe until Roy is dead," Susan Bradford Huff said with her brother Chad taking notice of what Susan was saying.

Mary Campbell said, "The school district has started a vigilant zero tolerance drug program. It will be in place at the beginning of the next school year thanks to Superintendent Harold Thomson, Mayor Sandra Martin, Pike County Sheriff Chad Bradford, and the community of Fort Henry. The zero drug programs will include drug testing for teachers, staff and anyone working with school students."

Mary Campbell continued, "The superintendent is serious about stopping drugs in the school district. He believes school is for education, not drugs."

"Yes, the Sheriff's Department will continue working with the school district as a part of the drug prevention program," Sheriff Chad Bradford said with pride.

Sandra Martin said, "I hate to say it but something good is coming out of the evil Grimms. We are taking our town, school, and farms back. We are becoming a community of neighbors again. It is like a very black cloud has been lifted from over Fort Henry. We have John to thank; his arrival has changed everything." Sandra Martin continued, "Some more good news: John Henry is here to stay, and he is going to take an active part in our community. John has been appointed constable of Fort Henry; he will surely bring law and order to our town."

"John Henry is also a deputy sheriff for Pike County. We should feel safe with John keeping a watchful eye on our town, county and all the people," Sheriff Chad Bradford said patting me on the back.

"There will be no running through stop signs or red lights," I said in humor.

"What red lights?" CherylAnn Swift questioned me, not catching my humor.

"We are a major metropolitan area now, so it is time for this town to have a traffic light and stop signs," I said continuing with my levity.

"Do we really need a traffic light? The next thing you will want is a round-about like they have in England," Mary Campbell said continuing the light heartedness.

I said kidding, "Progress, progress."

"On a happier note, we have the Fort Henry Fourth of July Celebration to prepare for. This will take place in a little over a month. I will be calling an organizational meeting next week and all of you will hopefully participate in the planning, preparation, and implementation of this festive community collaboration. I want this to be the most electrifying Fourth of July Celebration Fort Henry has ever had, for we are not only celebrating the Fourth of July, but we are also celebrating getting our community back. I want Fort Henry to start the celebration with a marvelous parade: this parade will heighten kicking off the celebration. A marching band will be a grand way to be at the head of the parade to start the Fourth of July Celebration," Sandra Martin the Mayor of Fort Henry said, with dramatic intense excitement.

Lady and Angel were getting restless. Angel kept rubbing against my legs and Lady was looking out the door. They wanted to go home and enjoy the day. It was time to leave. I said good-bye to all and said I had official business to take care of now that I was the town constable.

On returning to the Henry house, which day-by-day was becoming more and more like home, I saw Poke Sally Kasey working in the garden; she was my protector and guardian angel. Lady and Angel, seeing Sally Kasey, were anxious to exit the pickup truck and they ran directly to Sally; she welcomed them with open arms. Sally Kasey was a very independent person. She would not come and live in the house, even though I had asked her many times. Sally Kasey was content with living in her small, shed building behind the barn. Lady and Angel loved Sally Kasey and they were spending a great deal of time with her. They knew her as family.

I had wondered where the fresh eggs were coming from until Sally Kasey told me that she was raising chickens. She was supplying our kitchen with eggs. I had heard the roosters crowing and saw chickens behind the barn to the far left. On seeing the chickens, I told myself these were my neighbors. Sally Kasey was the one keeping the garden up, the yard clean, the house in good repair and making repairs to the outbuildings, plus providing eggs for breakfast. I was incredibly happy that I found Sally Kasey again… or did she find me?

Later that day, I took Lady and Angel to the veterinarian for a check-up and shots, they were not happy, but I believe they understood. I also stopped by the clinic to have my arm checked out; it was OK.

CHAPTER THIRTY-SEVEN

SUNDAY

A Morning of Celebration

It was late Saturday when we received word that Roy Grimm had hanged himself in the state prison. All traces of Roy disappeared; it was as if the state was erasing the Grimms and their associates from the face of the earth. I saw Susan Bradford Huff on Sunday morning; she was all smiles. We did not celebrate Roy's death. It was not a time of celebration. We were all drawn to the Catholic church that morning even though we were not all Catholics. We were sitting together holding hands giving thanks to God for a peaceful Fort Henry.

It was a Monday the next day, after all the excitement, when I came downstairs at about seven in the morning. Seated at the kitchen table were Susan Bradford Huff the assistant mayor of Fort Henry and my unofficial sister, Chad Bradford the Pike County Sheriff and Susan's brother, Sandra Martin the mayor of Fort Henry and my friend since I was eight, Mary Campbell my first love, Sally Kasey my guardian angel, Byron Shelley Keats, my next-door neighbor, and Vietnam veteran and at the stove was CherylAnn Swift my ex-wife. A place for me at the head of the table was vacant. Coffee was poured, and Mary Campbell seated to my right gestured for me to have a seat. I sat and CherylAnn Swift served me a plate full of breakfast culinary delights.

Sheriff Chad Bradford raised his coffee cup and made a toast, "To John the slaver of dragons and the builder of kingdoms." We all raised our coffee cups and recognized the toast; this was a morning of celebration.

After the celebration breakfast, Lady, Angel, and I went to the Henry farm and walked the land making sure to stop by the red oak tree that caught me and kept me from going to heaven. I was there to show my respect and give thanks to God and the mighty red oak tree that had saved me. I was sure my sister Alice, my wife Jacquelyn, Granny Ruth, my parents, and my great-many-times grandfather were looking down upon me. The three of us sat under the tree for some time. It was as if Lady and Angel knew this place and this tree were especially important to me.

The Fort Henry Town Council was made up of four people, Sandra Martin the Mayor; Susan Bradford Huff the assistant mayor; Mary Campbell the Council-At-Large; and CherylAnn Swift Council Member. It was nice to know people in power. The Fort Henry Town Council met on the first and third Wednesday of the month at 7:00 p.m. This being the third Wednesday of the month, at this council meeting I was officially appointed constable for Fort Henry. I was given the authority to hire assistant constables, which I used to hire Sally Kasey and Byron Keats. Fort Henry had received a grant of one hundred and twenty thousand dollars a year for five years for the safety and welfare of Fort Henry, because Fort Henry was a recognized historical site. The constable cost for the three of us would be around forty thousand dollars, this was going to be paid from the one hundred and twenty thousand dollar grant. I was only going to charge the town my expenses. Major John Anthony Henry and Granny Ruth would have been proud of the improvements to date and the planned improvements for the future of Fort Henry.

Accepting the position of constable of Fort Henry was in concert with my deputy sheriff position with the Pike County Sheriff's Department, that Sheriff Chad Bradford had awarded me. Fort Henry was not the Wild West or a rampant lawless town. It was a very peaceful people oriented civic minded community. The town folk looked out for each other, did you need a ride? Did you need something fixed? Did you need someone to talk to? Did you need some money? Basically, this was a community that cared about one another.

A cat stuck in a tree or a boy falling off his bike were the most adventurous events happening in town. My duties as constable of Fort Henry were more community relations spreading goodwill.

I was sitting on the front porch taking time to review all that had happened in the last few days, when: Bryon Keats walked up the front steps and said "You look like you are in deep concentration. What are you thinking?"

"I'm not thinking, I'm trying to remember," I replied.

"Remember what?" Byron said.

"Was that a blue Ford truck?" I said, questioning myself.

This is not the end, only the beginning....

Look for another John Anthony Henry adventure!